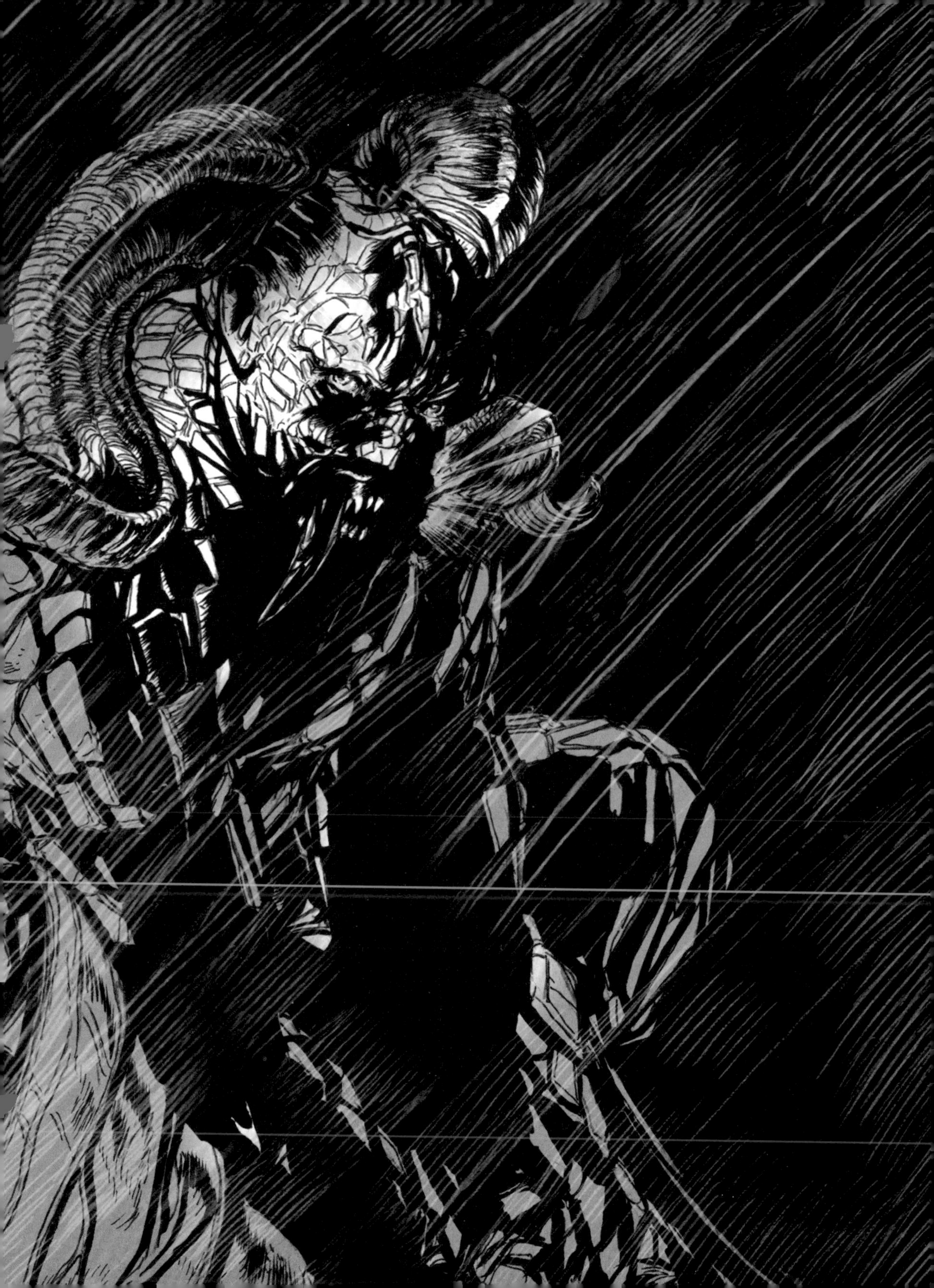

For David, who loves graphic novels and Scotland. —JY

For Ari, who's been bugging me to write this one from the moment she finished the first. —AS

To my beautiful wife, Katie Zangara, who is the light of my life. I love you. —OZ

Story by Jane Yolen and Adam Stemple
Illustrations by Orion Zangara
Lettering by Bill Hauser

Graphic Universe™
A division of Lerner Publishing Group, Inc.
241 First Avenue North
Minneapolis, MN 55401 USA

For reading levels and more information, look up this title at www.lernerbooks.com.

Main body text set in CCWildWords 7/8. Typeface provided by Comicraft.

Library of Congress Cataloging-in-Publication Data

Names: Yolen, Jane, author. | Stemple, Adam, author. | Zangara, Orion, illustrator.
Title: Sanctuary / written by Jane Yolen and Adam Stemple ; illustrated by Orion Zangara.
Description: Minneapolis : Graphic Universe, [2018] | Series: The Stone Man mysteries ; book two | Summary: "When a mysterious young woman takes refuge within Silex's Edinburgh church, it brings supernatural trouble for the gargoyle and his assistant, Craig" —Provided by publisher. | Identifiers: LCCN 2017006471 (print) | LCCN 2017033758 (ebook) | ISBN 9781512498585 (eb pdf) | ISBN 9781467741972 (lb : alk. paper) | ISBN 9781541510432 (pbk.)
Subjects: LCSH: Graphic novels. | CYAC: Graphic novels. | Gargoyles—Fiction. | Supernatural—Fiction. | Demonology—Fiction. | Scotland—History—20th century—Fiction. | Mystery and detective stories.
Classification: LCC PZ7.7.Y65 (ebook) | LCC PZ7.7.Y65 San 2018 (print) | DDC 741.5/973—dc23

LC record available at https://lccn.loc.gov/2017006471

Manufactured in the United States of America
1-36194-16978-10/6/2017

THE STONE MAN MYSTERIES

BOOK TWO

Sanctuary

JANE YOLEN AND ADAM STEMPLE

ILLUSTRATED BY ORION ZANGARA

GRAPHIC UNIVERSE™ • MINNEAPOLIS

Edinburgh, Scotland. The early 1930s. Young Craig, a desperate runaway, goes to the top of a church to throw himself off. But he is saved by a strange stone man, a gargoyle named Silex, who can move and speak but cannot leave the church parapet. Silex runs a detective agency and hires Craig to be his chief clue finder, since his last assistant has mysteriously disappeared and the church's priest, Father Harris, is getting too old and sick to help.

Shocked, yet happy to have important work to do, Craig signs on. Together, the gargoyle and the young lad solve the mysterious murder of an earl, as well as the deaths of several street people. But the solution points to a deeper, uglier scenario. One that involves freeing the Stone Man from his bonds, which will turn him from a force for good back into the evil demon he once was. In that form, he would threaten not only the church, Edinburgh, and Scotland, but indeed the entire world.

Silex doesn't want that. Craig doesn't want that. Father Harris dies to see that it can never happen. And yet the terror might well be starting up all over again.

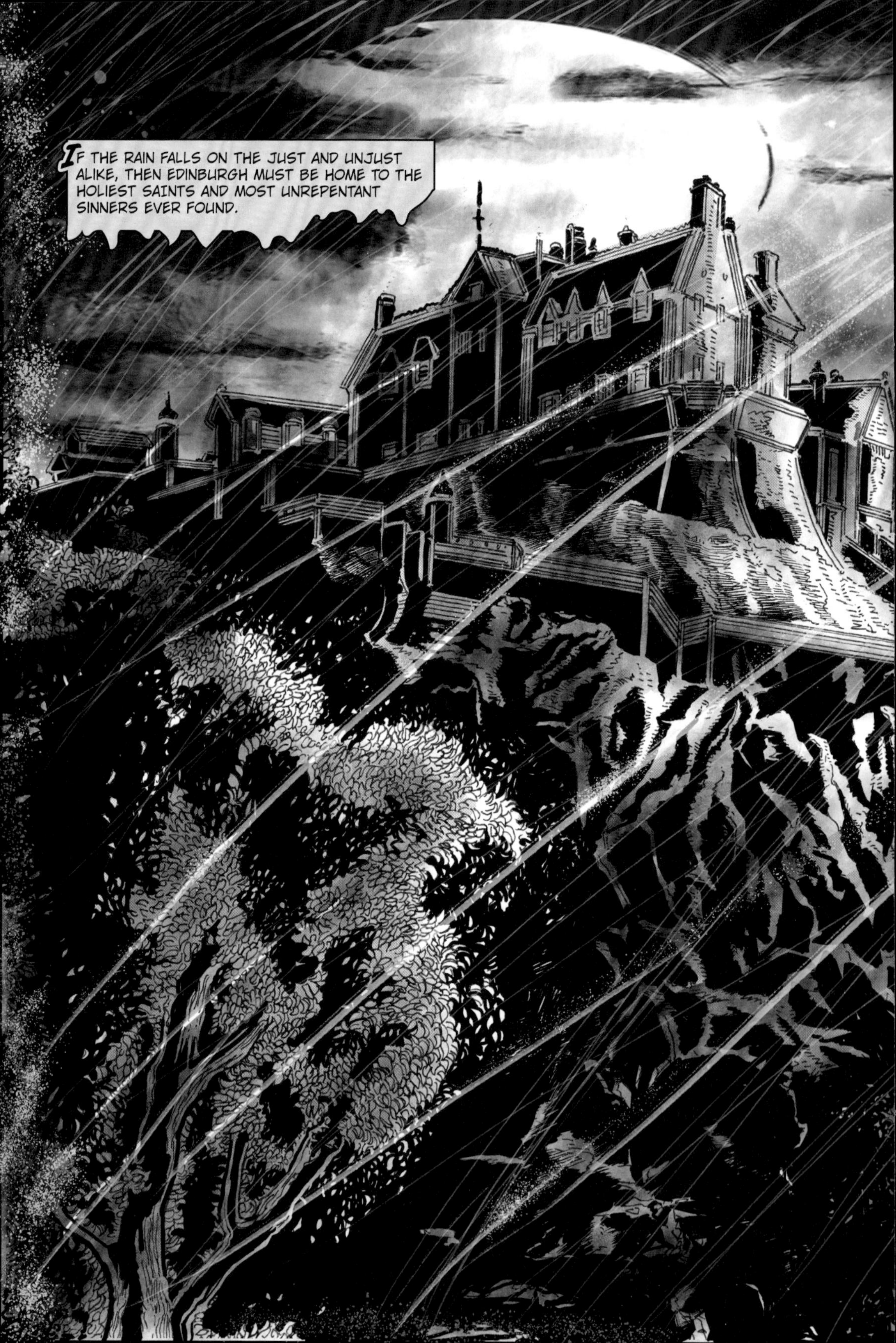
IF THE RAIN FALLS ON THE JUST AND UNJUST ALIKE, THEN EDINBURGH MUST BE HOME TO THE HOLIEST SAINTS AND MOST UNREPENTANT SINNERS EVER FOUND.

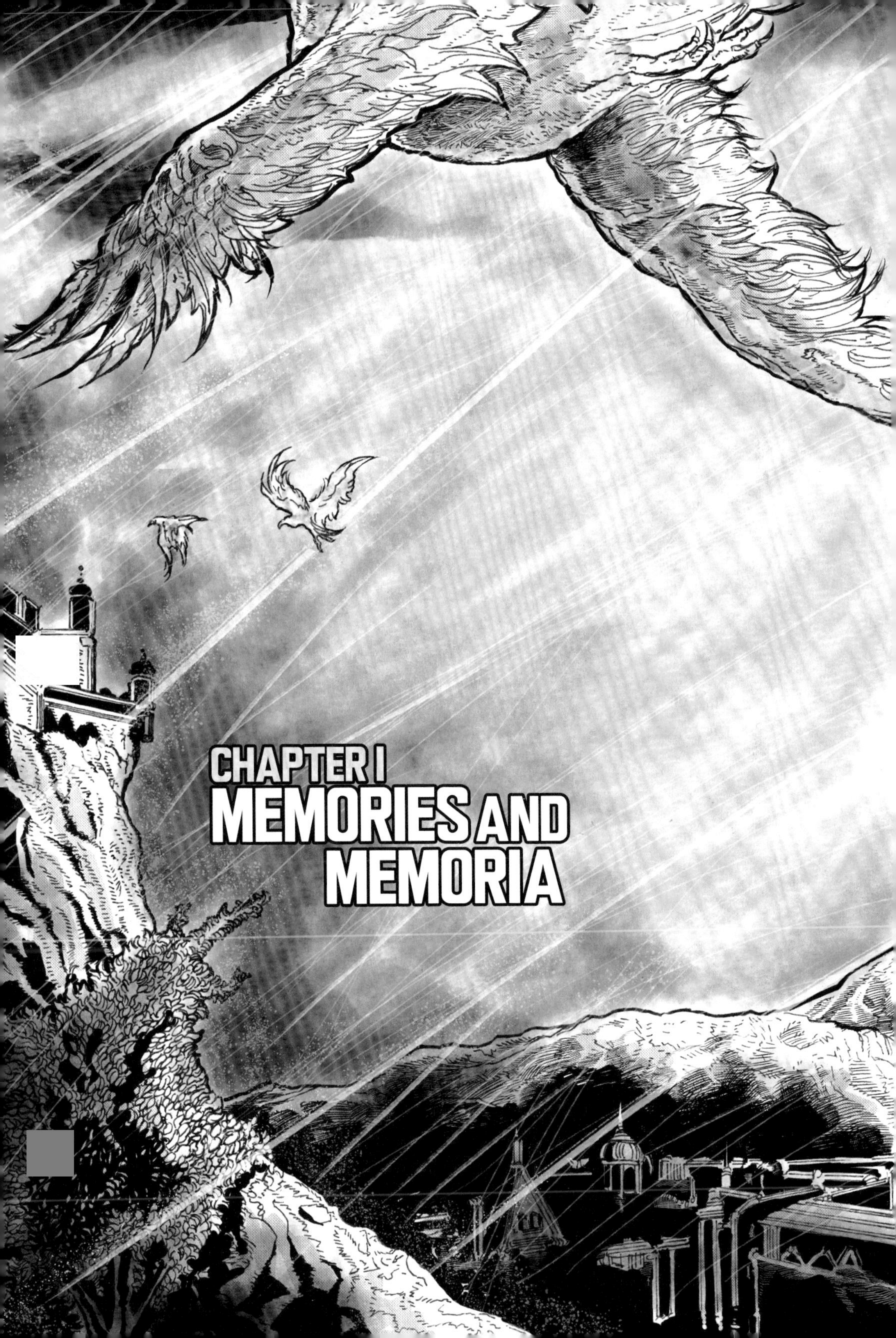
CHAPTER I
MEMORIES AND MEMORIA

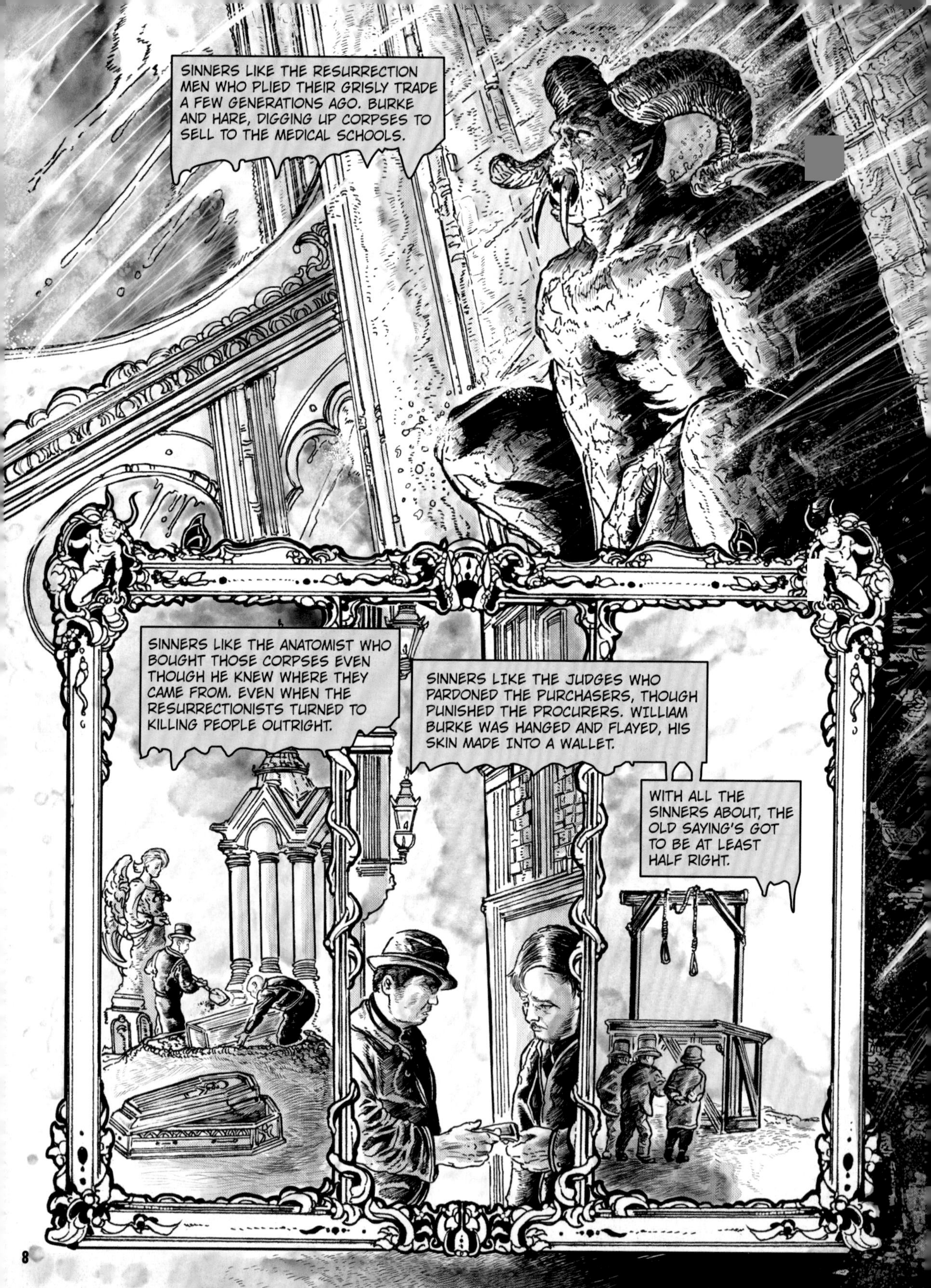
SINNERS LIKE THE RESURRECTION MEN WHO PLIED THEIR GRISLY TRADE A FEW GENERATIONS AGO. BURKE AND HARE, DIGGING UP CORPSES TO SELL TO THE MEDICAL SCHOOLS.
SINNERS LIKE THE ANATOMIST WHO BOUGHT THOSE CORPSES EVEN THOUGH HE KNEW WHERE THEY CAME FROM. EVEN WHEN THE RESURRECTIONISTS TURNED TO KILLING PEOPLE OUTRIGHT.
SINNERS LIKE THE JUDGES WHO PARDONED THE PURCHASERS, THOUGH PUNISHED THE PROCURERS. WILLIAM BURKE WAS HANGED AND FLAYED, HIS SKIN MADE INTO A WALLET.
WITH ALL THE SINNERS ABOUT, THE OLD SAYING'S GOT TO BE AT LEAST HALF RIGHT.

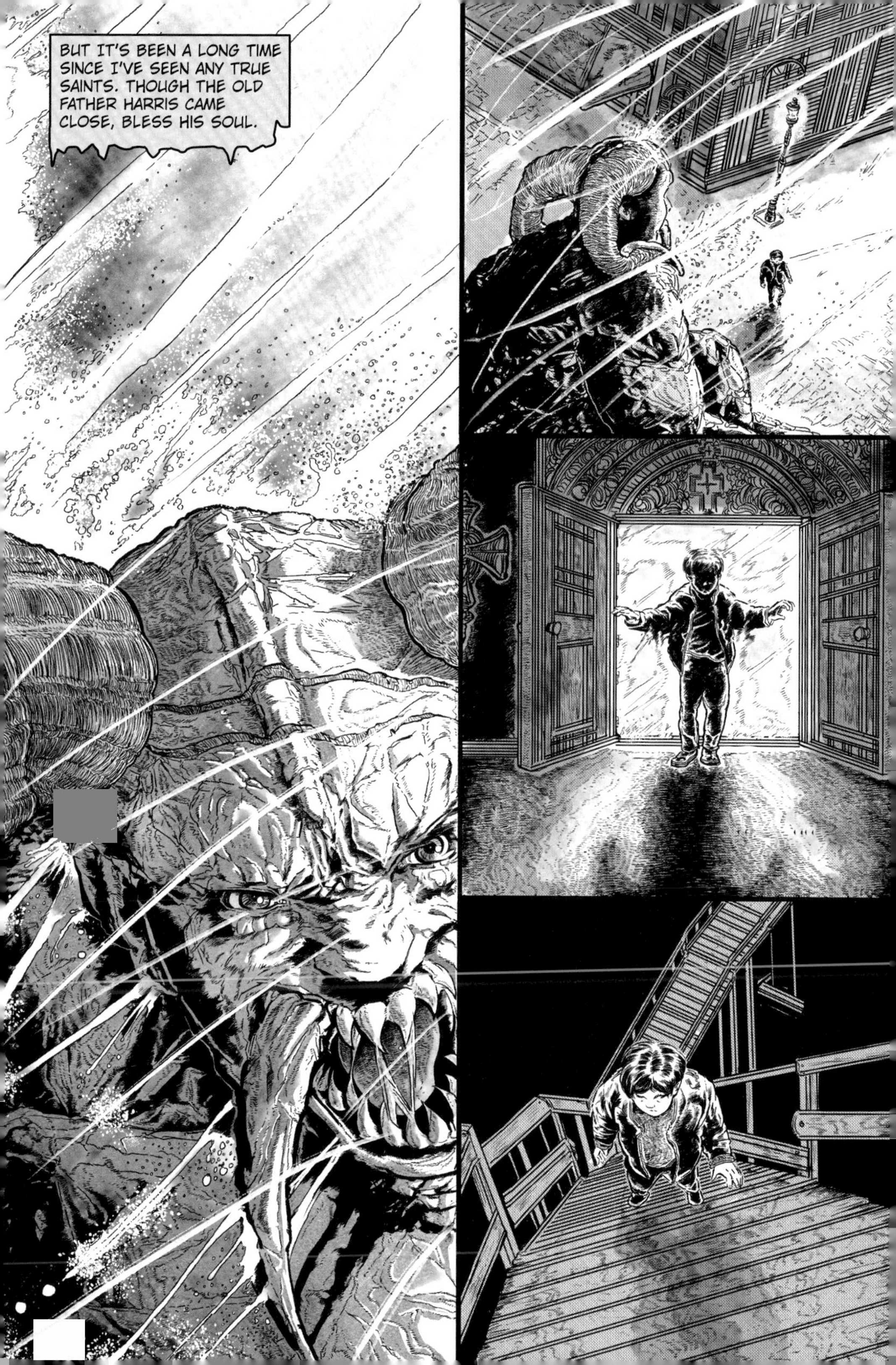
BUT IT'S BEEN A LONG TIME SINCE I'VE SEEN ANY TRUE SAINTS. THOUGH THE OLD FATHER HARRIS CAME CLOSE, BLESS HIS SOUL.

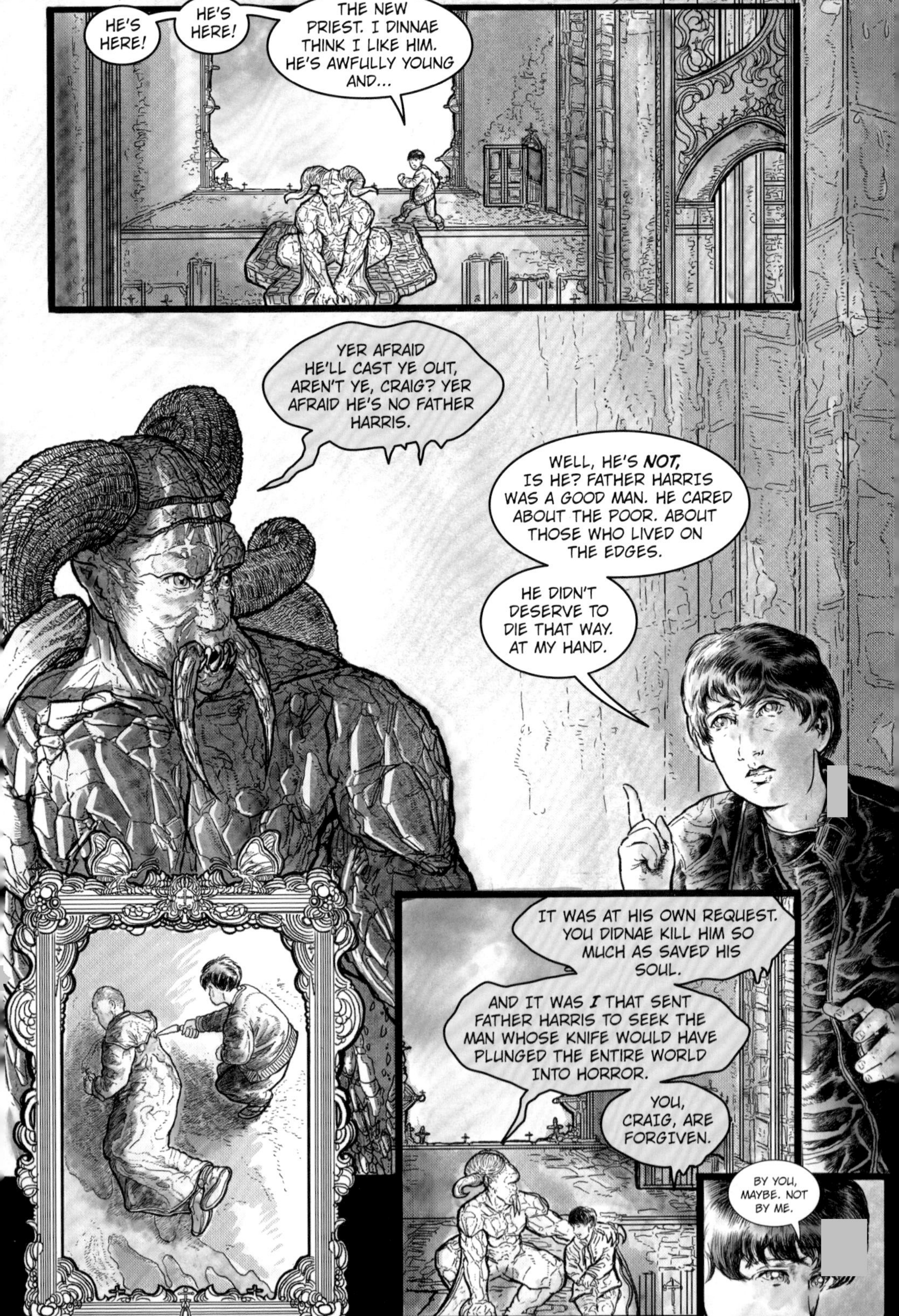
HE'S HERE!
HE'S HERE!
THE NEW PRIEST. I DINNAE THINK I LIKE HIM. HE'S AWFULLY YOUNG AND...
YER AFRAID HE'LL CAST YE OUT, AREN'T YE, CRAIG? YER AFRAID HE'S NO FATHER HARRIS.
WELL, HE'S *NOT,* IS HE? FATHER HARRIS WAS A GOOD MAN. HE CARED ABOUT THE POOR. ABOUT THOSE WHO LIVED ON THE EDGES.
HE DIDN'T DESERVE TO DIE THAT WAY. AT MY HAND.
IT WAS AT HIS OWN REQUEST. YOU DIDNAE KILL HIM SO MUCH AS SAVED HIS SOUL.
AND IT WAS *I* THAT SENT FATHER HARRIS TO SEEK THE MAN WHOSE KNIFE WOULD HAVE PLUNGED THE ENTIRE WORLD INTO HORROR.
YOU, CRAIG, ARE FORGIVEN.
BY YOU, MAYBE. NOT BY ME.

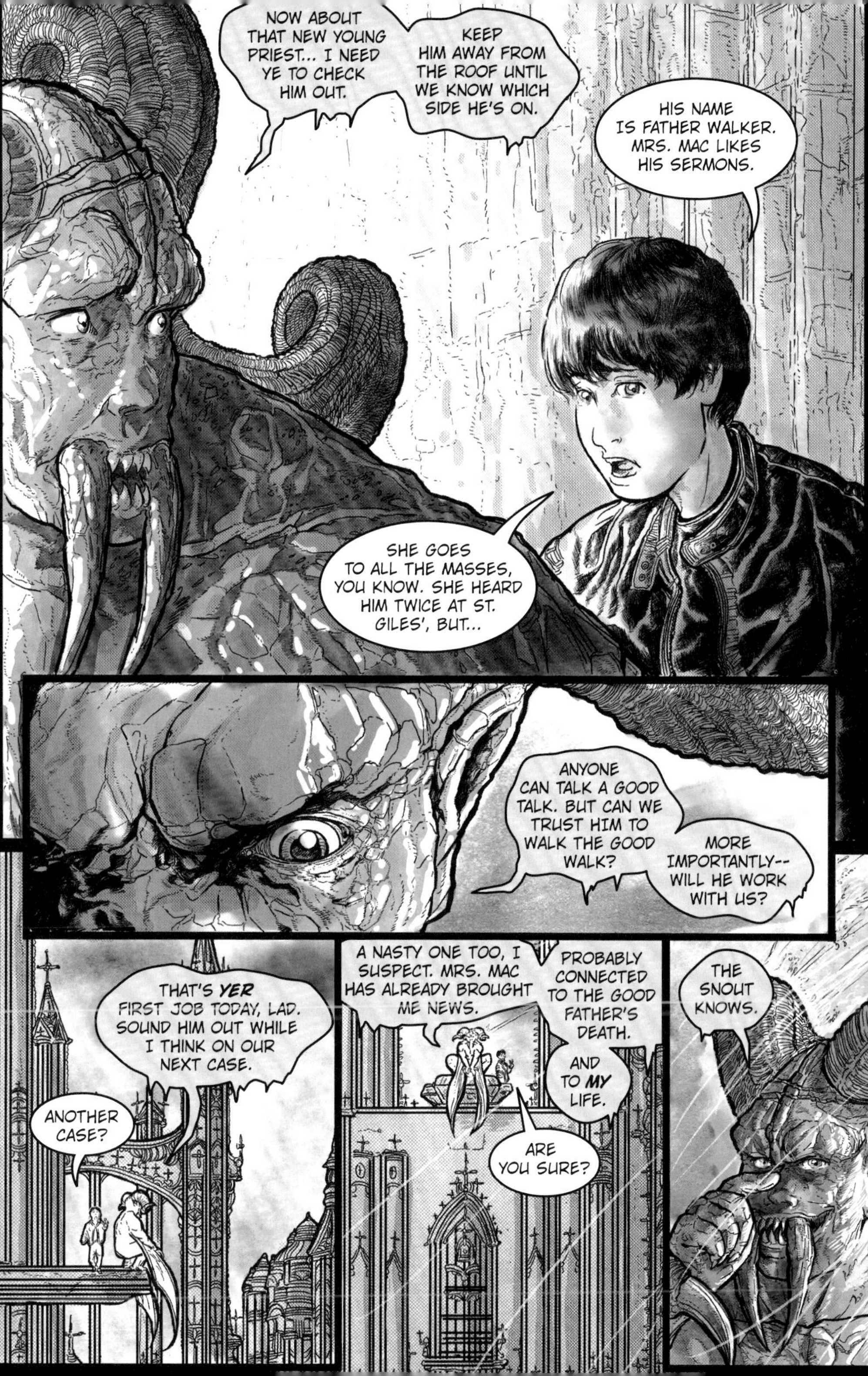
NOW ABOUT THAT NEW YOUNG PRIEST... I NEED YE TO CHECK HIM OUT.
KEEP HIM AWAY FROM THE ROOF UNTIL WE KNOW WHICH SIDE HE'S ON.
HIS NAME IS FATHER WALKER. MRS. MAC LIKES HIS SERMONS.
SHE GOES TO ALL THE MASSES, YOU KNOW. SHE HEARD HIM TWICE AT ST. GILES', BUT...
ANYONE CAN TALK A GOOD TALK. BUT CAN WE TRUST HIM TO WALK THE GOOD WALK?
MORE IMPORTANTLY-- WILL HE WORK WITH US?
THAT'S *YER* FIRST JOB TODAY, LAD. SOUND HIM OUT WHILE I THINK ON OUR NEXT CASE.
ANOTHER CASE?
A NASTY ONE TOO, I SUSPECT. MRS. MAC HAS ALREADY BROUGHT ME NEWS.
PROBABLY CONNECTED TO THE GOOD FATHER'S DEATH.
ARE YOU SURE?
AND TO *MY* LIFE.
THE SNOUT KNOWS.

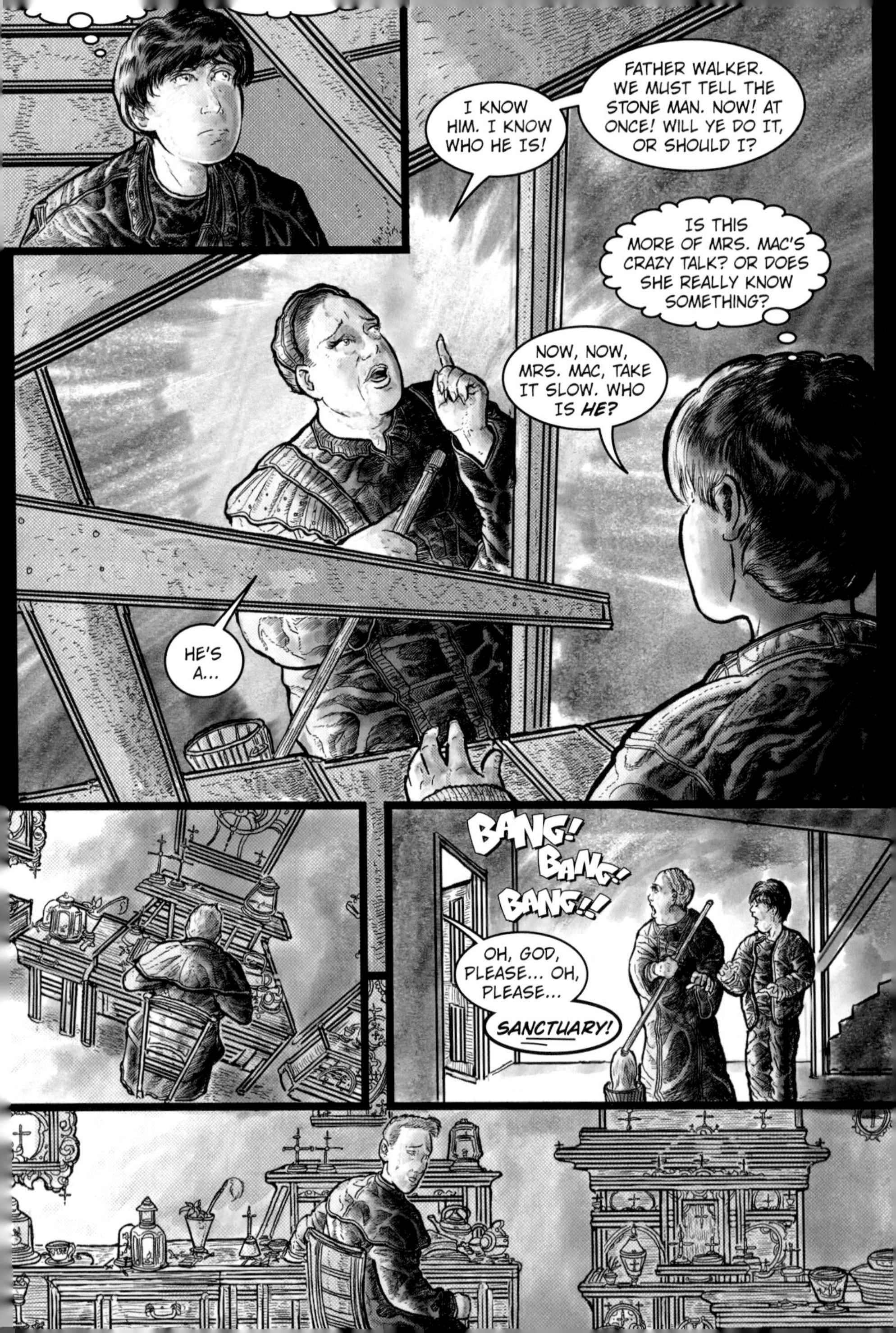
I KNOW HIM. I KNOW WHO HE IS!
FATHER WALKER. WE MUST TELL THE STONE MAN. NOW! AT ONCE! WILL YE DO IT, OR SHOULD I?
IS THIS MORE OF MRS. MAC'S CRAZY TALK? OR DOES SHE REALLY KNOW SOMETHING?
NOW, NOW, MRS. MAC, TAKE IT SLOW. WHO IS HE?
HE'S A...
BANG! BANG! BANG!!
OH, GOD, PLEASE... OH, PLEASE...
SANCTUARY!

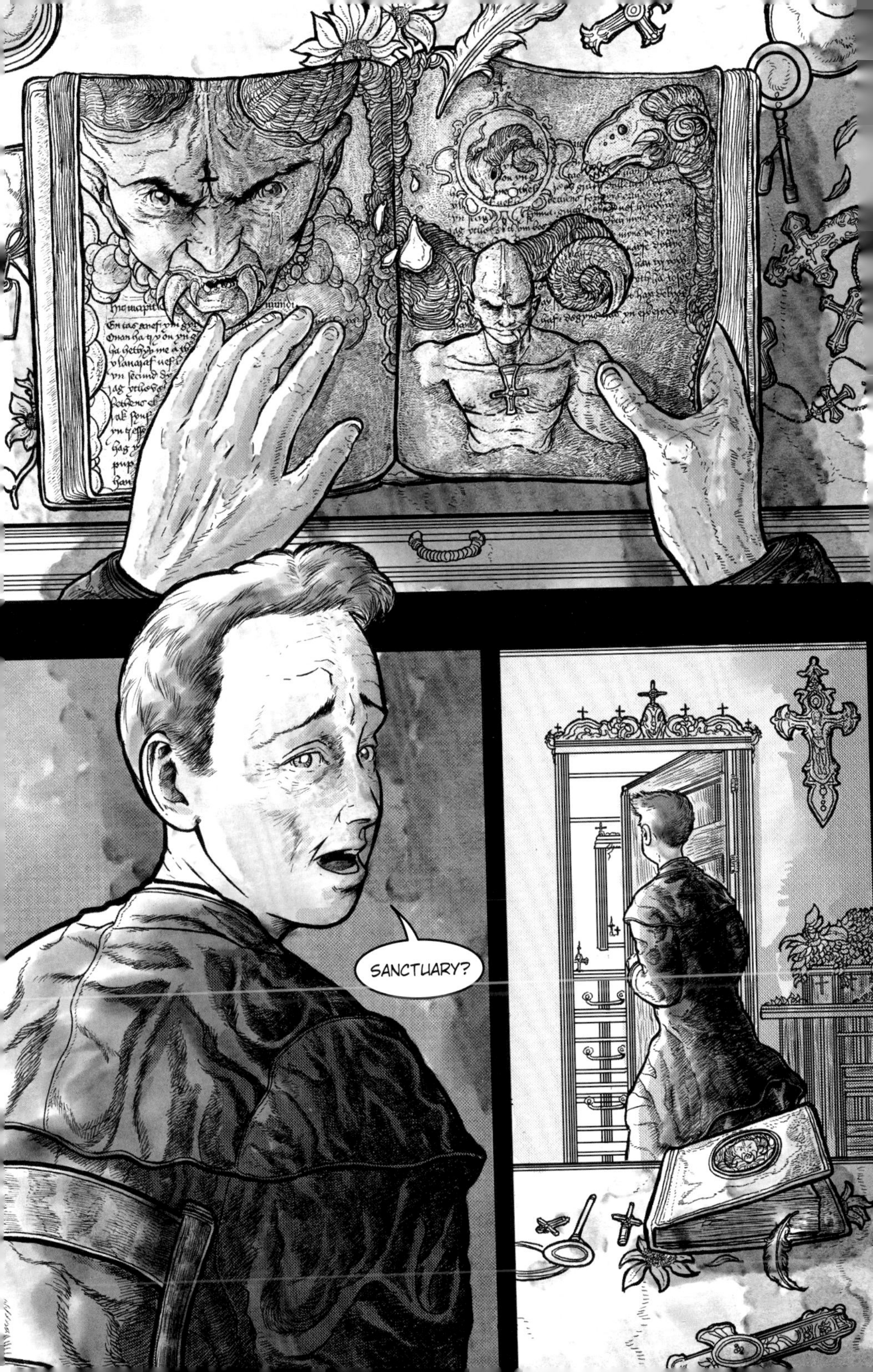
SANCTUARY?

CHAPTER 2
SANCTUARY LAW

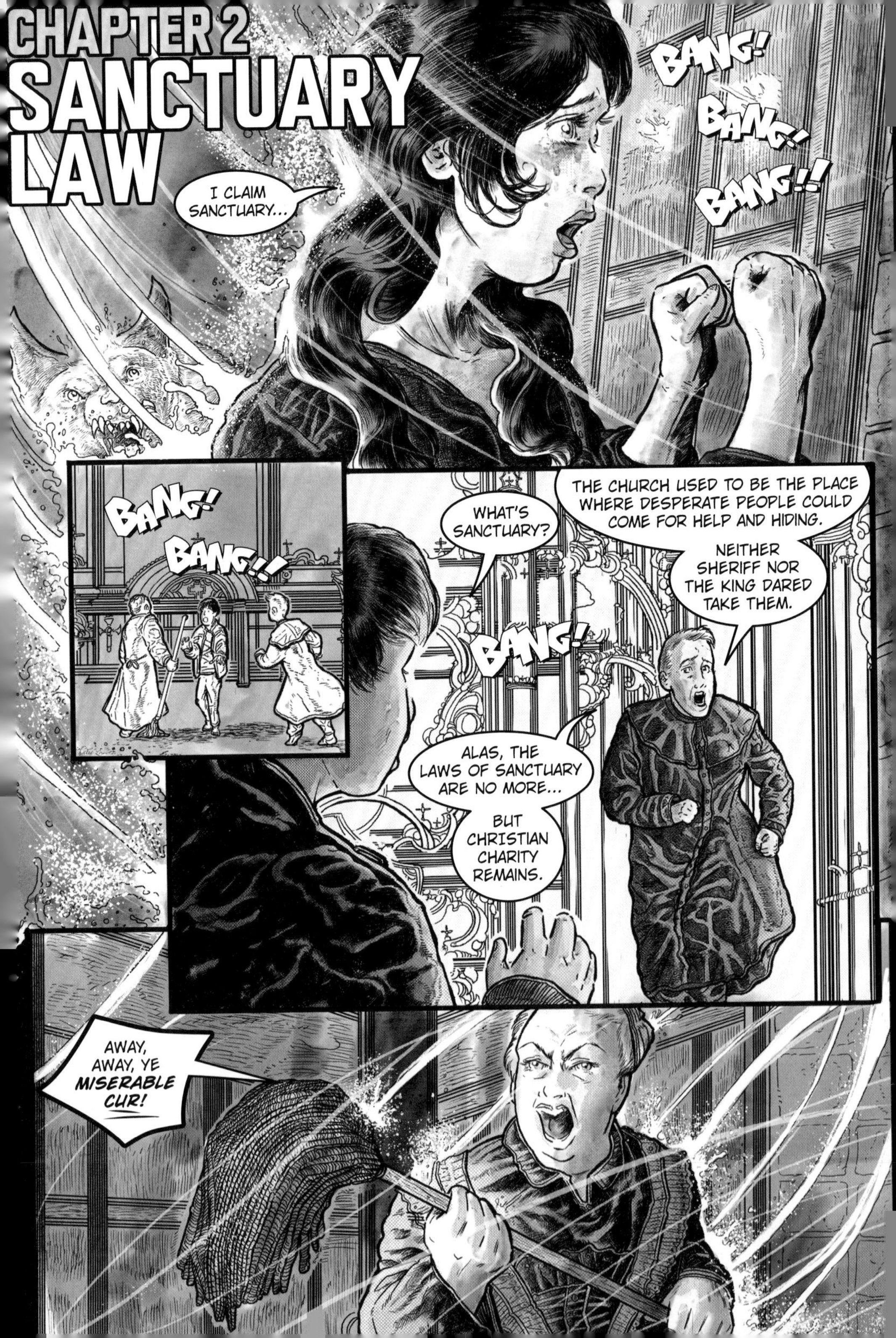

I CLAIM SANCTUARY...
BANG!
BANG!
BANG!!
BANG!
BANG!!
WHAT'S SANCTUARY?
THE CHURCH USED TO BE THE PLACE WHERE DESPERATE PEOPLE COULD COME FOR HELP AND HIDING.
NEITHER SHERIFF NOR THE KING DARED TAKE THEM.
BANG!
ALAS, THE LAWS OF SANCTUARY ARE NO MORE...
BUT CHRISTIAN CHARITY REMAINS.
AWAY, AWAY, YE *MISERABLE CUR!*

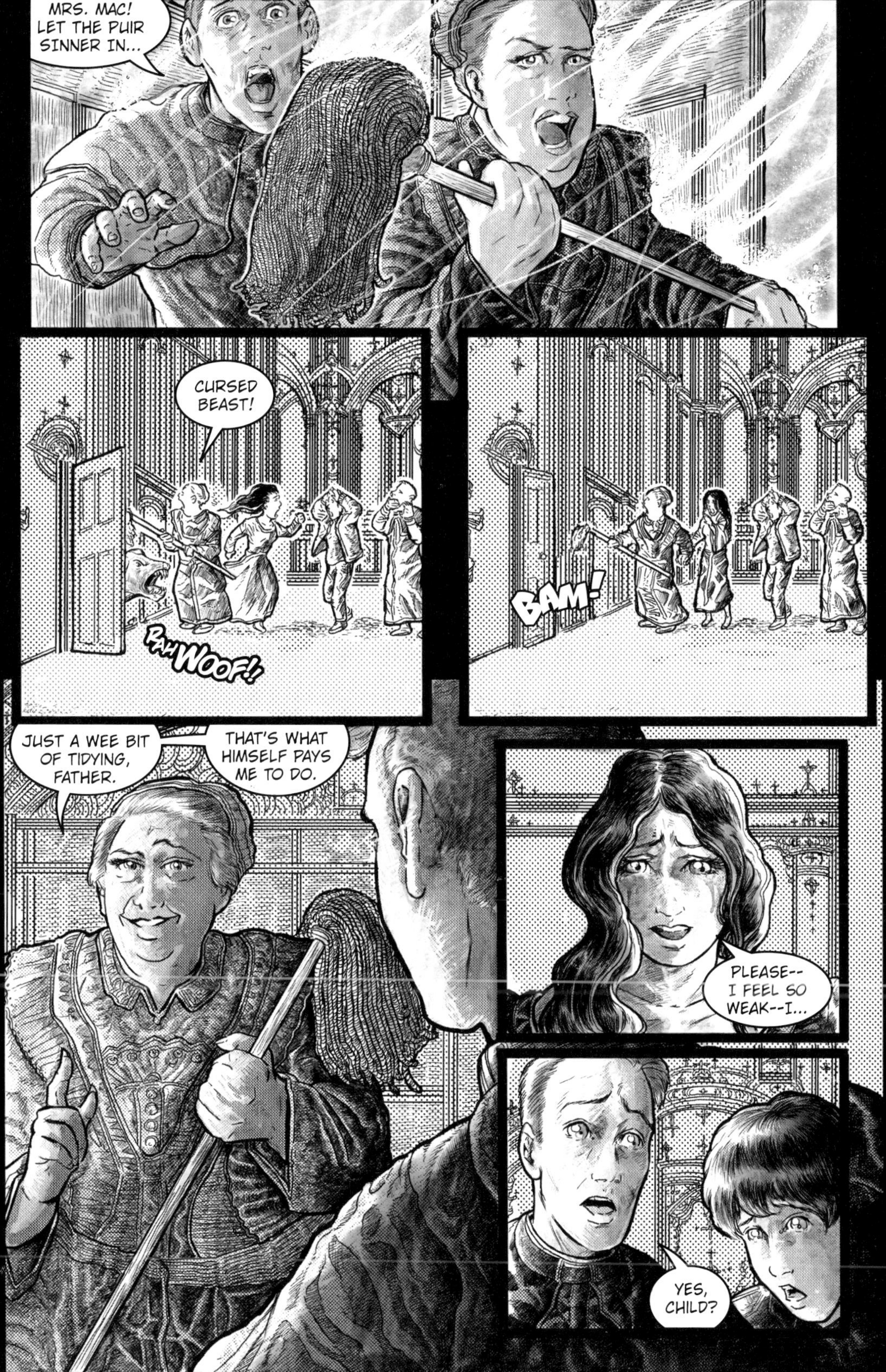
MRS. MAC! LET THE PUIR SINNER IN...
CURSED BEAST!
RAH WOOF!
BAM!
JUST A WEE BIT OF TIDYING, FATHER.
THAT'S WHAT HIMSELF PAYS ME TO DO.
PLEASE-- I FEEL SO WEAK--I...
YES, CHILD?

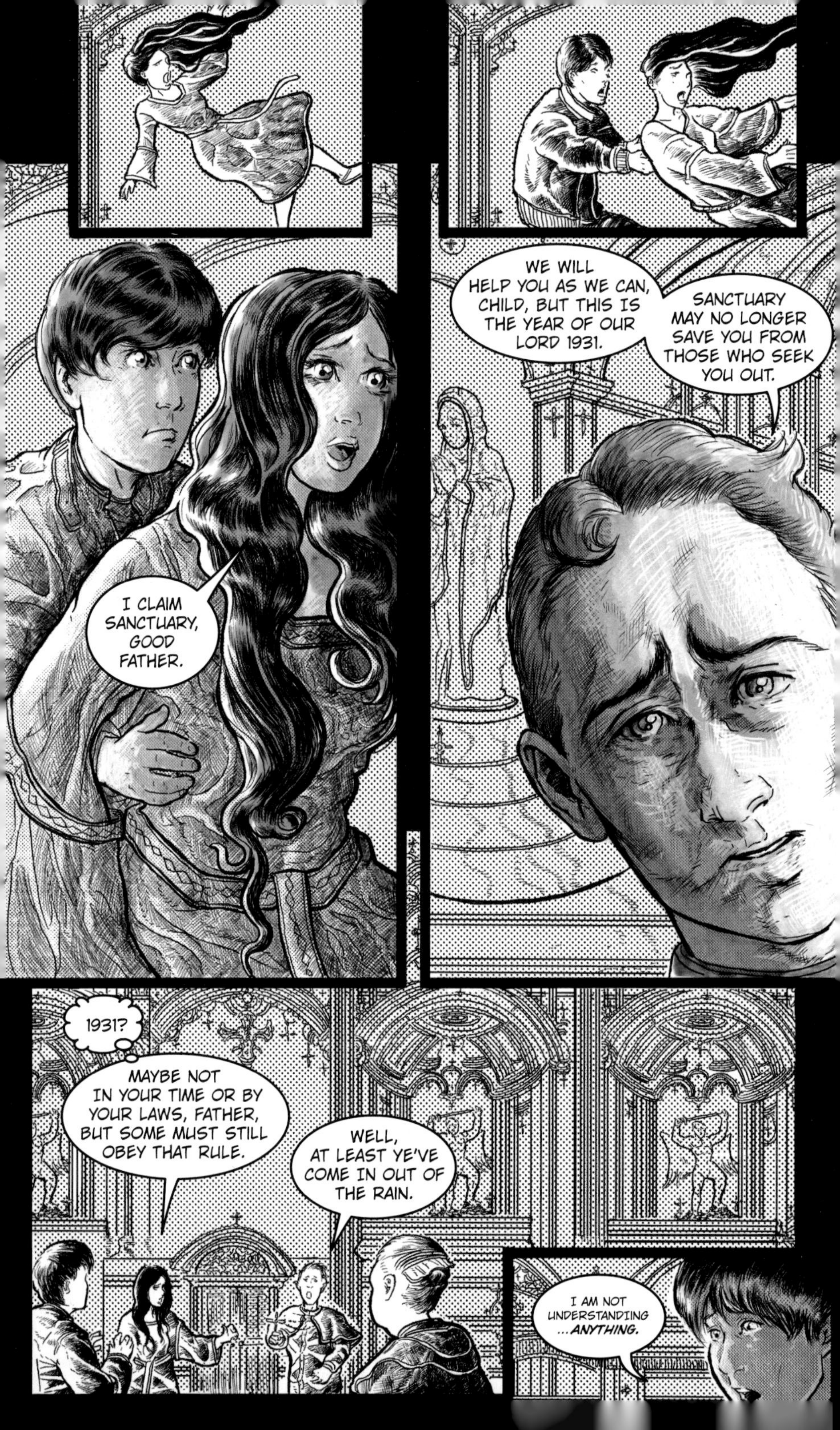
I CLAIM SANCTUARY, GOOD FATHER.
WE WILL HELP YOU AS WE CAN, CHILD, BUT THIS IS THE YEAR OF OUR LORD 1931.
SANCTUARY MAY NO LONGER SAVE YOU FROM THOSE WHO SEEK YOU OUT.
1931?
MAYBE NOT IN YOUR TIME OR BY YOUR LAWS, FATHER, BUT SOME MUST STILL OBEY THAT RULE.
WELL, AT LEAST YE'VE COME IN OUT OF THE RAIN.
I AM NOT UNDERSTANDING ...ANYTHING.

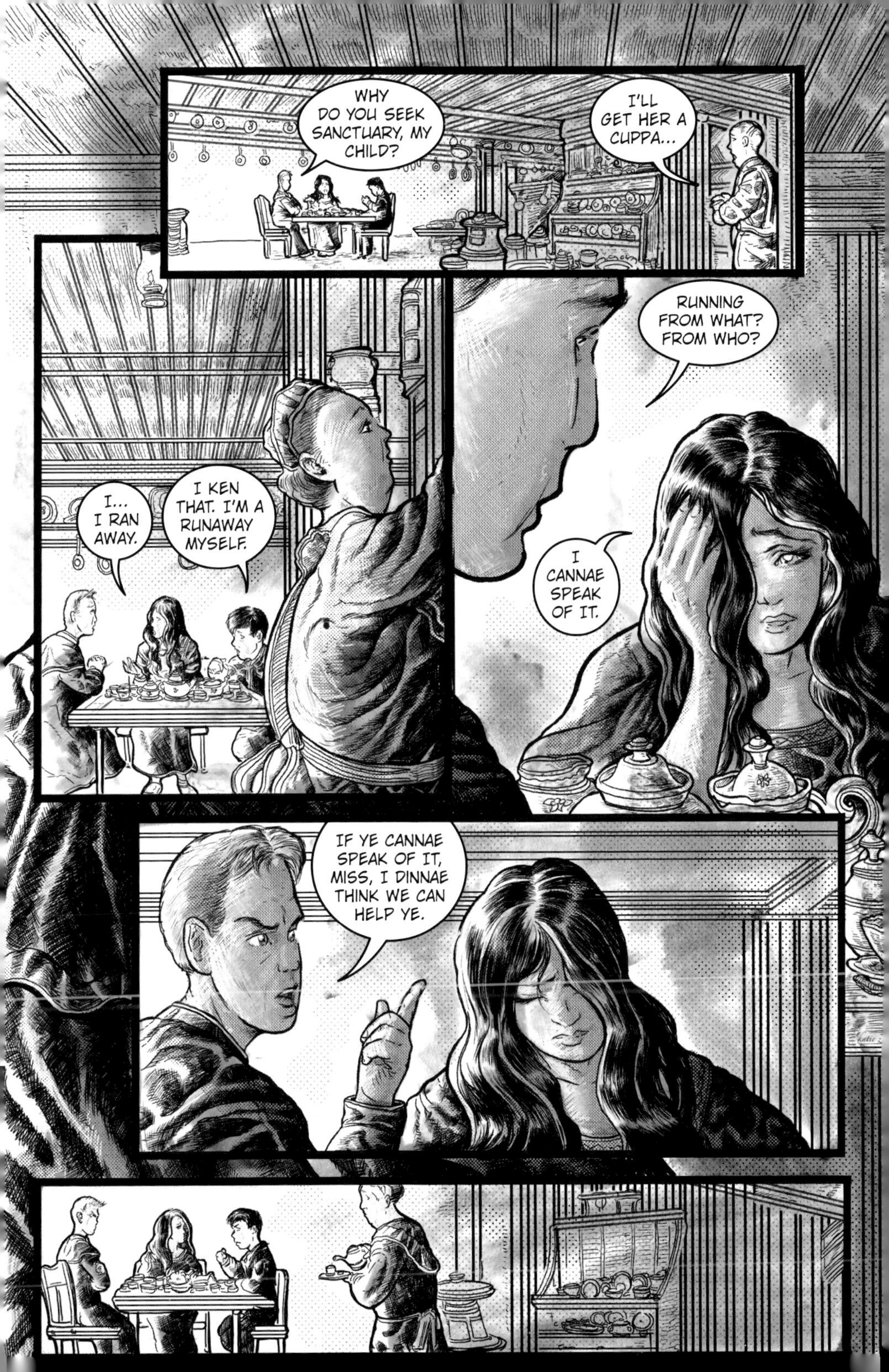
WHY DO YOU SEEK SANCTUARY, MY CHILD?
I'LL GET HER A CUPPA...
I... I RAN AWAY.
I KEN THAT. I'M A RUNAWAY MYSELF.
RUNNING FROM WHAT? FROM WHO?
I CANNAE SPEAK OF IT.
IF YE CANNAE SPEAK OF IT, MISS, I DINNAE THINK WE CAN HELP YE.

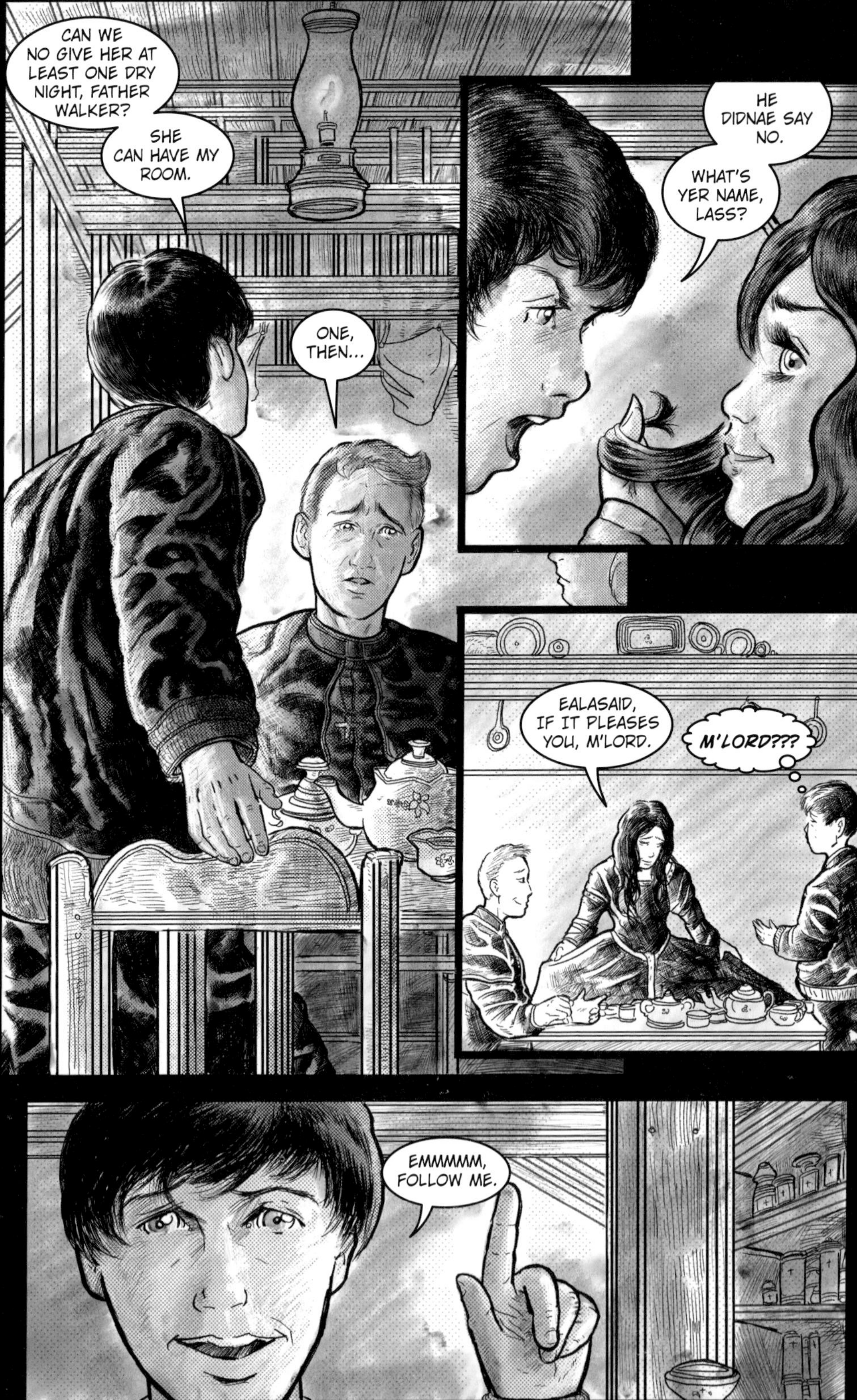
CAN WE NO GIVE HER AT LEAST ONE DRY NIGHT, FATHER WALKER?
SHE CAN HAVE MY ROOM.
ONE, THEN...
HE DIDNAE SAY NO.
WHAT'S YER NAME, LASS?
EALASAID, IF IT PLEASES YOU, M'LORD.
M'LORD???
EMMMMM, FOLLOW ME.

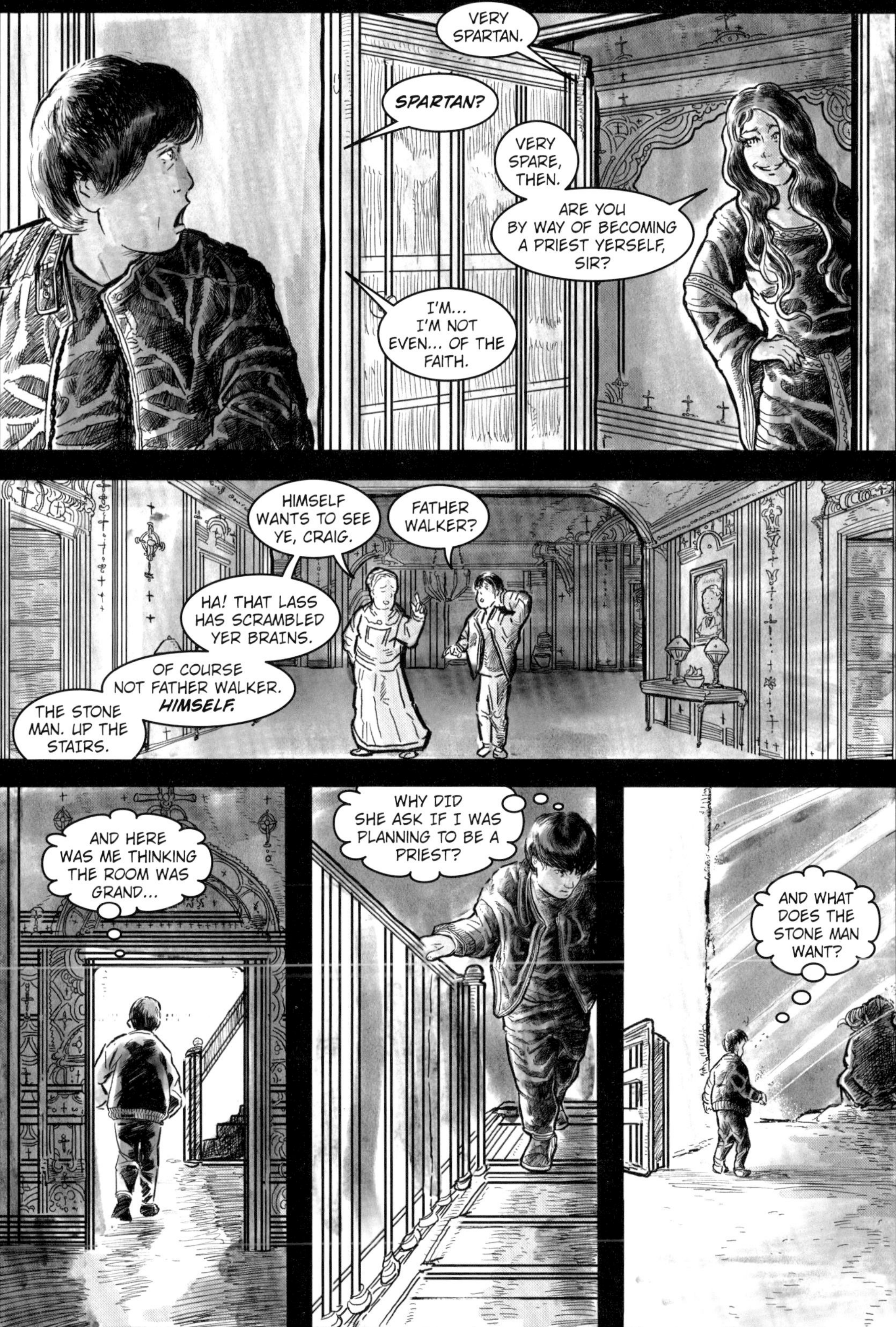
VERY SPARTAN.
SPARTAN?
VERY SPARE, THEN.
ARE YOU BY WAY OF BECOMING A PRIEST YERSELF, SIR?
I'M... I'M NOT EVEN... OF THE FAITH.
HIMSELF WANTS TO SEE YE, CRAIG.
FATHER WALKER?
HA! THAT LASS HAS SCRAMBLED YER BRAINS.
OF COURSE NOT FATHER WALKER. *HIMSELF.*
THE STONE MAN. UP THE STAIRS.
AND HERE WAS ME THINKING THE ROOM WAS GRAND...
WHY DID SHE ASK IF I WAS PLANNING TO BE A PRIEST?
AND WHAT DOES THE STONE MAN WANT?

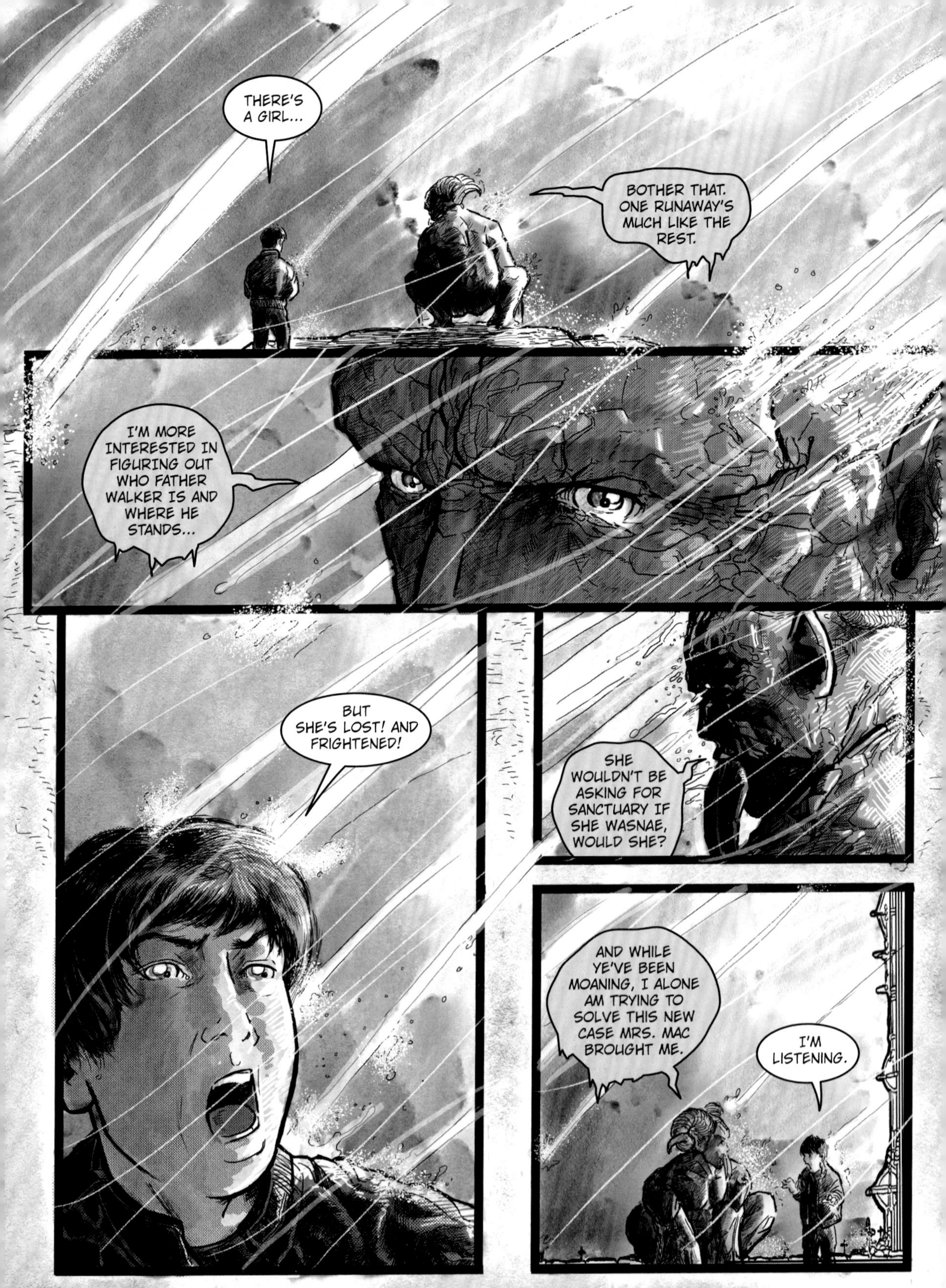
THERE'S A GIRL...
BOTHER THAT. ONE RUNAWAY'S MUCH LIKE THE REST.
I'M MORE INTERESTED IN FIGURING OUT WHO FATHER WALKER IS AND WHERE HE STANDS...
BUT SHE'S LOST! AND FRIGHTENED!
SHE WOULDN'T BE ASKING FOR SANCTUARY IF SHE WASNAE, WOULD SHE?
AND WHILE YE'VE BEEN MOANING, I ALONE AM TRYING TO SOLVE THIS NEW CASE MRS. MAC BROUGHT ME.
I'M LISTENING.

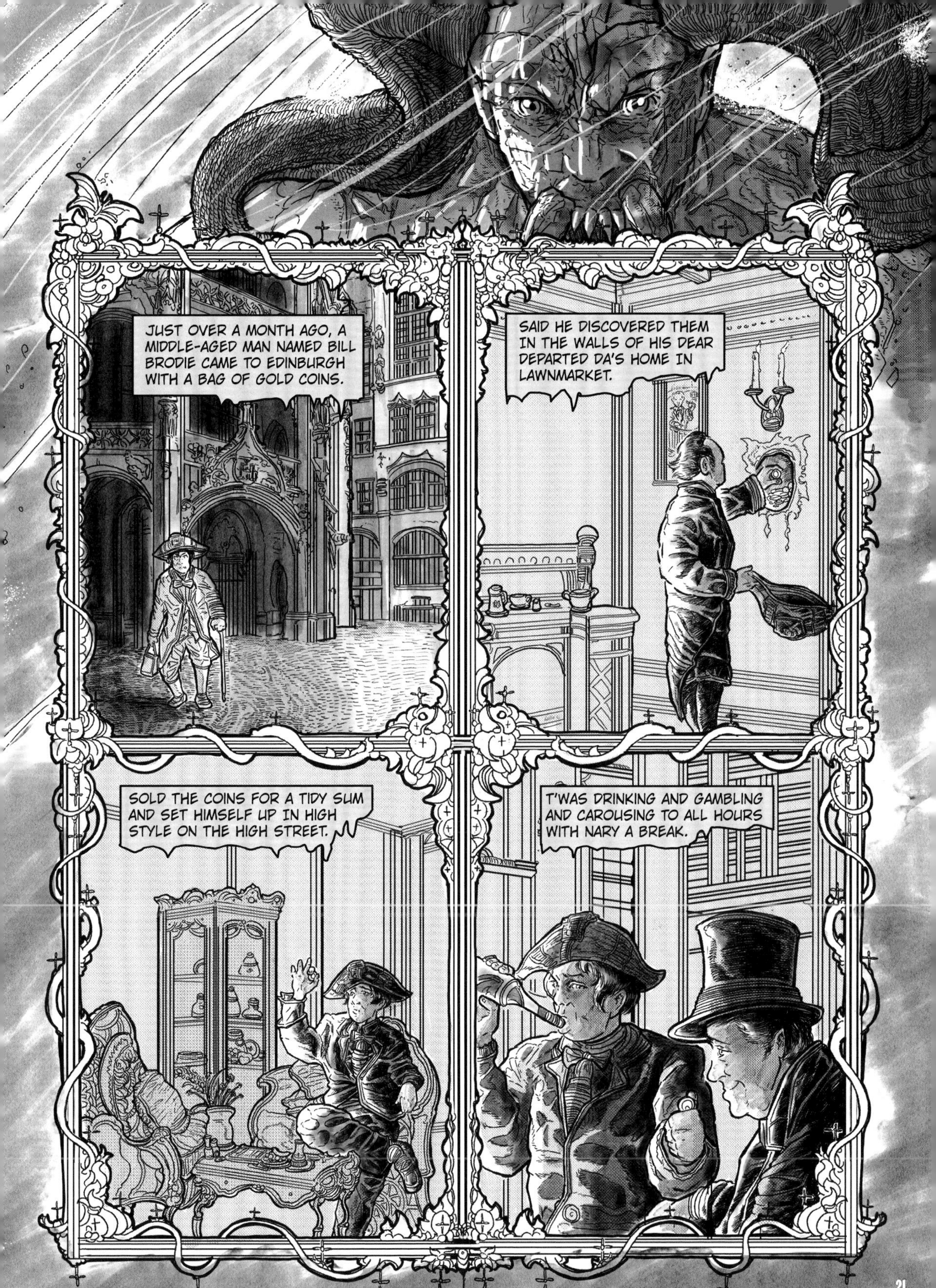
JUST OVER A MONTH AGO, A MIDDLE-AGED MAN NAMED BILL BRODIE CAME TO EDINBURGH WITH A BAG OF GOLD COINS.
SAID HE DISCOVERED THEM IN THE WALLS OF HIS DEAR DEPARTED DA'S HOME IN LAWNMARKET.
SOLD THE COINS FOR A TIDY SUM AND SET HIMSELF UP IN HIGH STYLE ON THE HIGH STREET.
T'WAS DRINKING AND GAMBLING AND CAROUSING TO ALL HOURS WITH NARY A BREAK.

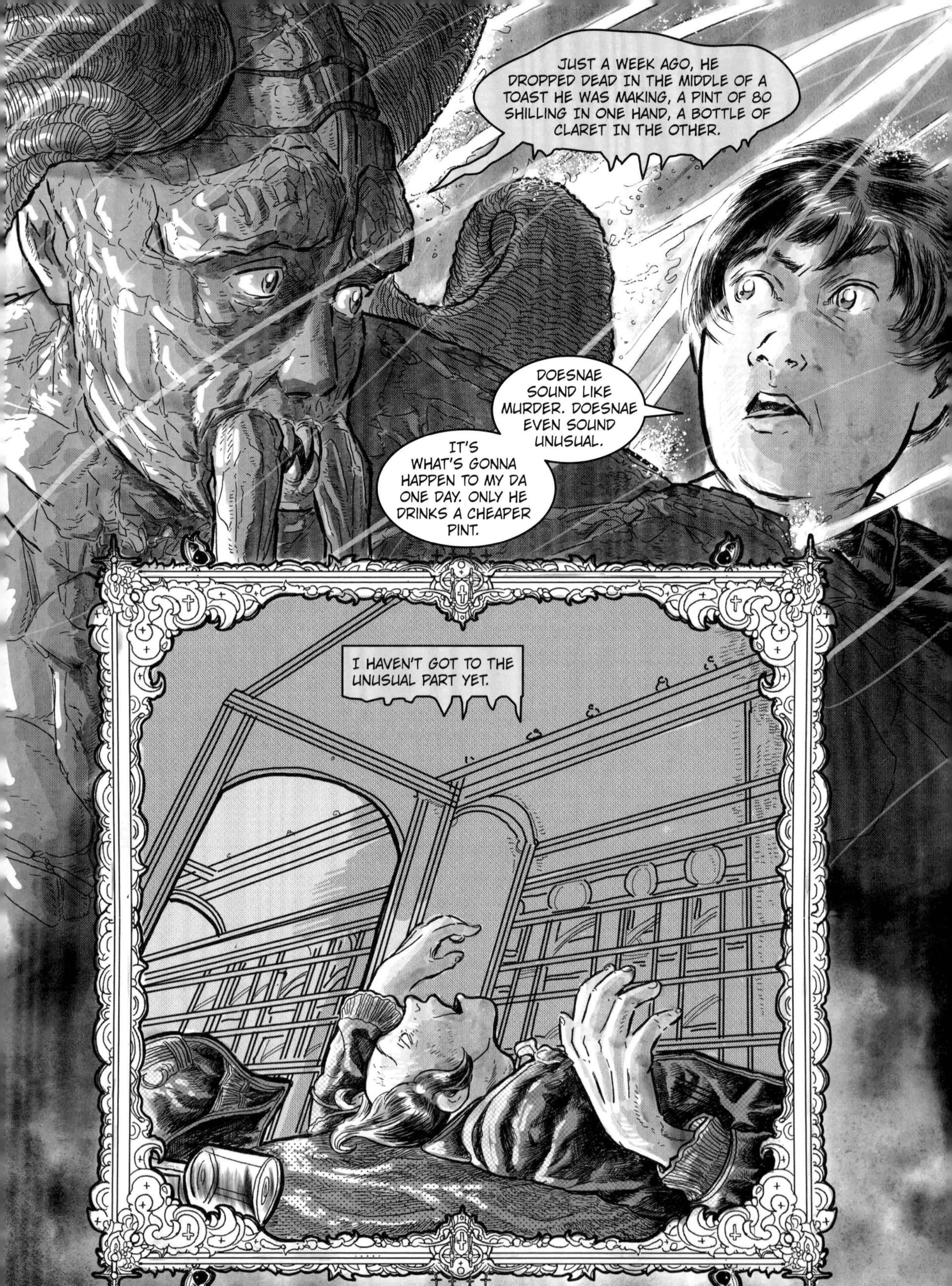
JUST A WEEK AGO, HE DROPPED DEAD IN THE MIDDLE OF A TOAST HE WAS MAKING, A PINT OF 80 SHILLING IN ONE HAND, A BOTTLE OF CLARET IN THE OTHER.
DOESNAE SOUND LIKE MURDER. DOESNAE EVEN SOUND UNUSUAL.
IT'S WHAT'S GONNA HAPPEN TO MY DA ONE DAY. ONLY HE DRINKS A CHEAPER PINT.
I HAVEN'T GOT TO THE UNUSUAL PART YET.

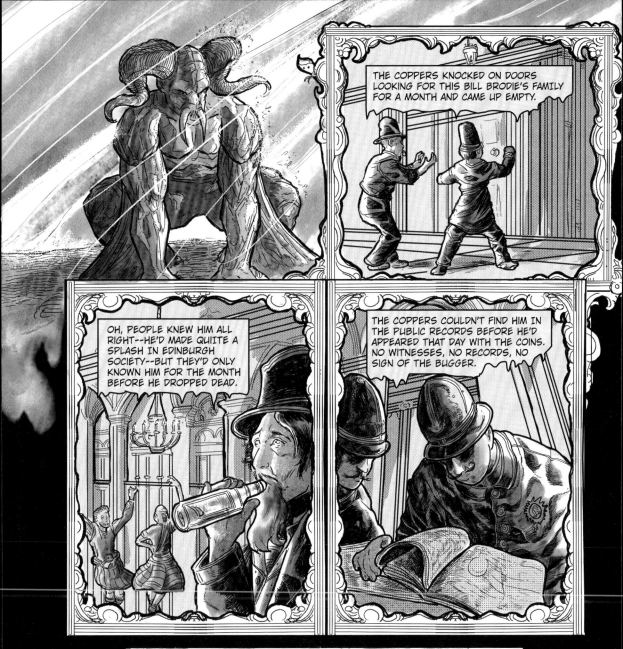

THE COPPERS KNOCKED ON DOORS LOOKING FOR THIS BILL BRODIE'S FAMILY FOR A MONTH AND CAME UP EMPTY.

OH, PEOPLE KNEW HIM ALL RIGHT--HE'D MADE QUITE A SPLASH IN EDINBURGH SOCIETY--BUT THEY'D ONLY KNOWN HIM FOR THE MONTH BEFORE HE DROPPED DEAD.

THE COPPERS COULDN'T FIND HIM IN THE PUBLIC RECORDS BEFORE HE'D APPEARED THAT DAY WITH THE COINS. NO WITNESSES, NO RECORDS, NO SIGN OF THE BUGGER.

SO DID THE COPPERS THINK THE NAME *BILL BRODIE* WAS A FAKE?

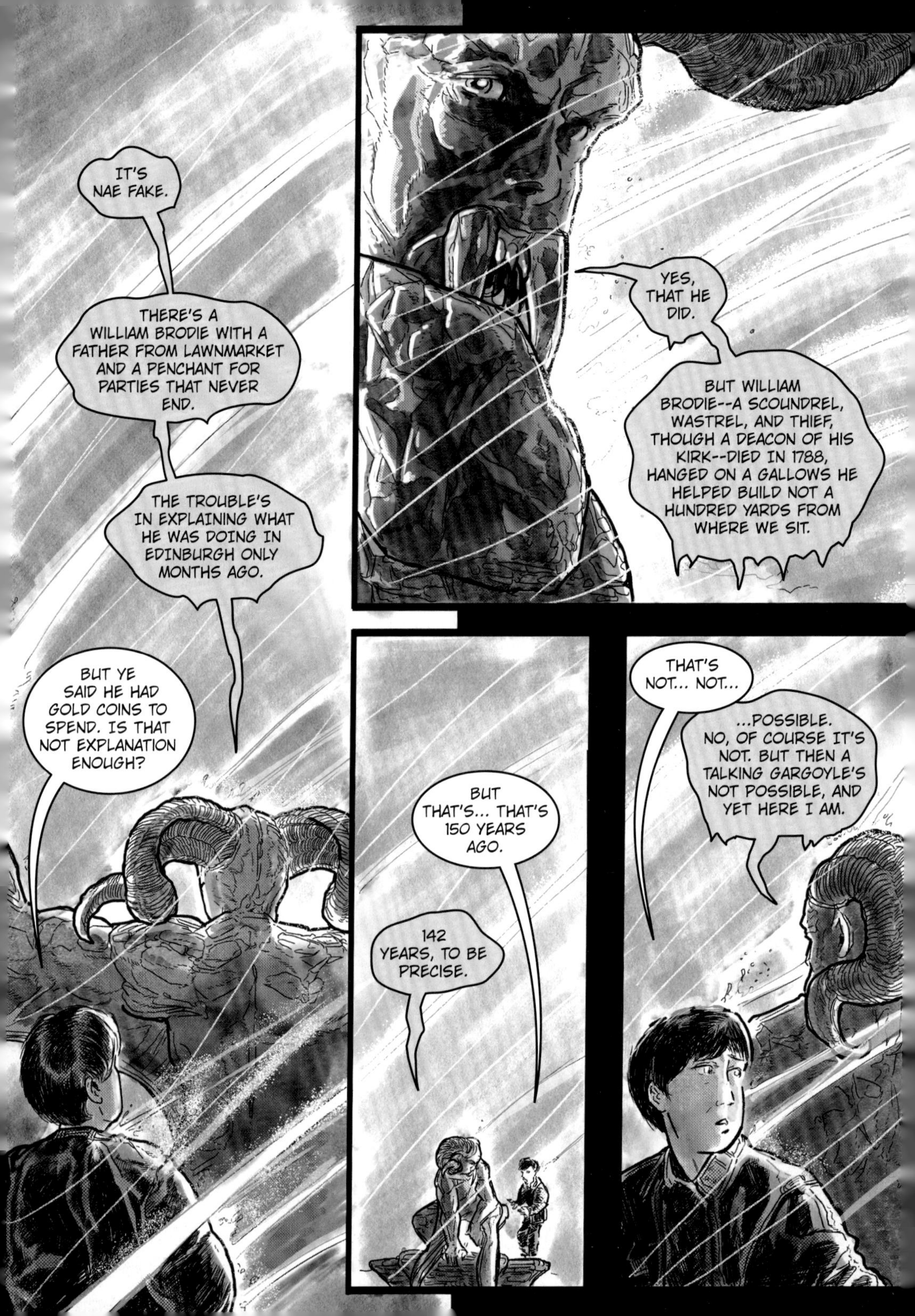
IT'S NAE FAKE.
THERE'S A WILLIAM BRODIE WITH A FATHER FROM LAWNMARKET AND A PENCHANT FOR PARTIES THAT NEVER END.
THE TROUBLE'S IN EXPLAINING WHAT HE WAS DOING IN EDINBURGH ONLY MONTHS AGO.
YES, THAT HE DID.
BUT WILLIAM BRODIE--A SCOUNDREL, WASTREL, AND THIEF, THOUGH A DEACON OF HIS KIRK--DIED IN 1788, HANGED ON A GALLOWS HE HELPED BUILD NOT A HUNDRED YARDS FROM WHERE WE SIT.
BUT YE SAID HE HAD GOLD COINS TO SPEND. IS THAT NOT EXPLANATION ENOUGH?
BUT THAT'S... THAT'S 150 YEARS AGO.
142 YEARS, TO BE PRECISE.
THAT'S NOT... NOT...
...POSSIBLE. NO, OF COURSE IT'S NOT. BUT THEN A TALKING GARGOYLE'S NOT POSSIBLE, AND YET HERE I AM.

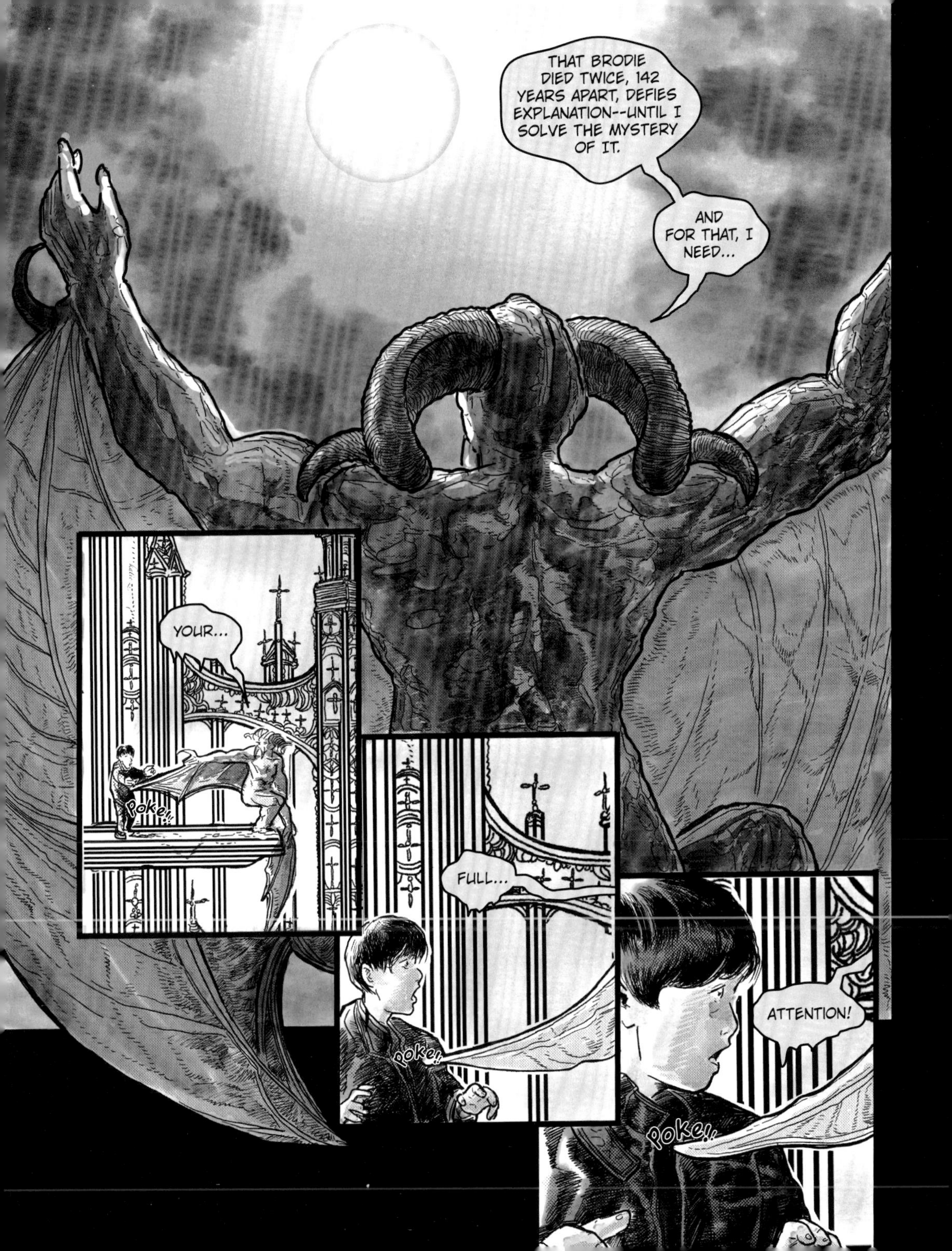
THAT BRODIE DIED TWICE, 142 YEARS APART, DEFIES EXPLANATION--UNTIL I SOLVE THE MYSTERY OF IT.
AND FOR THAT, I NEED...
YOUR...
POKE!!
FULL...
POKE!!
ATTENTION!
POKE!!

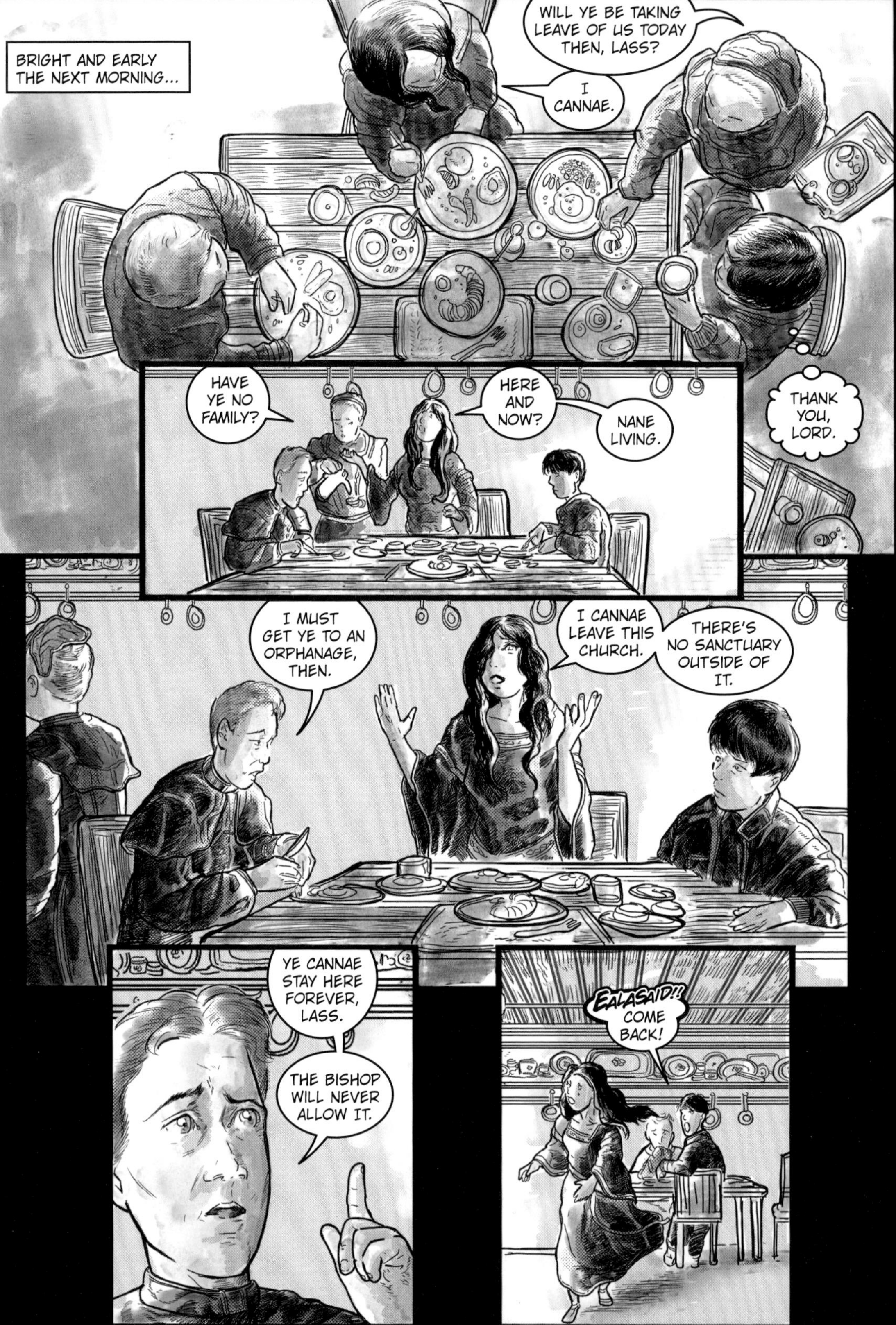
BRIGHT AND EARLY THE NEXT MORNING...
WILL YE BE TAKING LEAVE OF US TODAY THEN, LASS?
I CANNAE.
THANK YOU, LORD.
HAVE YE NO FAMILY?
HERE AND NOW?
NANE LIVING.
I MUST GET YE TO AN ORPHANAGE, THEN.
I CANNAE LEAVE THIS CHURCH.
THERE'S NO SANCTUARY OUTSIDE OF IT.
YE CANNAE STAY HERE FOREVER, LASS.
THE BISHOP WILL NEVER ALLOW IT.
EALASAID!! COME BACK!

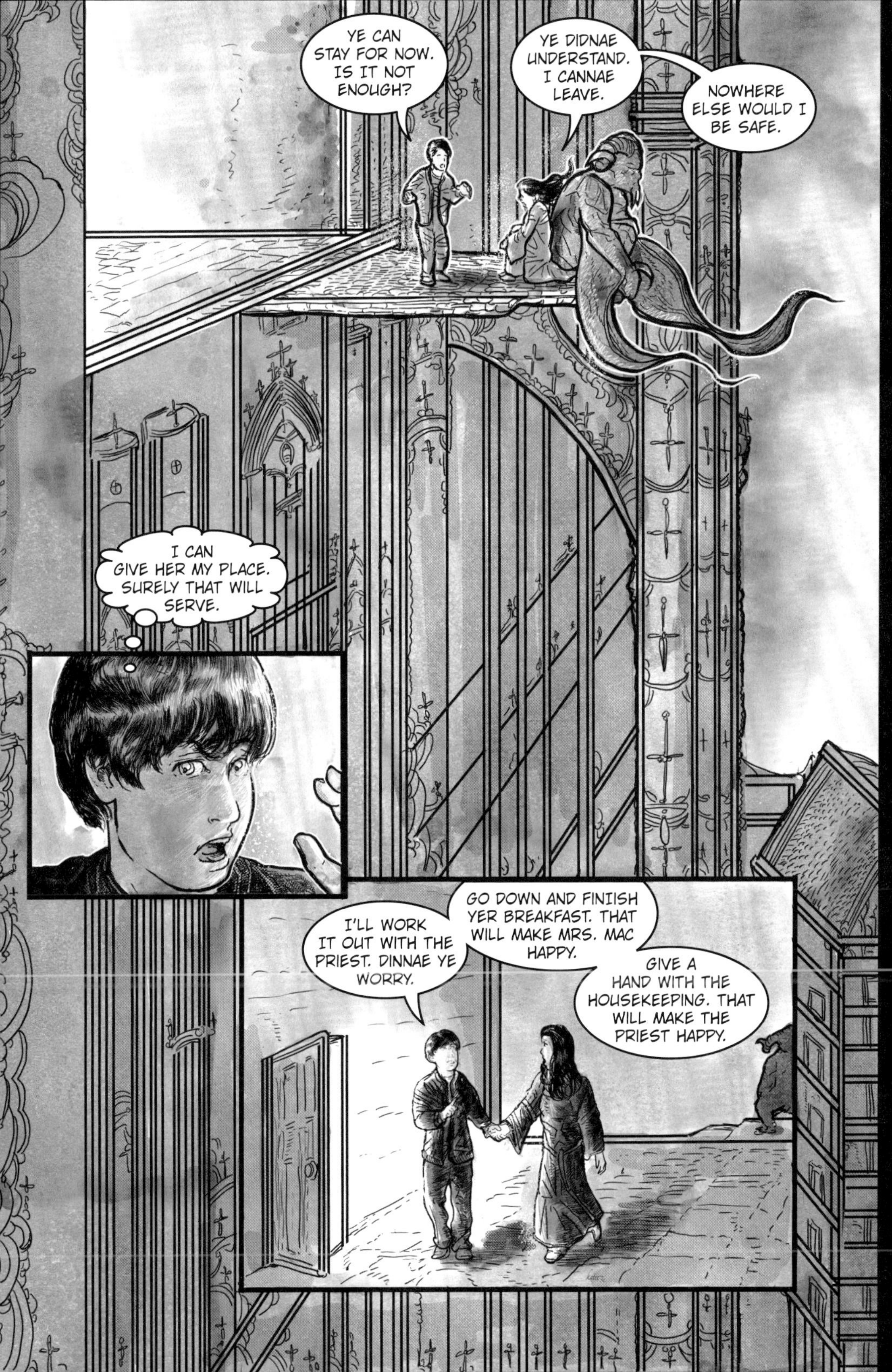
YE CAN STAY FOR NOW. IS IT NOT ENOUGH?
YE DIDNAE UNDERSTAND. I CANNAE LEAVE.
NOWHERE ELSE WOULD I BE SAFE.
I CAN GIVE HER MY PLACE. SURELY THAT WILL SERVE.
I'LL WORK IT OUT WITH THE PRIEST. DINNAE YE WORRY.
GO DOWN AND FINISH YER BREAKFAST. THAT WILL MAKE MRS. MAC HAPPY.
GIVE A HAND WITH THE HOUSEKEEPING. THAT WILL MAKE THE PRIEST HAPPY.

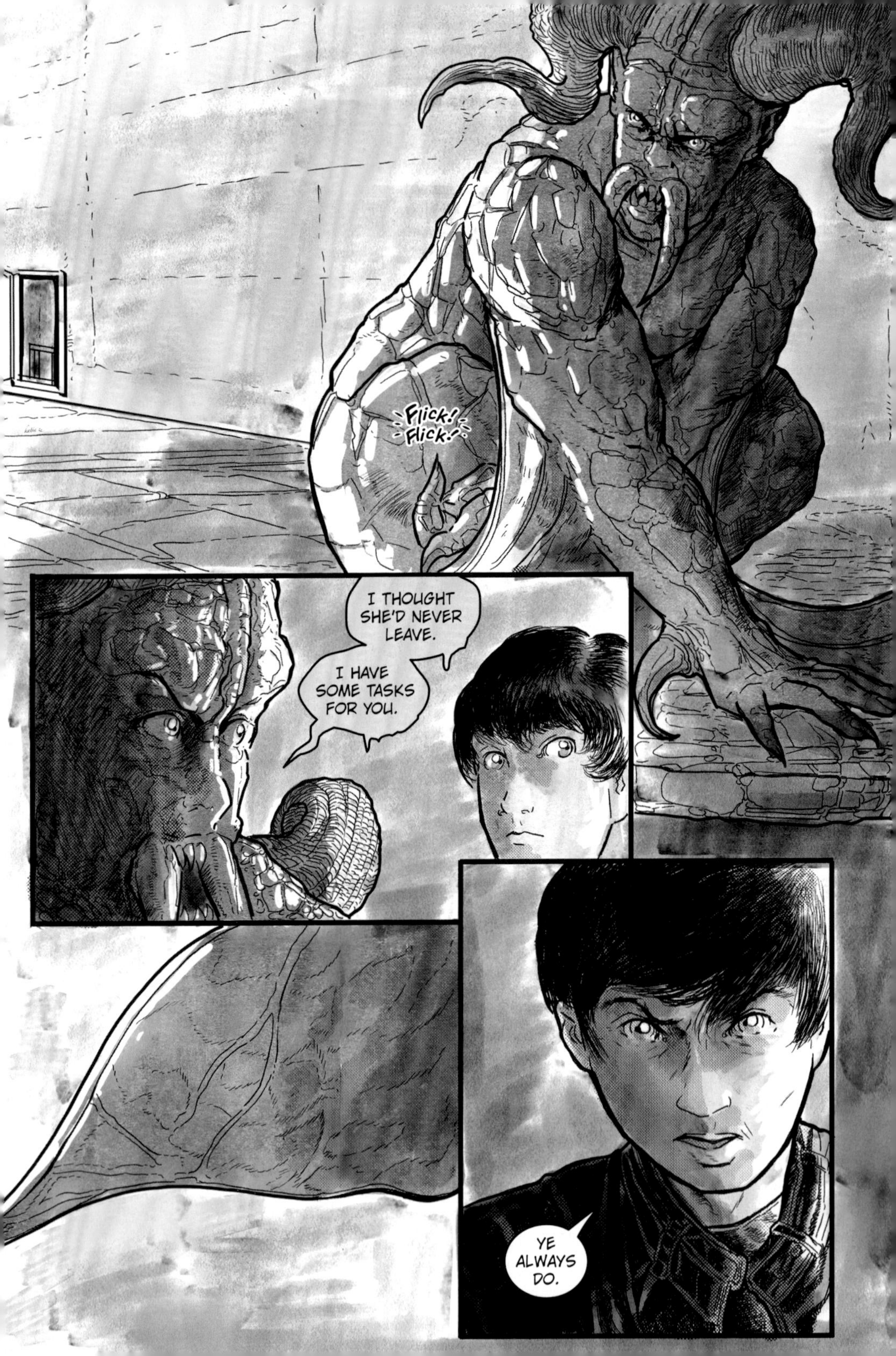

FLICK! FLICK!
I THOUGHT SHE'D NEVER LEAVE.
I HAVE SOME TASKS FOR YOU.
YE ALWAYS DO.

CHAPTER 3 GATHERING INFORMATION

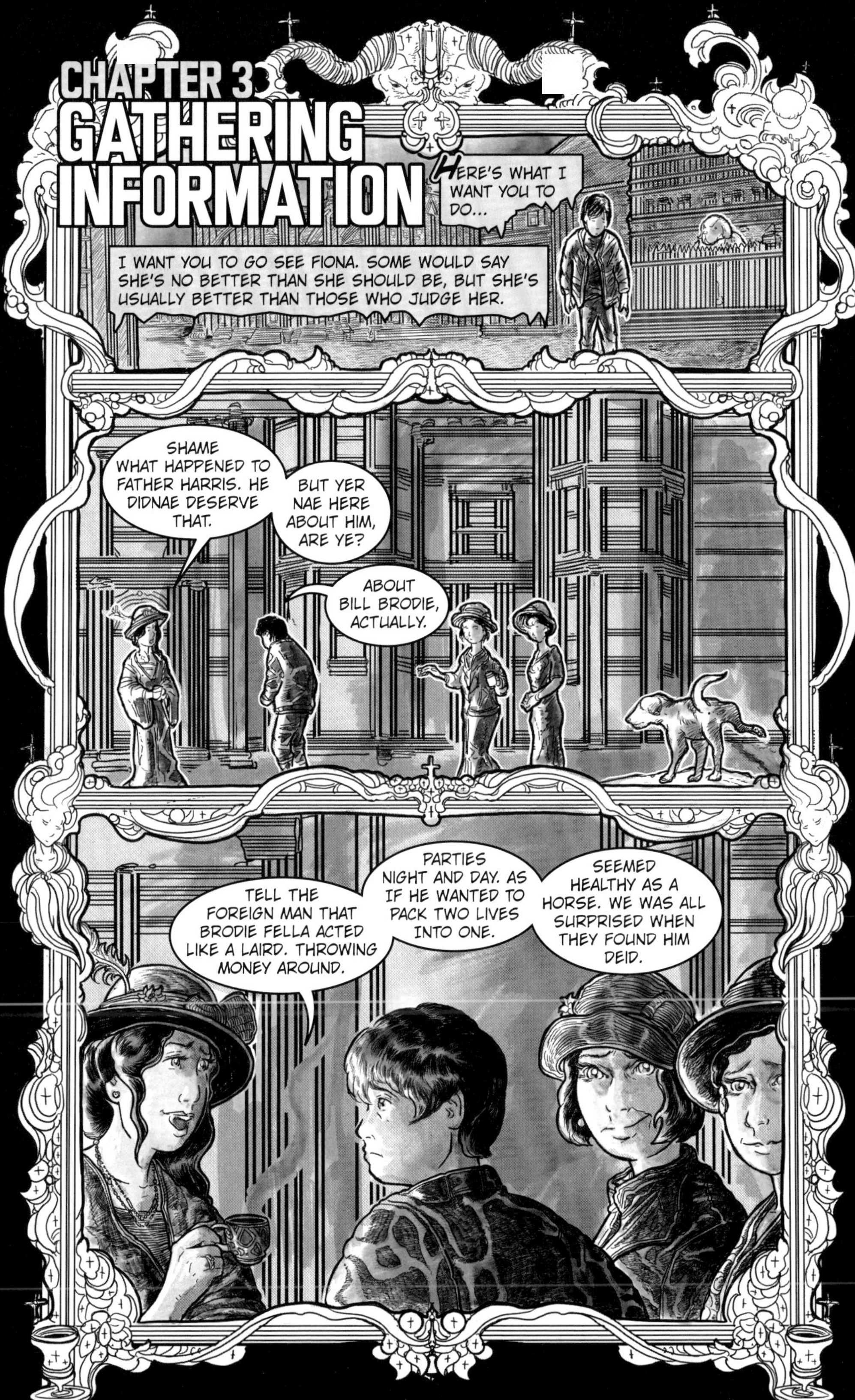

HERE'S WHAT I WANT YOU TO DO...
I WANT YOU TO GO SEE FIONA. SOME WOULD SAY SHE'S NO BETTER THAN SHE SHOULD BE, BUT SHE'S USUALLY BETTER THAN THOSE WHO JUDGE HER.
SHAME WHAT HAPPENED TO FATHER HARRIS. HE DIDNAE DESERVE THAT.
BUT YER NAE HERE ABOUT HIM, ARE YE?
ABOUT BILL BRODIE, ACTUALLY.
TELL THE FOREIGN MAN THAT BRODIE FELLA ACTED LIKE A LAIRD. THROWING MONEY AROUND.
PARTIES NIGHT AND DAY. AS IF HE WANTED TO PACK TWO LIVES INTO ONE.
SEEMED HEALTHY AS A HORSE. WE WAS ALL SURPRISED WHEN THEY FOUND HIM DEID.

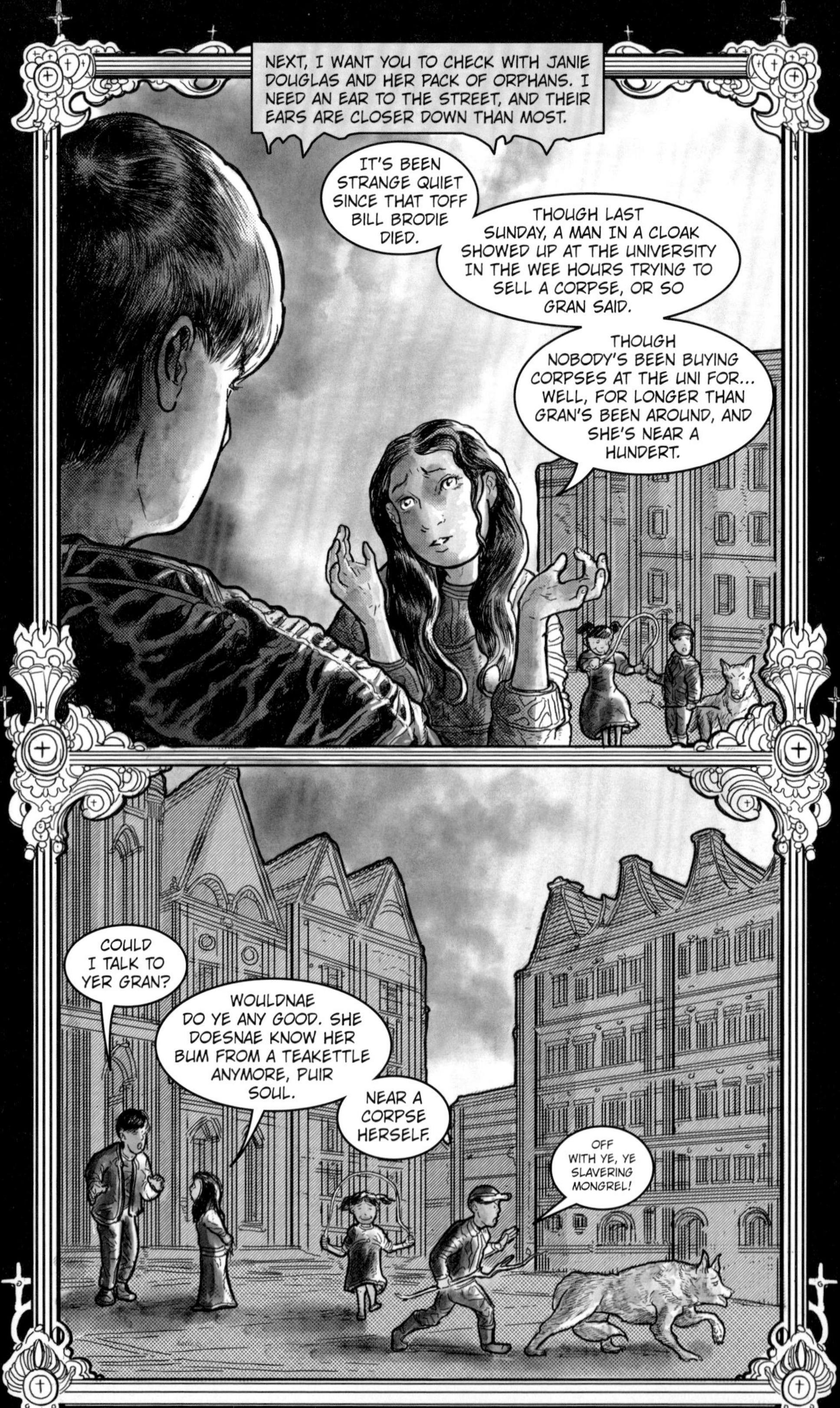
NEXT, I WANT YOU TO CHECK WITH JANIE DOUGLAS AND HER PACK OF ORPHANS. I NEED AN EAR TO THE STREET, AND THEIR EARS ARE CLOSER DOWN THAN MOST.
IT'S BEEN STRANGE QUIET SINCE THAT TOFF BILL BRODIE DIED.
THOUGH LAST SUNDAY, A MAN IN A CLOAK SHOWED UP AT THE UNIVERSITY IN THE WEE HOURS TRYING TO SELL A CORPSE, OR SO GRAN SAID.
THOUGH NOBODY'S BEEN BUYING CORPSES AT THE UNI FOR... WELL, FOR LONGER THAN GRAN'S BEEN AROUND, AND SHE'S NEAR A HUNDERT.
COULD I TALK TO YER GRAN?
WOULDNAE DO YE ANY GOOD. SHE DOESNAE KNOW HER BUM FROM A TEAKETTLE ANYMORE, PUIR SOUL.
NEAR A CORPSE HERSELF.
OFF WITH YE, YE SLAVERING MONGREL!

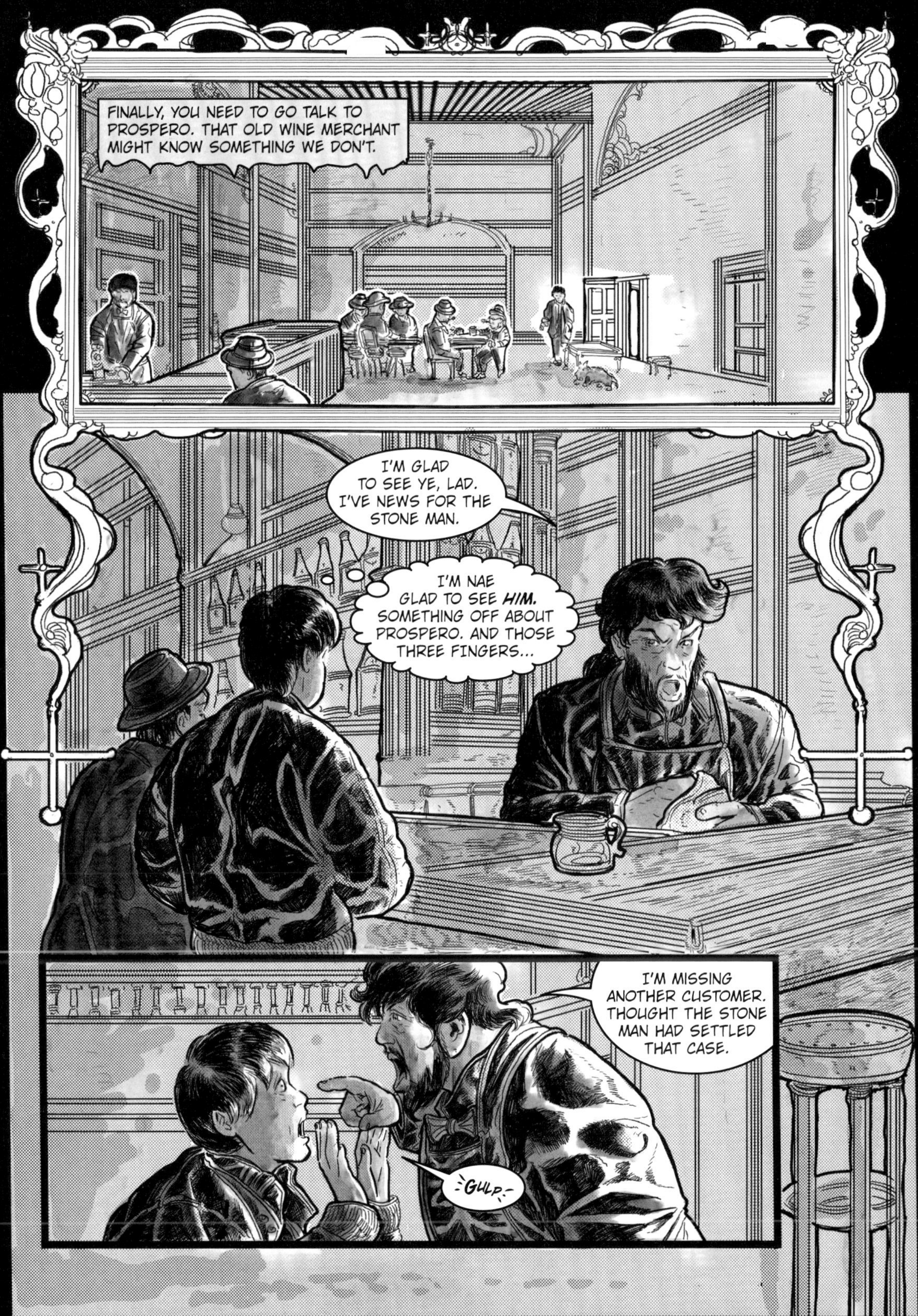

FINALLY, YOU NEED TO GO TALK TO PROSPERO. THAT OLD WINE MERCHANT MIGHT KNOW SOMETHING WE DON'T.
I'M GLAD TO SEE YE, LAD. I'VE NEWS FOR THE STONE MAN.
I'M NAE GLAD TO SEE ***HIM.*** SOMETHING OFF ABOUT PROSPERO. AND THOSE THREE FINGERS...
I'M MISSING ANOTHER CUSTOMER. THOUGHT THE STONE MAN HAD SETTLED THAT CASE.
GULP

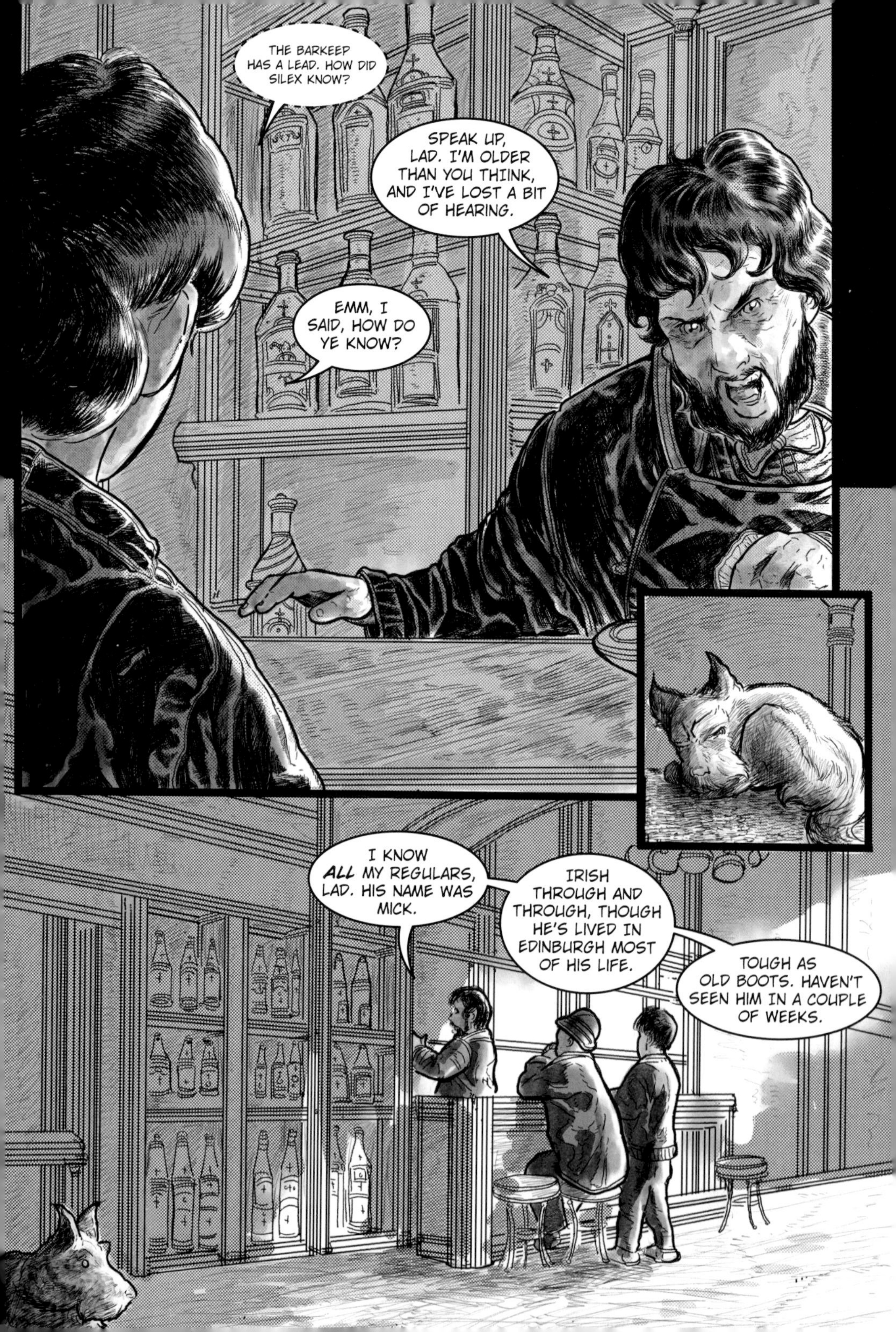
THE BARKEEP HAS A LEAD. HOW DID SILEX KNOW?
SPEAK UP, LAD. I'M OLDER THAN YOU THINK, AND I'VE LOST A BIT OF HEARING.
EMM, I SAID, HOW DO YE KNOW?
I KNOW ALL MY REGULARS, LAD. HIS NAME WAS MICK.
IRISH THROUGH AND THROUGH, THOUGH HE'S LIVED IN EDINBURGH MOST OF HIS LIFE.
TOUGH AS OLD BOOTS. HAVEN'T SEEN HIM IN A COUPLE OF WEEKS.

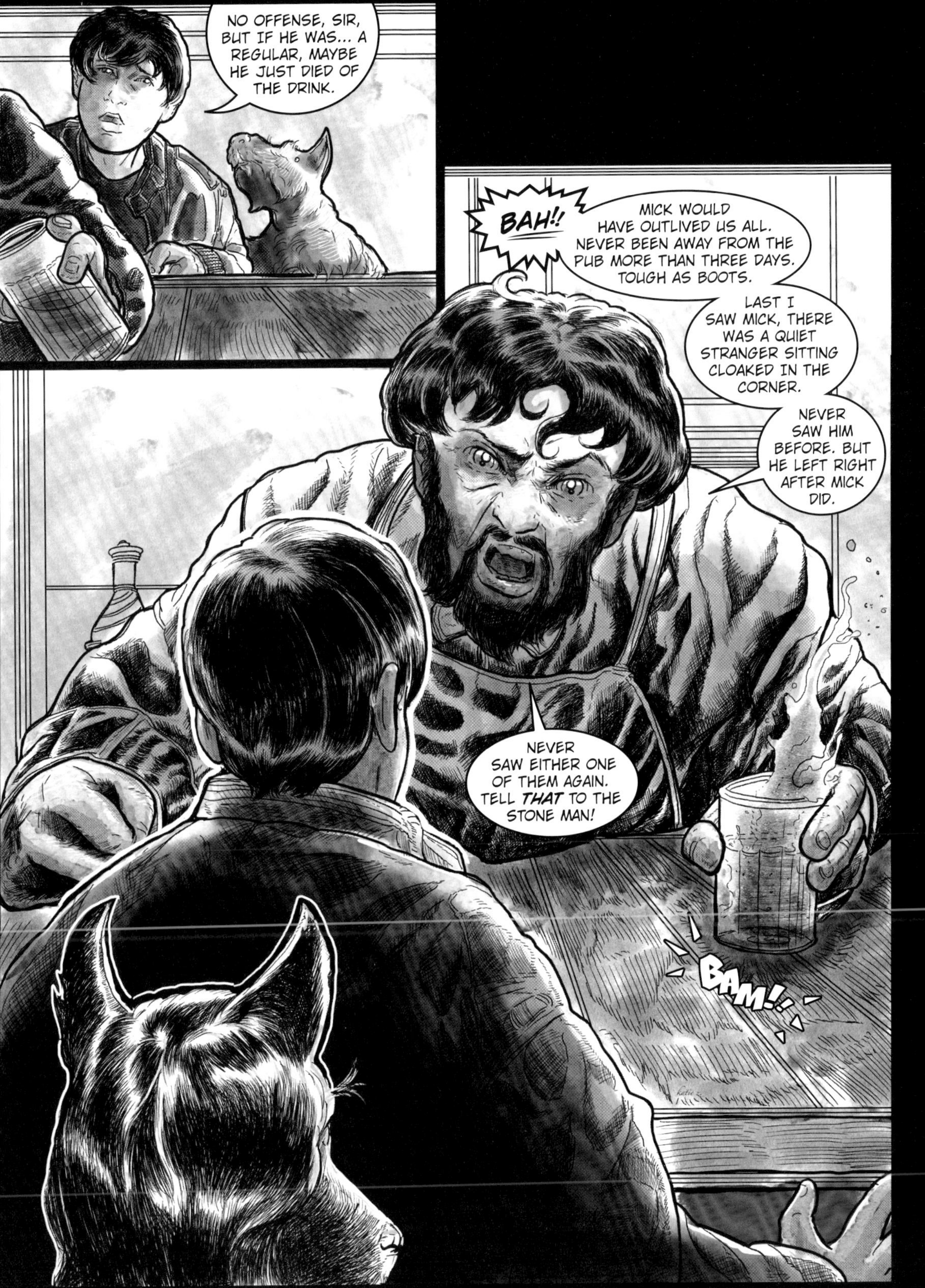
NO OFFENSE, SIR, BUT IF HE WAS... A REGULAR, MAYBE HE JUST DIED OF THE DRINK.
BAH!!
MICK WOULD HAVE OUTLIVED US ALL. NEVER BEEN AWAY FROM THE PUB MORE THAN THREE DAYS. TOUGH AS BOOTS.
LAST I SAW MICK, THERE WAS A QUIET STRANGER SITTING CLOAKED IN THE CORNER.
NEVER SAW HIM BEFORE. BUT HE LEFT RIGHT AFTER MICK DID.
NEVER SAW EITHER ONE OF THEM AGAIN. TELL *THAT* TO THE STONE MAN!
BAM!!

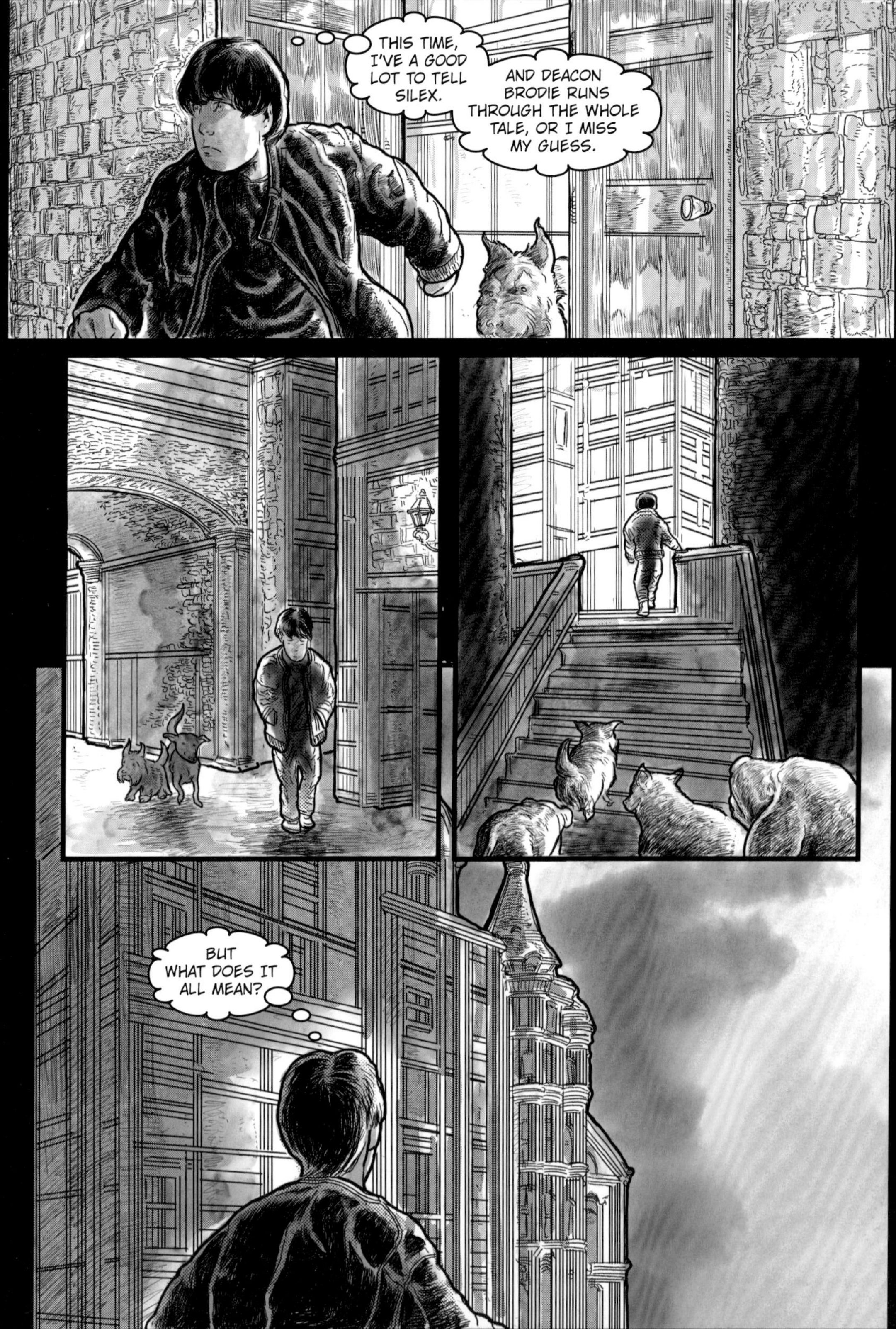
THIS TIME, I'VE A GOOD LOT TO TELL SILEX.
AND DEACON BRODIE RUNS THROUGH THE WHOLE TALE, OR I MISS MY GUESS.
BUT WHAT DOES IT ALL MEAN?

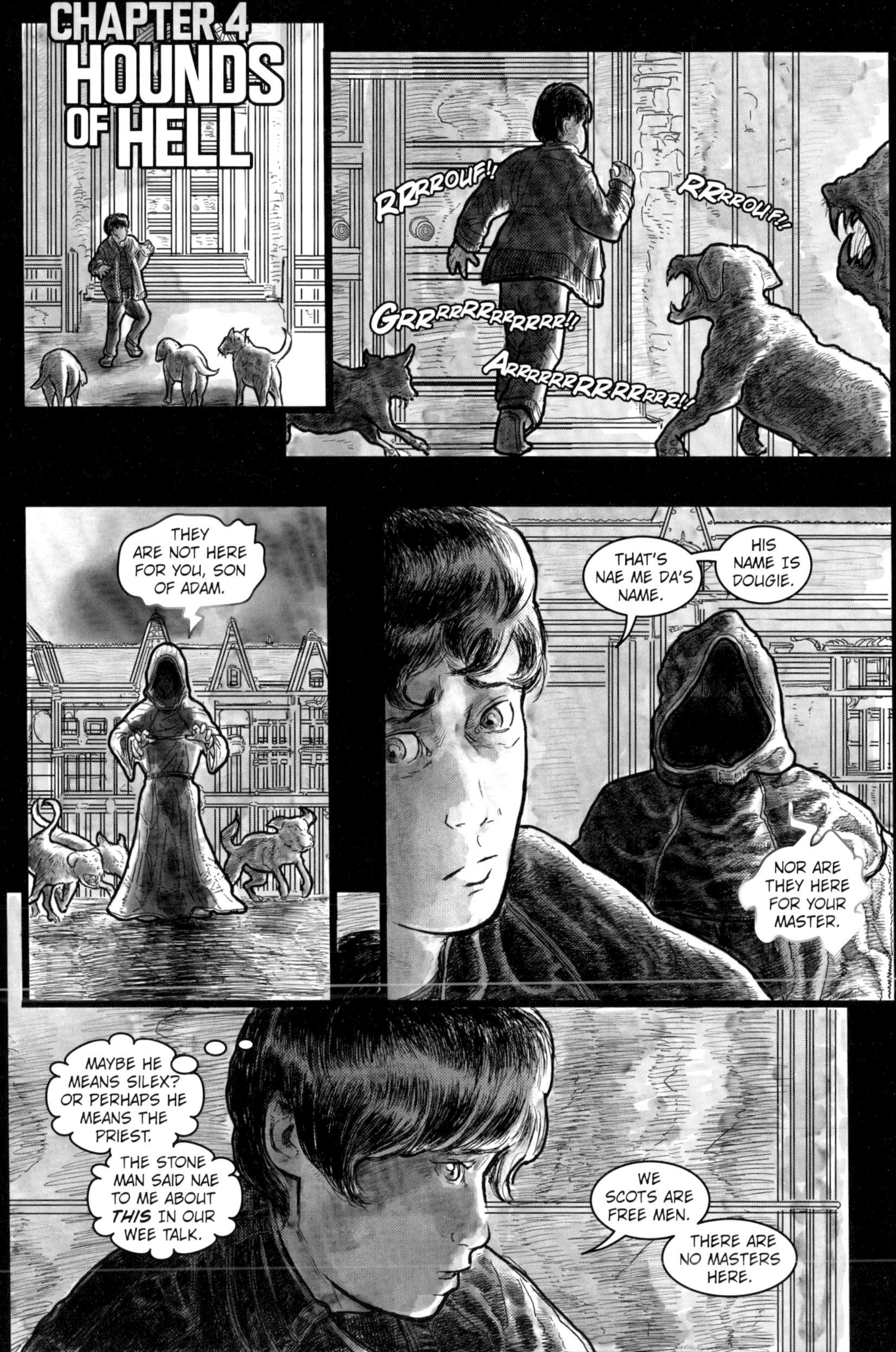
CHAPTER 4
HOUNDS OF HELL
RRRROUF!!
RRRROUF?!!
GRRRRRRRRRRRR!!
ARRRRRRRRRRRRR!!
THEY ARE NOT HERE FOR YOU, SON OF ADAM.
THAT'S NAE ME DA'S NAME.
HIS NAME IS DOUGIE.
NOR ARE THEY HERE FOR YOUR MASTER.
MAYBE HE MEANS SILEX? OR PERHAPS HE MEANS THE PRIEST.
THE STONE MAN SAID NAE TO ME ABOUT THIS IN OUR WEE TALK.
WE SCOTS ARE FREE MEN.
THERE ARE NO MASTERS HERE.

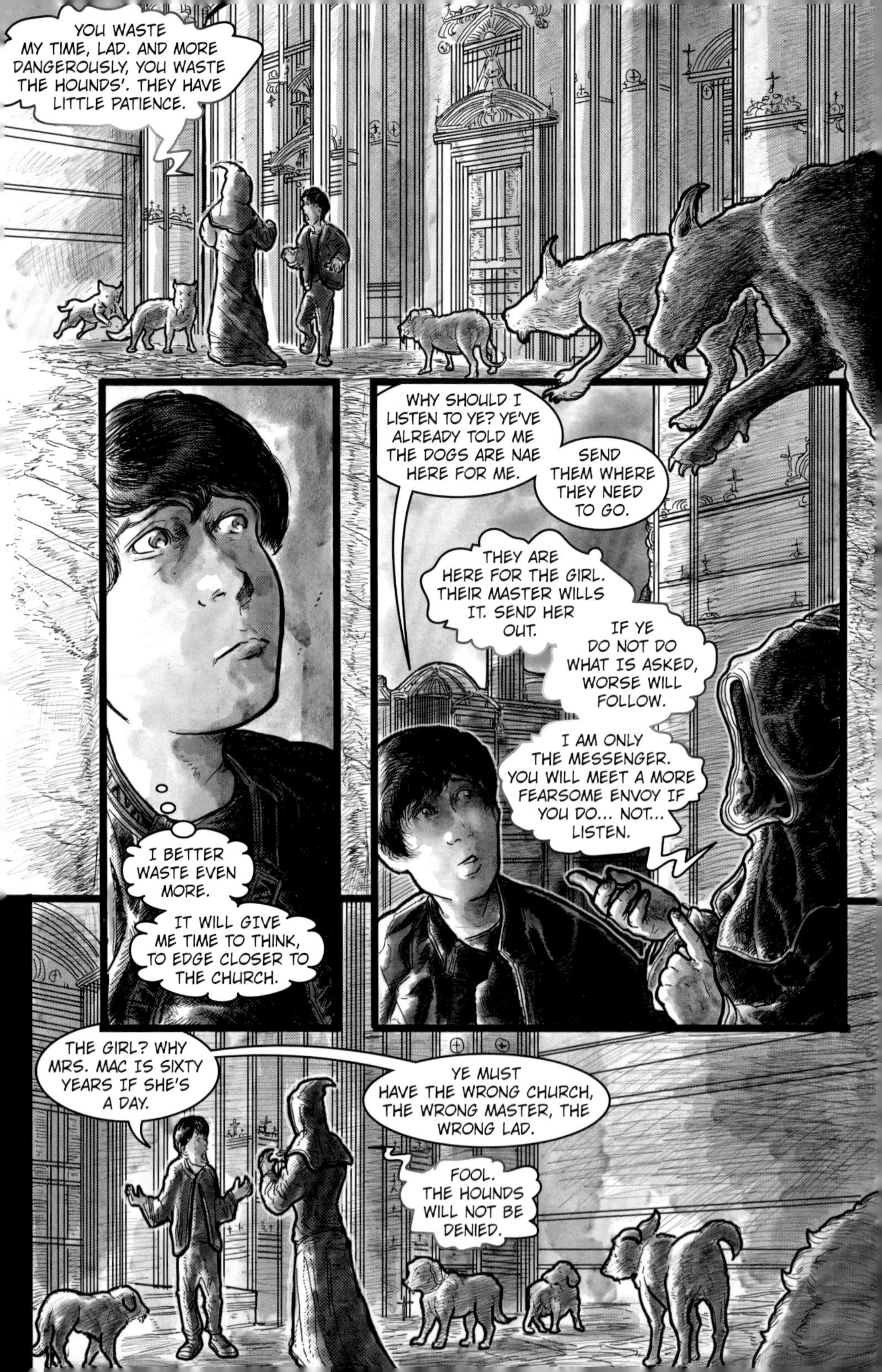
YOU WASTE MY TIME, LAD. AND MORE DANGEROUSLY, YOU WASTE THE HOUNDS'. THEY HAVE LITTLE PATIENCE.
I BETTER WASTE EVEN MORE.
IT WILL GIVE ME TIME TO THINK, TO EDGE CLOSER TO THE CHURCH.
WHY SHOULD I LISTEN TO YE? YE'VE ALREADY TOLD ME THE DOGS ARE NAE HERE FOR ME.
SEND THEM WHERE THEY NEED TO GO.
THEY ARE HERE FOR THE GIRL. THEIR MASTER WILLS IT. SEND HER OUT.
IF YE DO NOT DO WHAT IS ASKED, WORSE WILL FOLLOW.
I AM ONLY THE MESSENGER. YOU WILL MEET A MORE FEARSOME ENVOY IF YOU DO... NOT... LISTEN.
THE GIRL? WHY MRS. MAC IS SIXTY YEARS IF SHE'S A DAY.
YE MUST HAVE THE WRONG CHURCH, THE WRONG MASTER, THE WRONG LAD.
FOOL. THE HOUNDS WILL NOT BE DENIED.

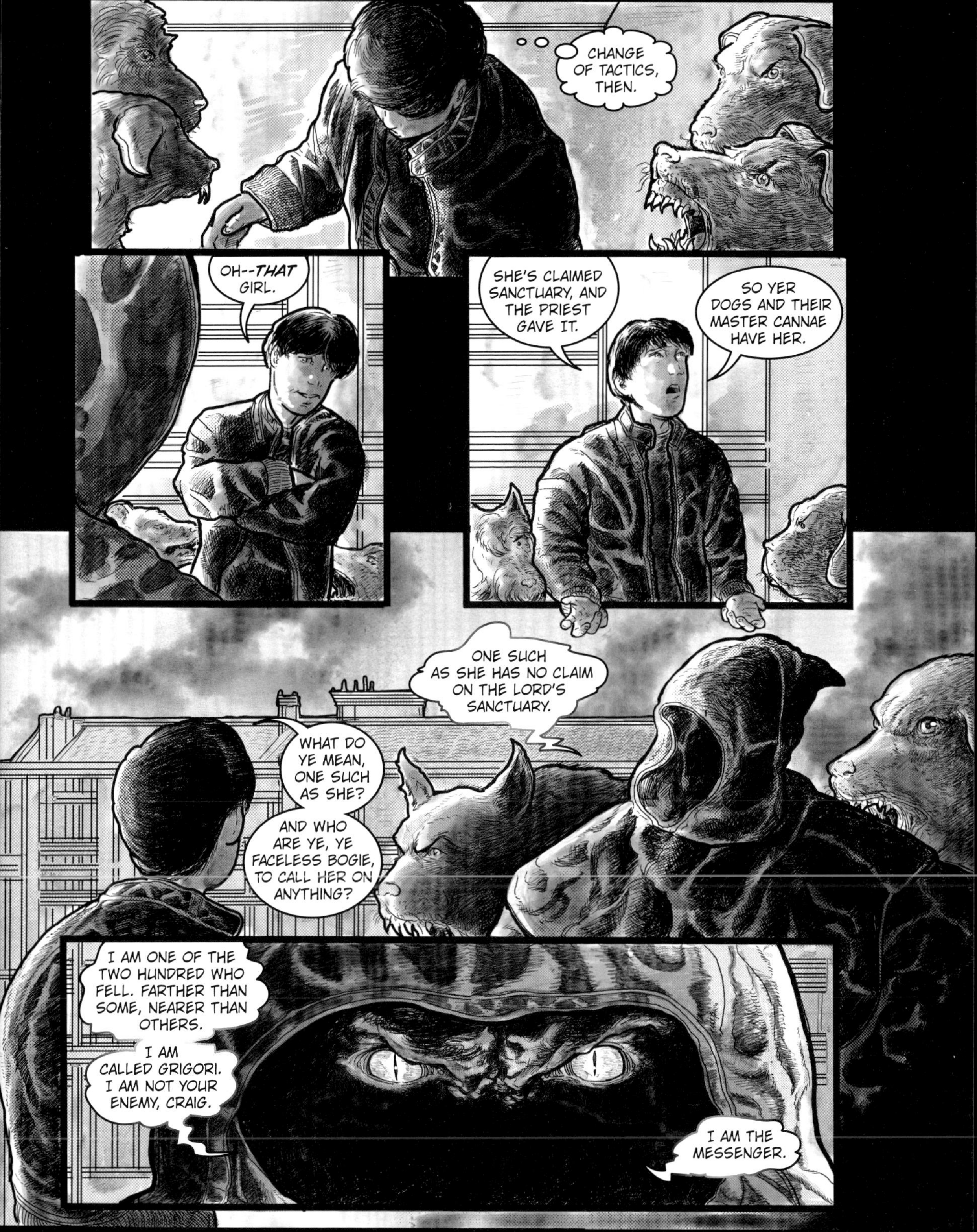
CHANGE OF TACTICS, THEN.
OH--*THAT* GIRL.
SHE'S CLAIMED SANCTUARY, AND THE PRIEST GAVE IT.
SO YER DOGS AND THEIR MASTER CANNAE HAVE HER.
ONE SUCH AS SHE HAS NO CLAIM ON THE LORD'S SANCTUARY.
WHAT DO YE MEAN, ONE SUCH AS SHE?
AND WHO ARE YE, YE FACELESS BOGIE, TO CALL HER ON ANYTHING?
I AM ONE OF THE TWO HUNDRED WHO FELL. FARTHER THAN SOME, NEARER THAN OTHERS.
I AM CALLED GRIGORI. I AM NOT YOUR ENEMY, CRAIG.
I AM THE MESSENGER.

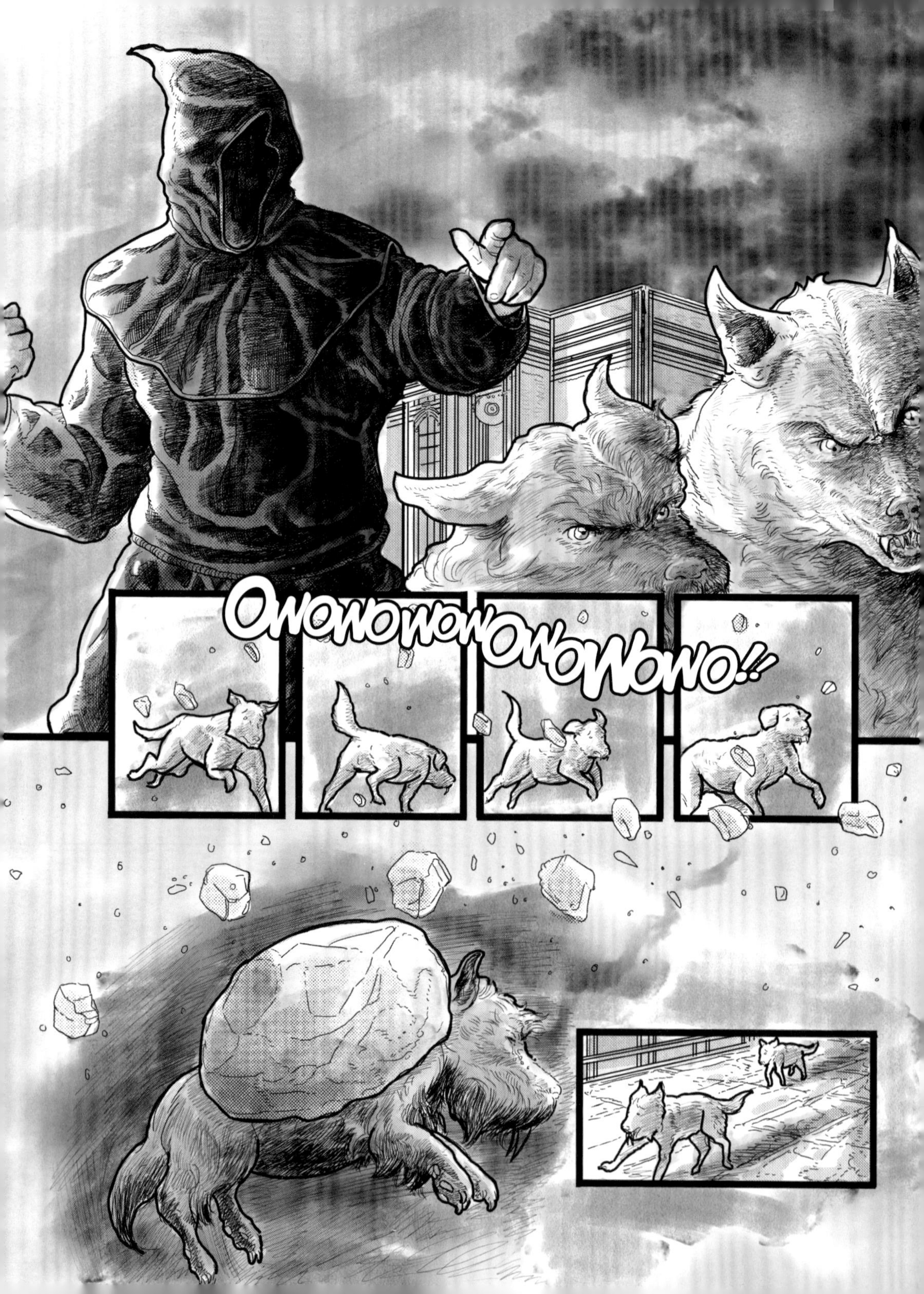
OWOWOWOWOWOWOWOWO!!

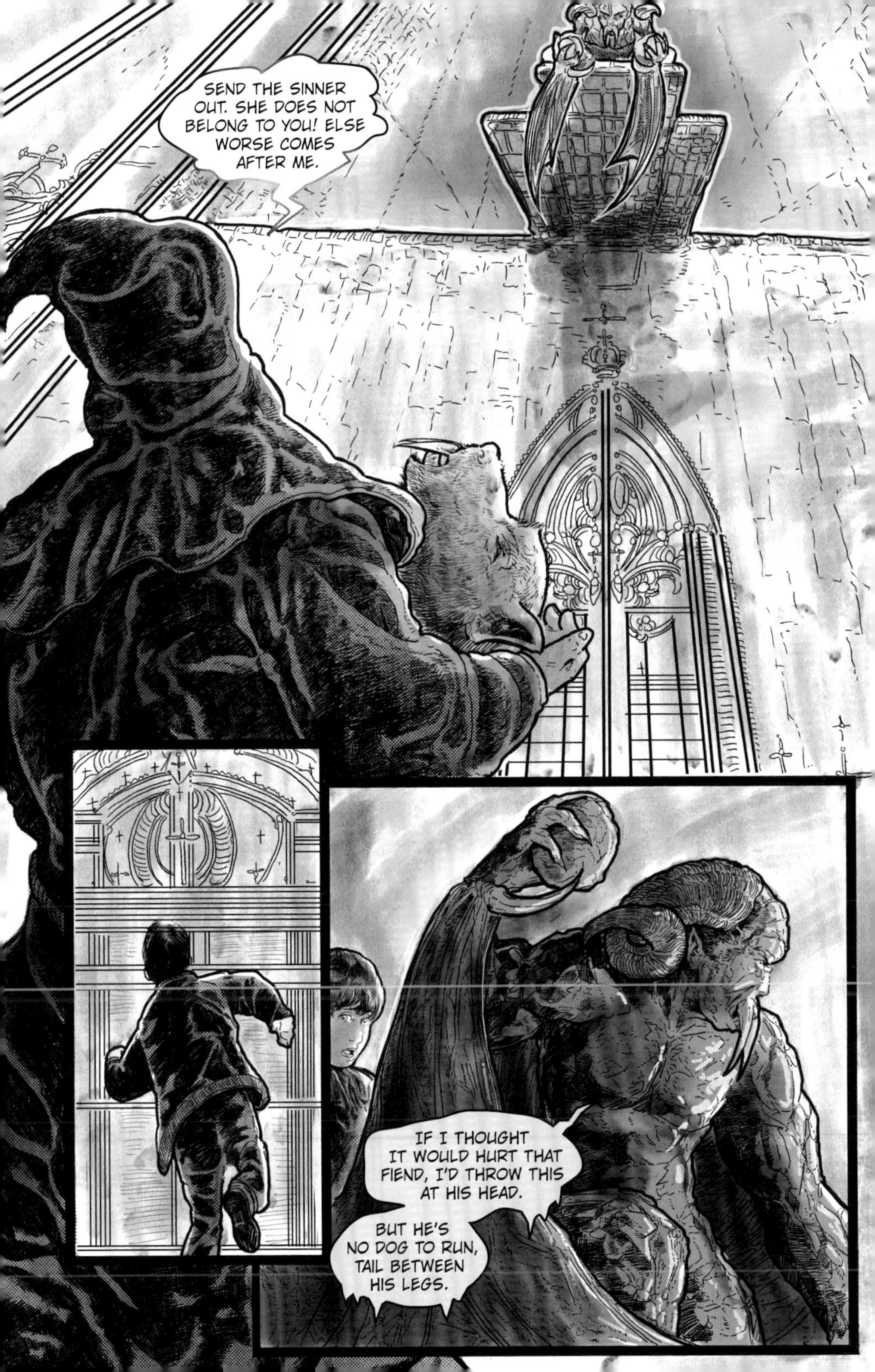
SEND THE SINNER OUT. SHE DOES NOT BELONG TO YOU! ELSE WORSE COMES AFTER ME.
IF I THOUGHT IT WOULD HURT THAT FIEND, I'D THROW THIS AT HIS HEAD.
BUT HE'S NO DOG TO RUN, TAIL BETWEEN HIS LEGS.

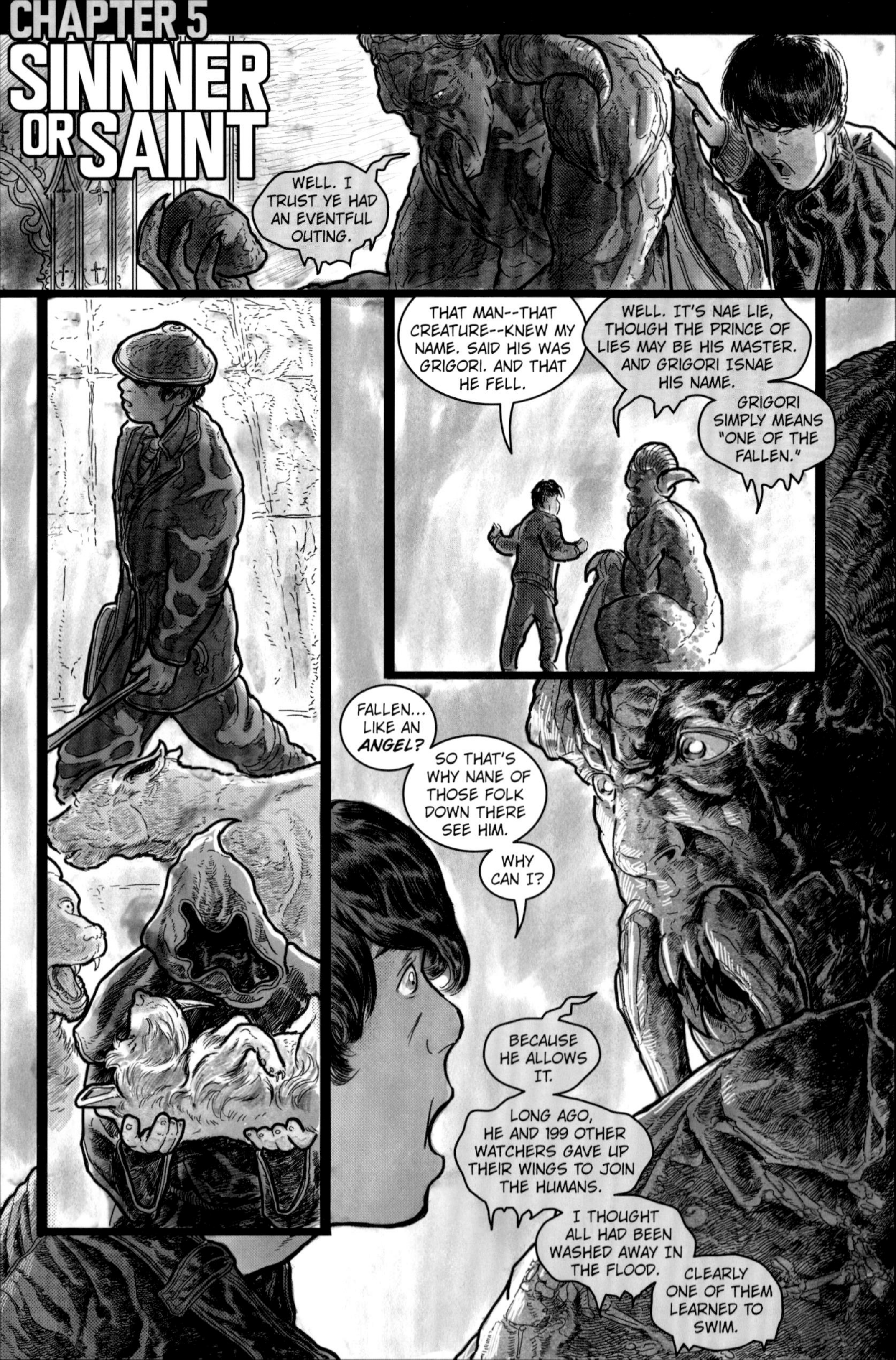
CHAPTER 5
SINNNER OR SAINT
WELL. I TRUST YE HAD AN EVENTFUL OUTING.
THAT MAN--THAT CREATURE--KNEW MY NAME. SAID HIS WAS GRIGORI. AND THAT HE FELL.
WELL. IT'S NAE LIE, THOUGH THE PRINCE OF LIES MAY BE HIS MASTER. AND GRIGORI ISNAE HIS NAME.
GRIGORI SIMPLY MEANS "ONE OF THE FALLEN."
FALLEN... LIKE AN *ANGEL*?
SO THAT'S WHY NANE OF THOSE FOLK DOWN THERE SEE HIM.
WHY CAN I?
BECAUSE HE ALLOWS IT.
LONG AGO, HE AND 199 OTHER WATCHERS GAVE UP THEIR WINGS TO JOIN THE HUMANS.
I THOUGHT ALL HAD BEEN WASHED AWAY IN THE FLOOD.
CLEARLY ONE OF THEM LEARNED TO SWIM.

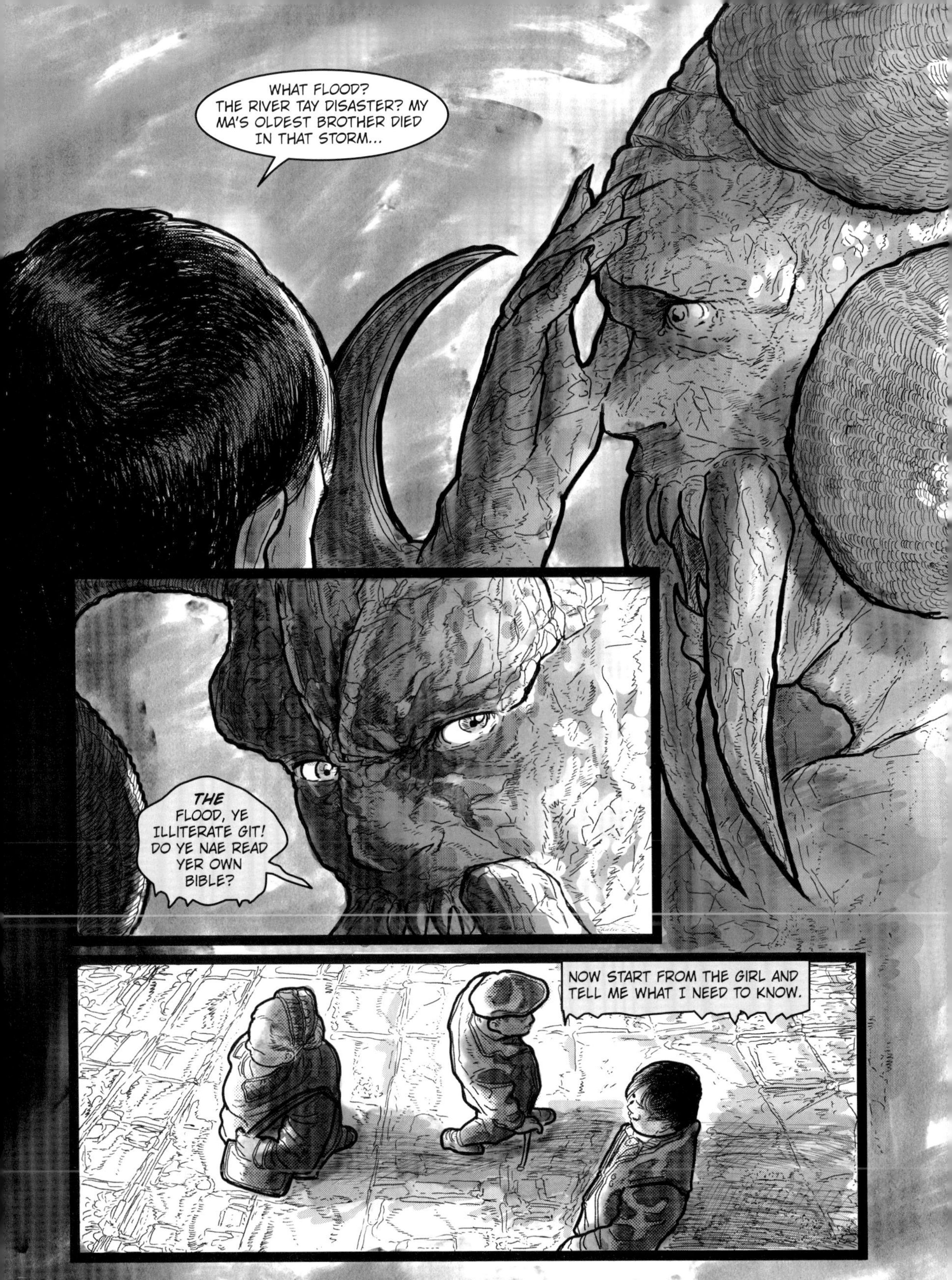

WHAT FLOOD? THE RIVER TAY DISASTER? MY MA'S OLDEST BROTHER DIED IN THAT STORM...
THE FLOOD, YE ILLITERATE GIT! DO YE NAE READ YER OWN BIBLE?
NOW START FROM THE GIRL AND TELL ME WHAT I NEED TO KNOW.

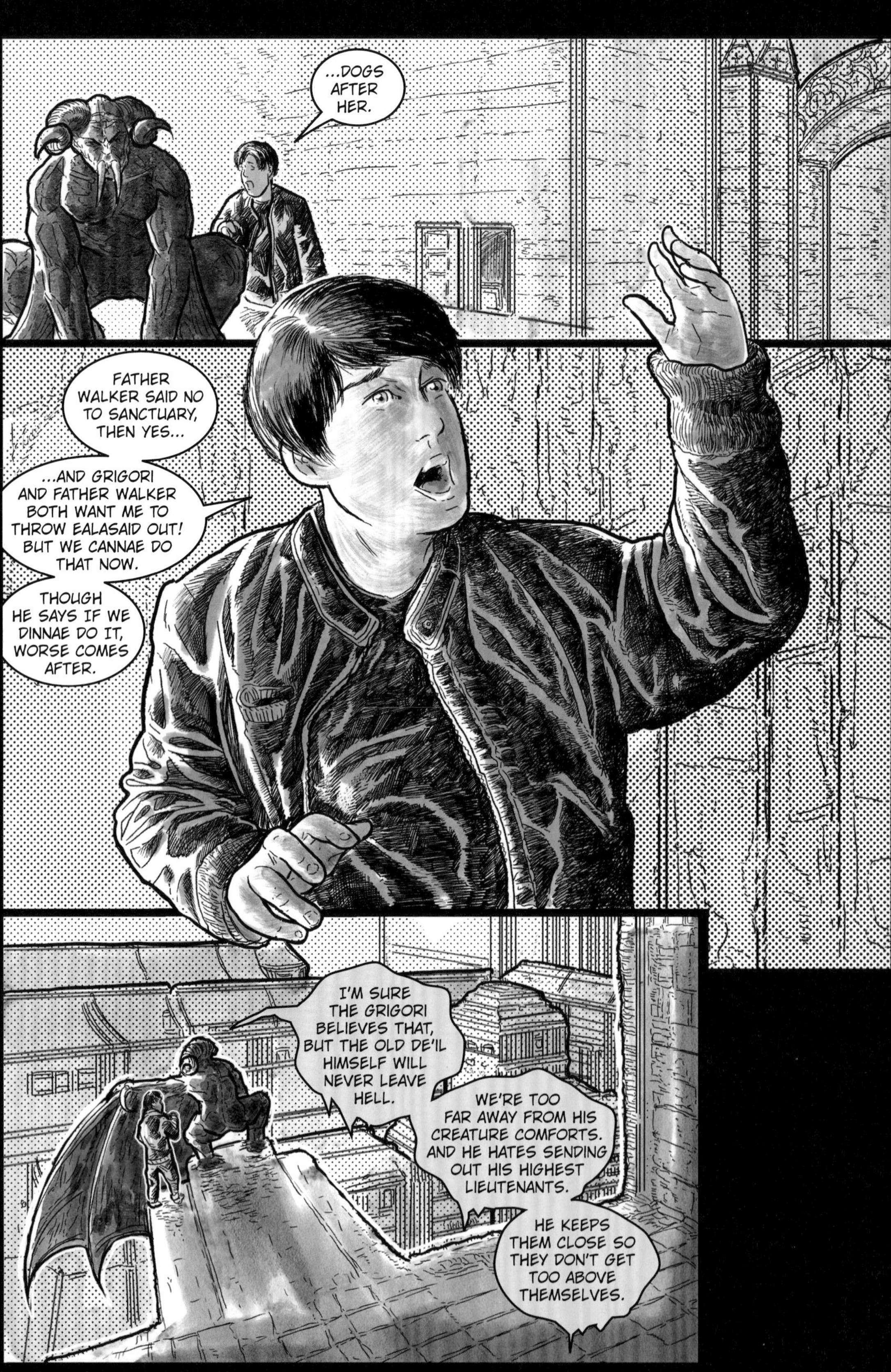
...DOGS AFTER HER.
FATHER WALKER SAID NO TO SANCTUARY, THEN YES...
...AND GRIGORI AND FATHER WALKER BOTH WANT ME TO THROW EALASAID OUT! BUT WE CANNAE DO THAT NOW.
THOUGH HE SAYS IF WE DINNAE DO IT, WORSE COMES AFTER.
I'M SURE THE GRIGORI BELIEVES THAT, BUT THE OLD DE'IL HIMSELF WILL NEVER LEAVE HELL.
WE'RE TOO FAR AWAY FROM HIS CREATURE COMFORTS. AND HE HATES SENDING OUT HIS HIGHEST LIEUTENANTS.
HE KEEPS THEM CLOSE SO THEY DON'T GET TOO ABOVE THEMSELVES.

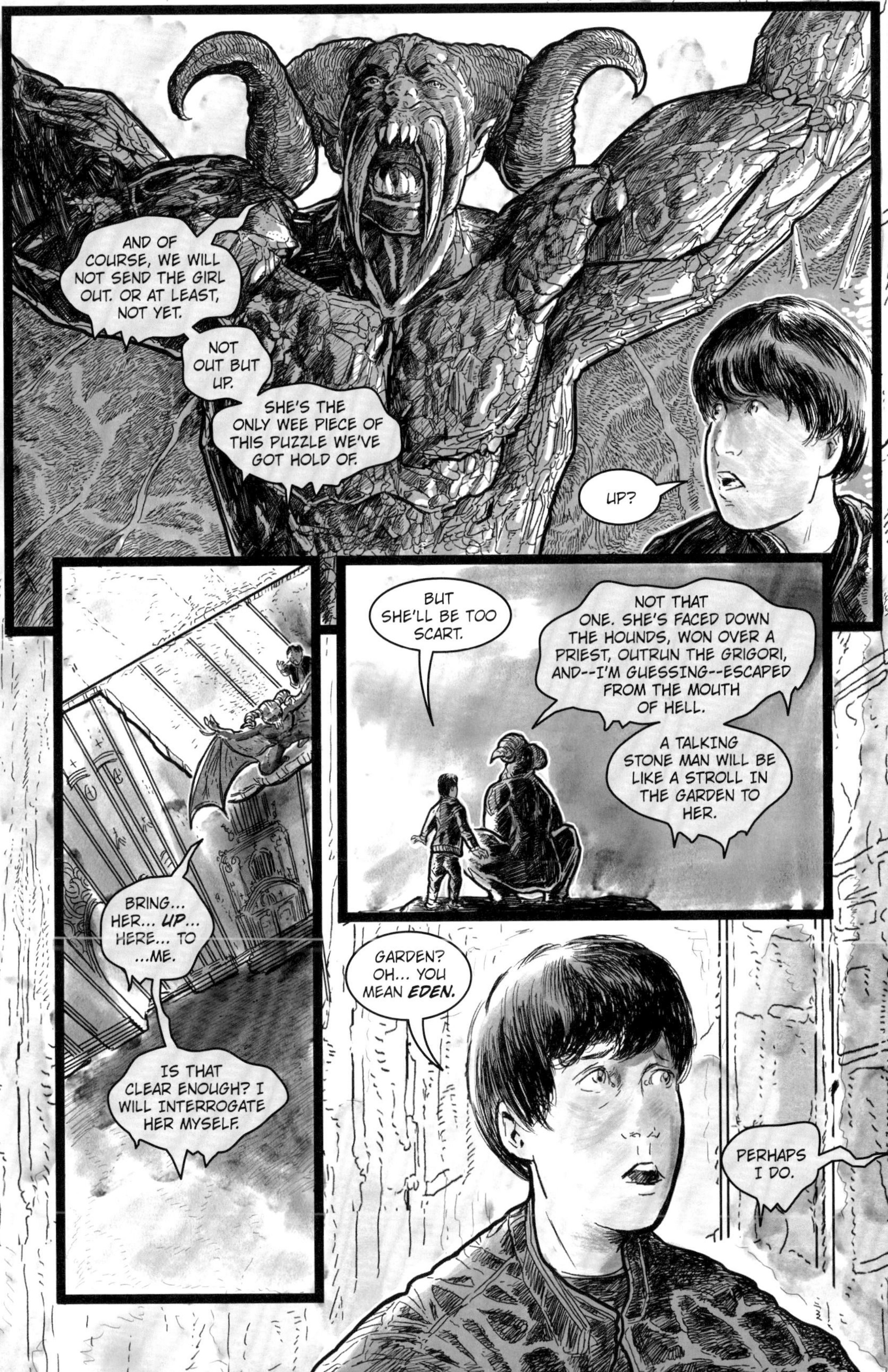
AND OF COURSE, WE WILL NOT SEND THE GIRL OUT. OR AT LEAST, NOT YET.
NOT OUT BUT UP.
SHE'S THE ONLY WEE PIECE OF THIS PUZZLE WE'VE GOT HOLD OF.
UP?
BRING... HER... *UP*... HERE... TO ...ME.
IS THAT CLEAR ENOUGH? I WILL INTERROGATE HER MYSELF.
BUT SHE'LL BE TOO SCART.
NOT THAT ONE. SHE'S FACED DOWN THE HOUNDS, WON OVER A PRIEST, OUTRUN THE GRIGORI, AND--I'M GUESSING--ESCAPED FROM THE MOUTH OF HELL.
A TALKING STONE MAN WILL BE LIKE A STROLL IN THE GARDEN TO HER.
GARDEN? OH... YOU MEAN *EDEN.*
PERHAPS I DO.

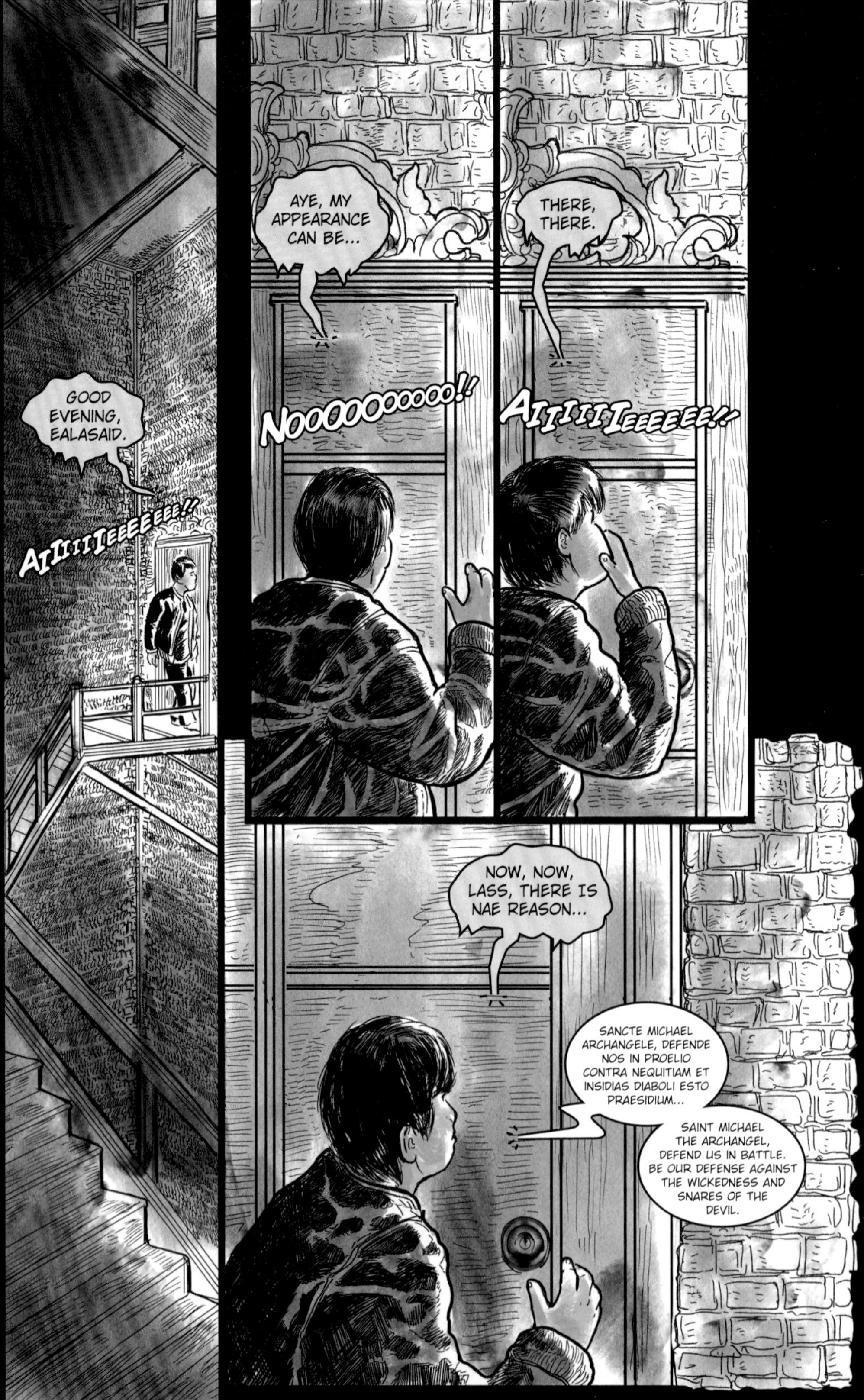
GOOD EVENING, EALASAID.
AIIIIIIeeeEEEEE!!
AYE, MY APPEARANCE CAN BE...
NOOOOOooooo!!
THERE, THERE.
AIIIIIIeeeEEE!!
NOW, NOW, LASS, THERE IS NAE REASON...
SANCTE MICHAEL ARCHANGELE, DEFENDE NOS IN PROELIO CONTRA NEQUITIAM ET INSIDIAS DIABOLI ESTO PRAESIDIUM...
SAINT MICHAEL THE ARCHANGEL, DEFEND US IN BATTLE. BE OUR DEFENSE AGAINST THE WICKEDNESS AND SNARES OF THE DEVIL.

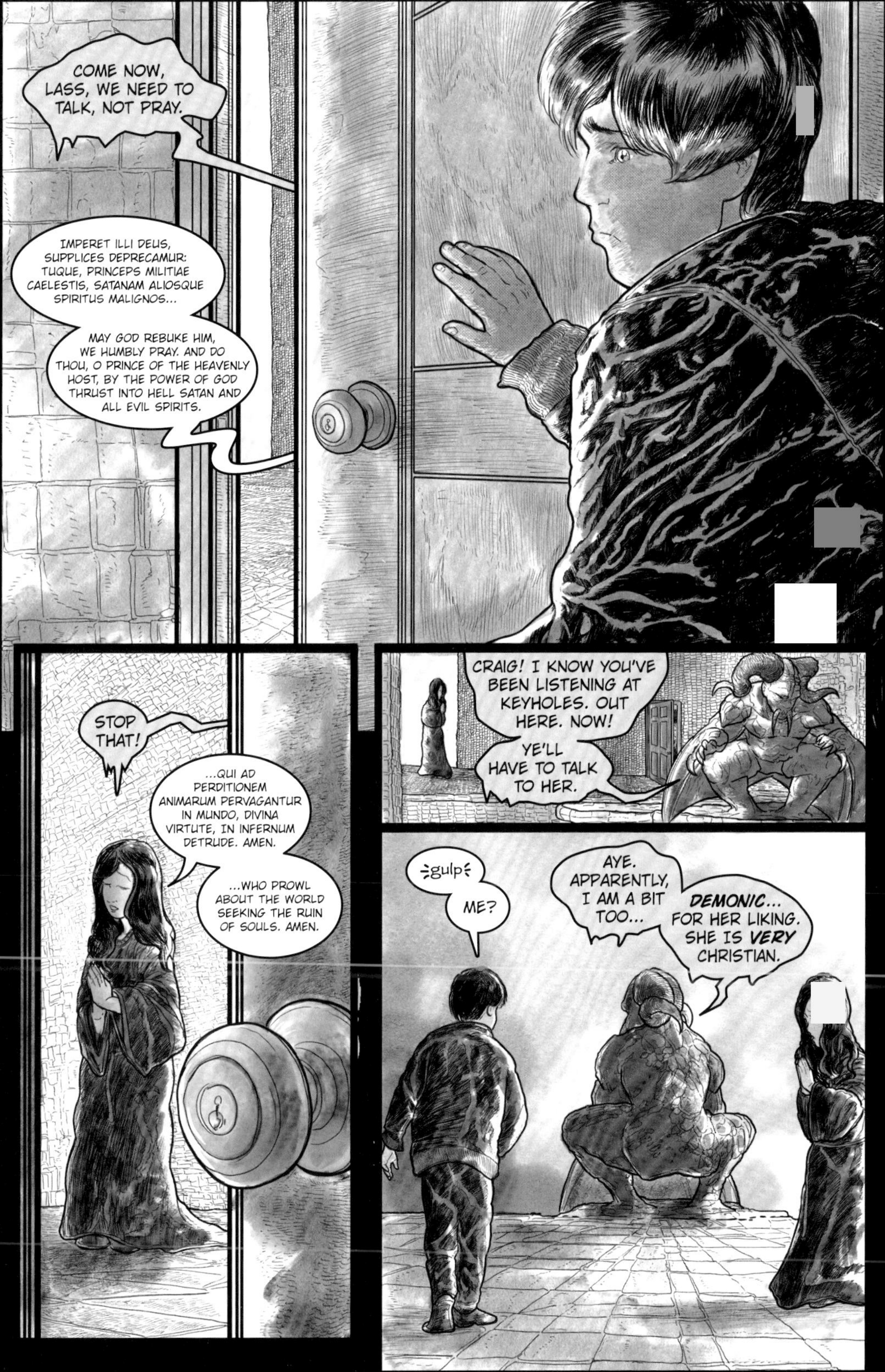
COME NOW, LASS, WE NEED TO TALK, NOT PRAY.
IMPERET ILLI DEUS, SUPPLICES DEPRECAMUR: TUQUE, PRINCEPS MILITIAE CAELESTIS, SATANAM ALIOSQUE SPIRITUS MALIGNOS...
MAY GOD REBUKE HIM, WE HUMBLY PRAY. AND DO THOU, O PRINCE OF THE HEAVENLY HOST, BY THE POWER OF GOD THRUST INTO HELL SATAN AND ALL EVIL SPIRITS.
STOP THAT!
...QUI AD PERDITIONEM ANIMARUM PERVAGANTUR IN MUNDO, DIVINA VIRTUTE, IN INFERNUM DETRUDE. AMEN.
...WHO PROWL ABOUT THE WORLD SEEKING THE RUIN OF SOULS. AMEN.
CRAIG! I KNOW YOU'VE BEEN LISTENING AT KEYHOLES. OUT HERE. NOW!
YE'LL HAVE TO TALK TO HER.
gulp
ME?
AYE. APPARENTLY, I AM A BIT TOO...
DEMONIC... FOR HER LIKING. SHE IS VERY CHRISTIAN.

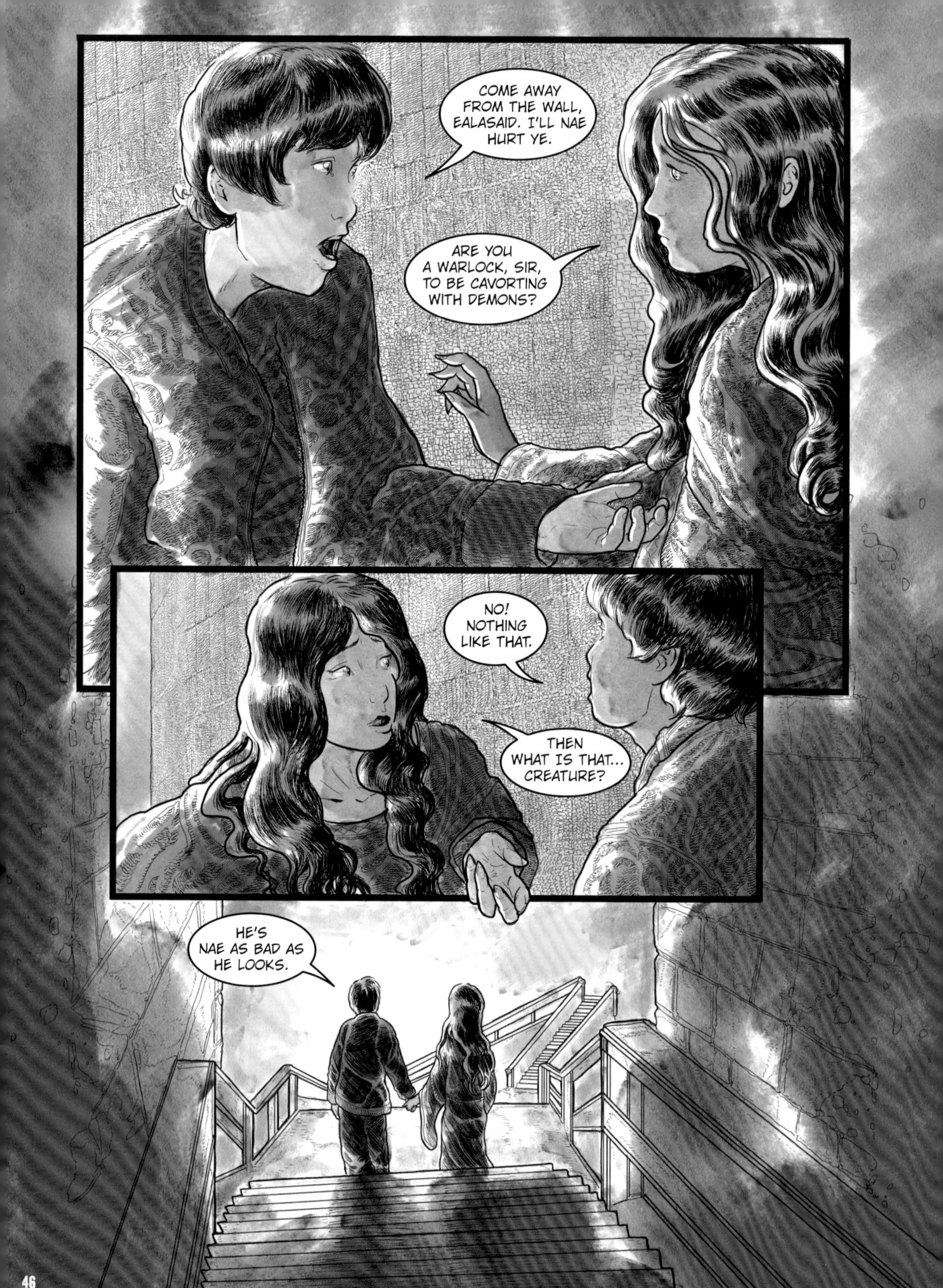
COME AWAY FROM THE WALL, EALASAID. I'LL NAE HURT YE.
ARE YOU A WARLOCK, SIR, TO BE CAVORTING WITH DEMONS?
NO! NOTHING LIKE THAT.
THEN WHAT IS THAT... CREATURE?
HE'S NAE AS BAD AS HE LOOKS.

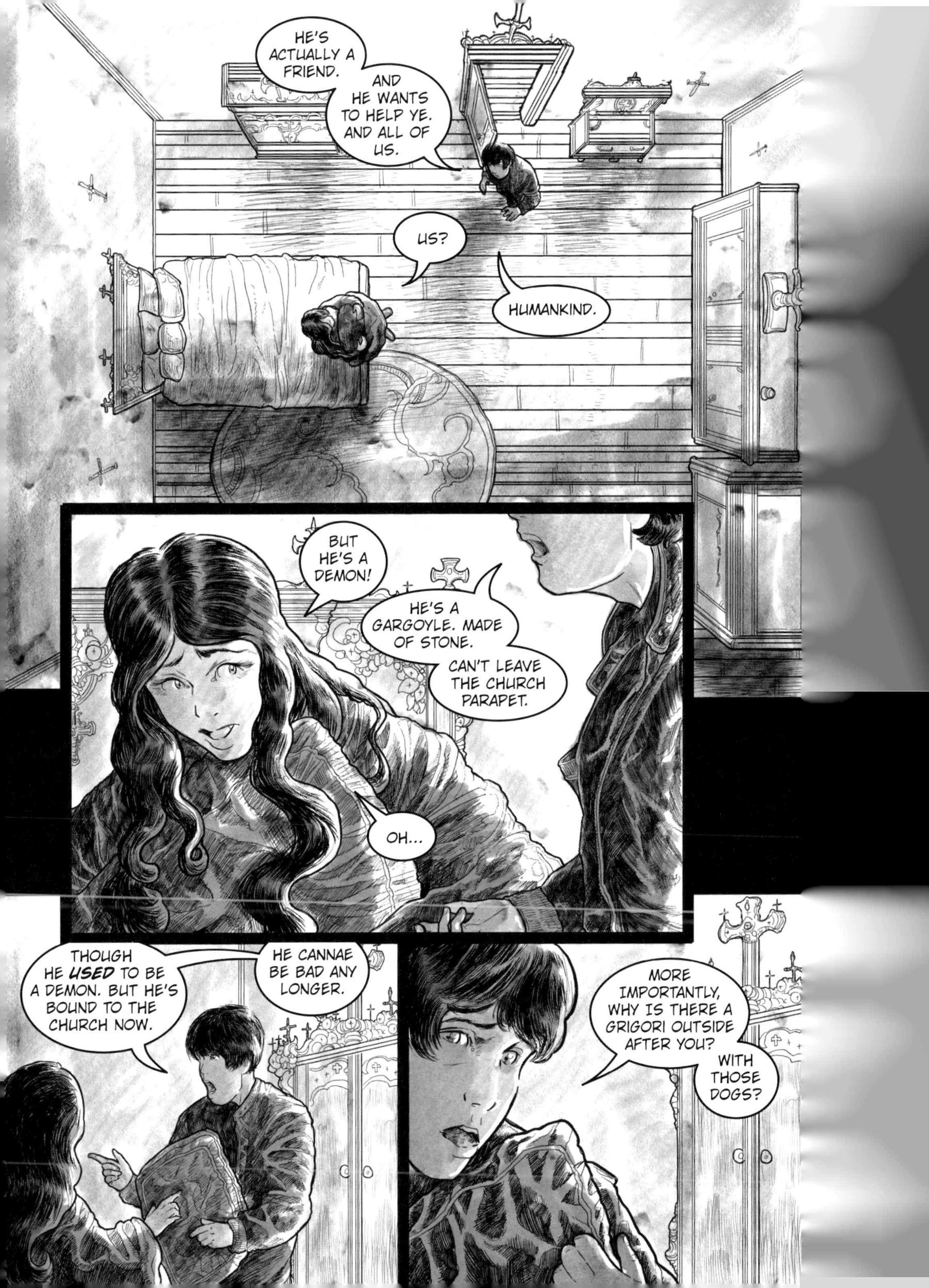
HE'S ACTUALLY A FRIEND.
AND HE WANTS TO HELP YE. AND ALL OF US.
US?
HUMANKIND.
BUT HE'S A DEMON!
HE'S A GARGOYLE. MADE OF STONE.
CAN'T LEAVE THE CHURCH PARAPET.
OH...
THOUGH HE USED TO BE A DEMON. BUT HE'S BOUND TO THE CHURCH NOW.
HE CANNAE BE BAD ANY LONGER.
MORE IMPORTANTLY, WHY IS THERE A GRIGORI OUTSIDE AFTER YOU?
WITH THOSE DOGS?

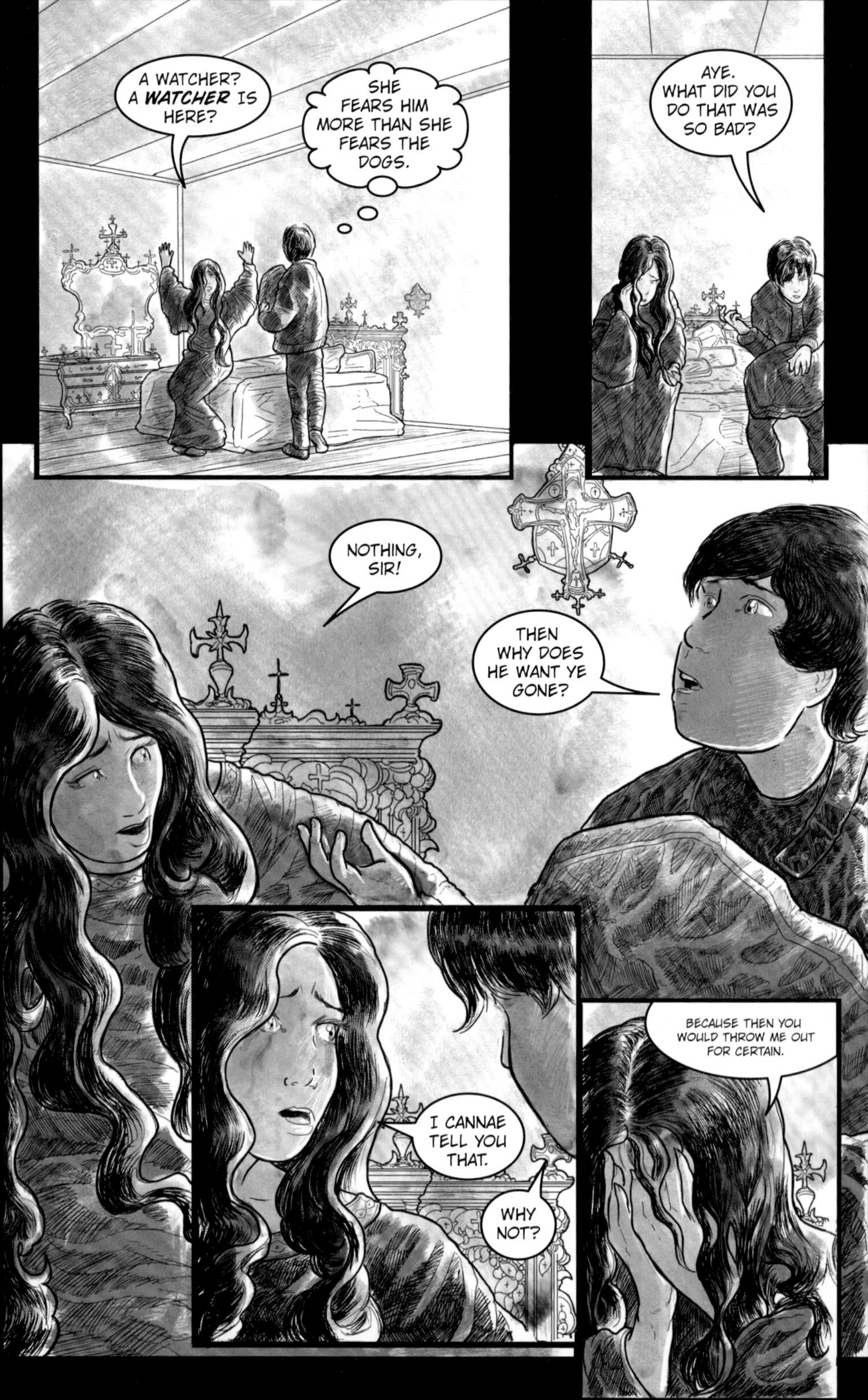
A WATCHER? A WATCHER IS HERE?
SHE FEARS HIM MORE THAN SHE FEARS THE DOGS.
AYE. WHAT DID YOU DO THAT WAS SO BAD?
NOTHING, SIR!
THEN WHY DOES HE WANT YE GONE?
I CANNAE TELL YOU THAT.
WHY NOT?
BECAUSE THEN YOU WOULD THROW ME OUT FOR CERTAIN.

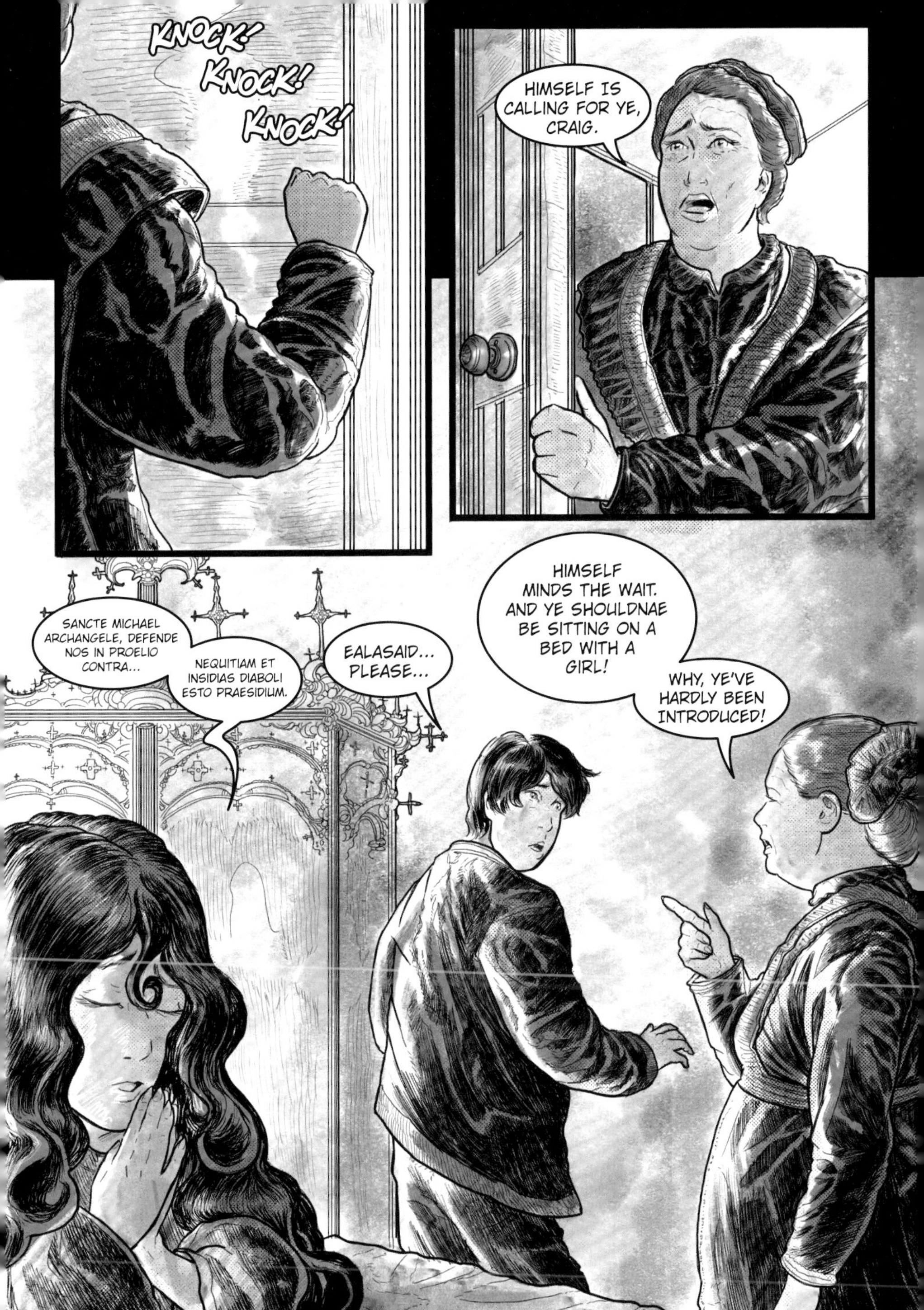
KNOCK! KNOCK! KNOCK!
HIMSELF IS CALLING FOR YE, CRAIG.
SANCTE MICHAEL ARCHANGELE, DEFENDE NOS IN PROELIO CONTRA...
NEQUITIAM ET INSIDIAS DIABOLI ESTO PRAESIDIUM.
EALASAID... PLEASE...
HIMSELF MINDS THE WAIT. AND YE SHOULDNAE BE SITTING ON A BED WITH A GIRL!
WHY, YE'VE HARDLY BEEN INTRODUCED!

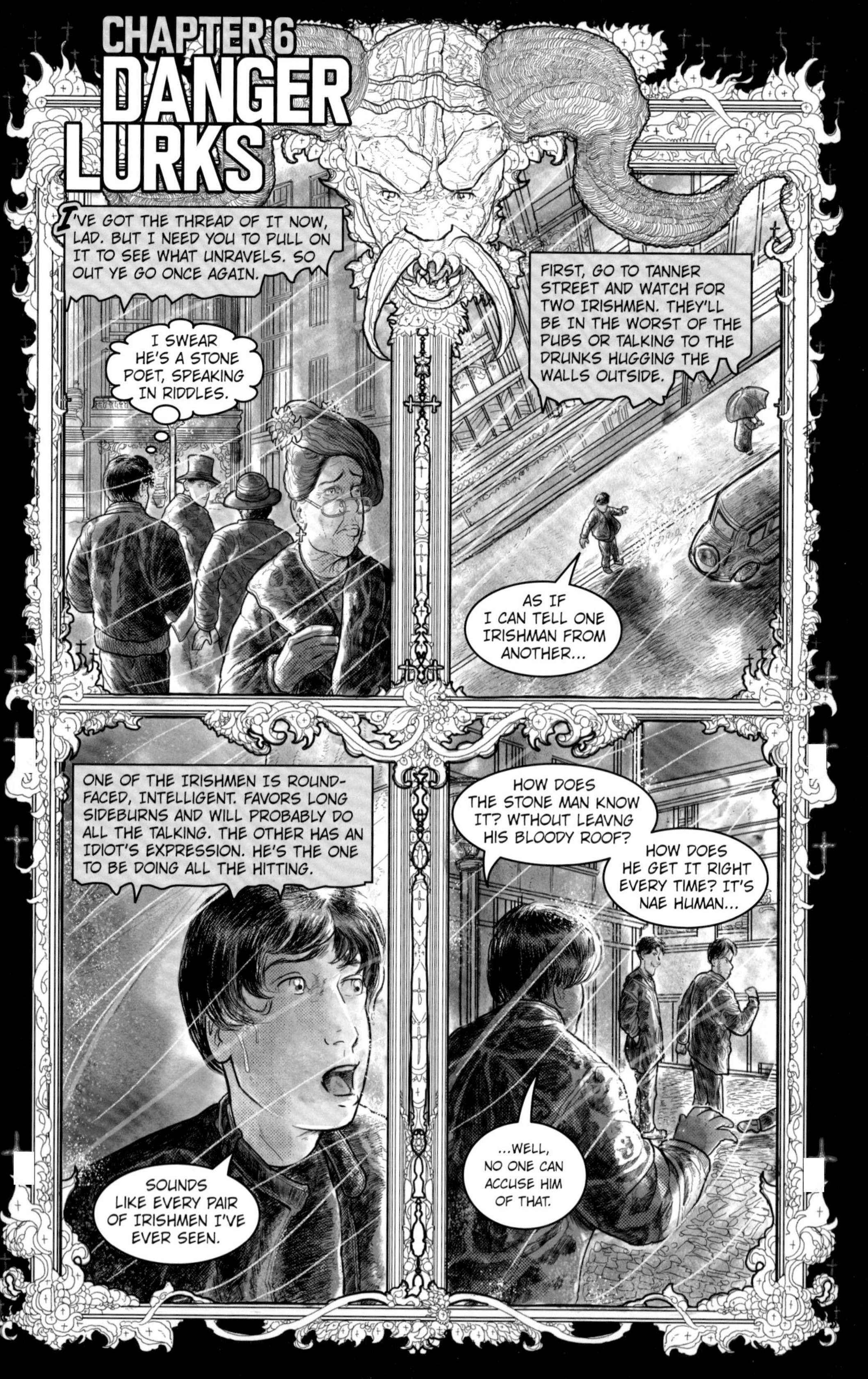
CHAPTER 6
DANGER LURKS
I'VE GOT THE THREAD OF IT NOW, LAD. BUT I NEED YOU TO PULL ON IT TO SEE WHAT UNRAVELS. SO OUT YE GO ONCE AGAIN.
I SWEAR HE'S A STONE POET, SPEAKING IN RIDDLES.
FIRST, GO TO TANNER STREET AND WATCH FOR TWO IRISHMEN. THEY'LL BE IN THE WORST OF THE PUBS OR TALKING TO THE DRUNKS HUGGING THE WALLS OUTSIDE.
AS IF I CAN TELL ONE IRISHMAN FROM ANOTHER...
ONE OF THE IRISHMEN IS ROUND-FACED, INTELLIGENT. FAVORS LONG SIDEBURNS AND WILL PROBABLY DO ALL THE TALKING. THE OTHER HAS AN IDIOT'S EXPRESSION. HE'S THE ONE TO BE DOING ALL THE HITTING.
SOUNDS LIKE EVERY PAIR OF IRISHMEN I'VE EVER SEEN.
HOW DOES THE STONE MAN KNOW IT? WTHOUT LEAVNG HIS BLOODY ROOF?
HOW DOES HE GET IT RIGHT EVERY TIME? IT'S NAE HUMAN...
...WELL, NO ONE CAN ACCUSE HIM OF THAT.

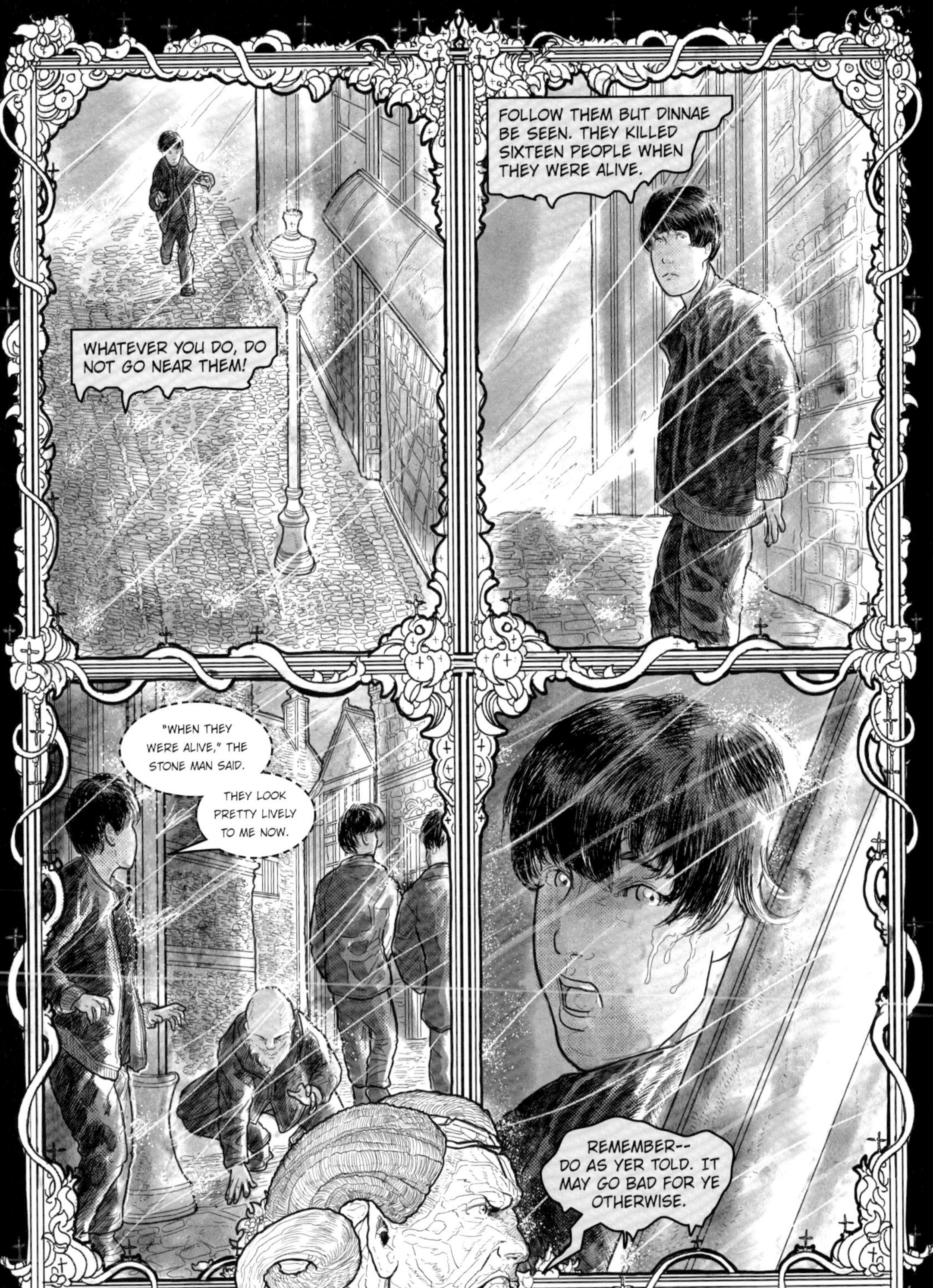
WHATEVER YOU DO, DO NOT GO NEAR THEM!
FOLLOW THEM BUT DINNAE BE SEEN. THEY KILLED SIXTEEN PEOPLE WHEN THEY WERE ALIVE.
"WHEN THEY WERE ALIVE," THE STONE MAN SAID.
THEY LOOK PRETTY LIVELY TO ME NOW.
REMEMBER-- DO AS YER TOLD. IT MAY GO BAD FOR YE OTHERWISE.

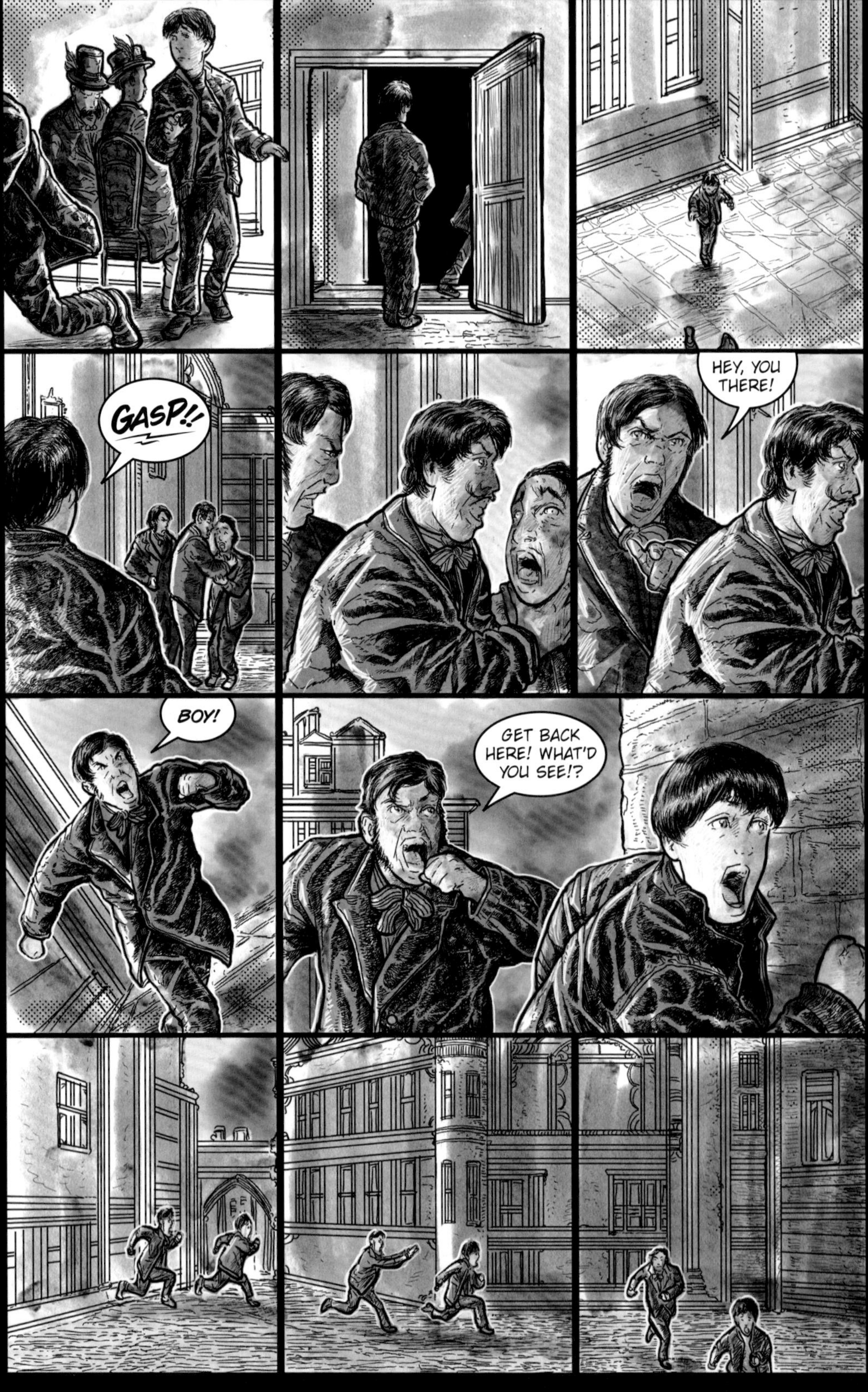
GASP!!
HEY, YOU THERE!
BOY!
GET BACK HERE! WHAT'D YOU SEE!?

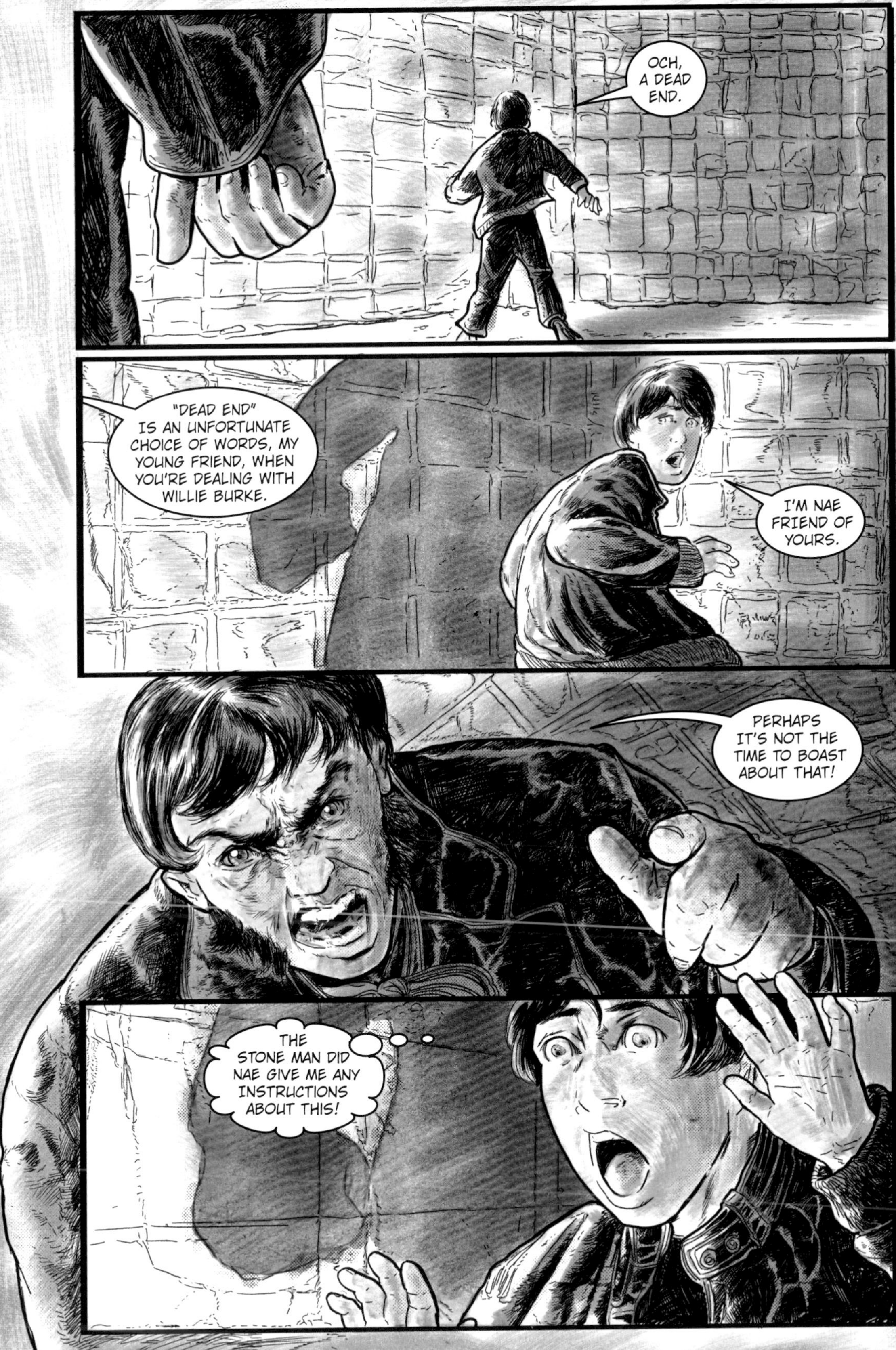
OCH, A DEAD END.
"DEAD END" IS AN UNFORTUNATE CHOICE OF WORDS, MY YOUNG FRIEND, WHEN YOU'RE DEALING WITH WILLIE BURKE.
I'M NAE FRIEND OF YOURS.
PERHAPS IT'S NOT THE TIME TO BOAST ABOUT THAT!
THE STONE MAN DID NAE GIVE ME ANY INSTRUCTIONS ABOUT THIS!

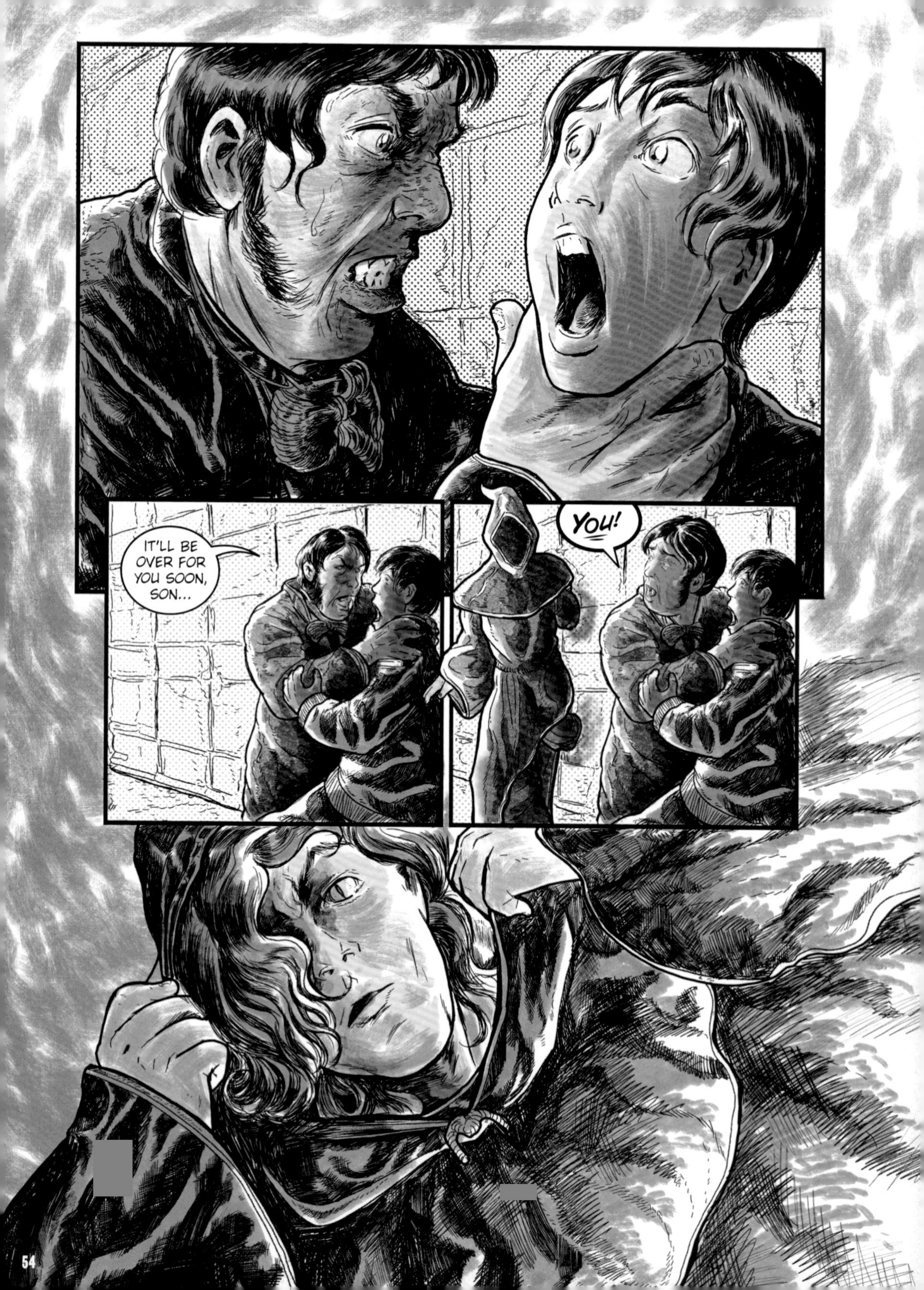
IT'LL BE OVER FOR YOU SOON, SON...
YOU!

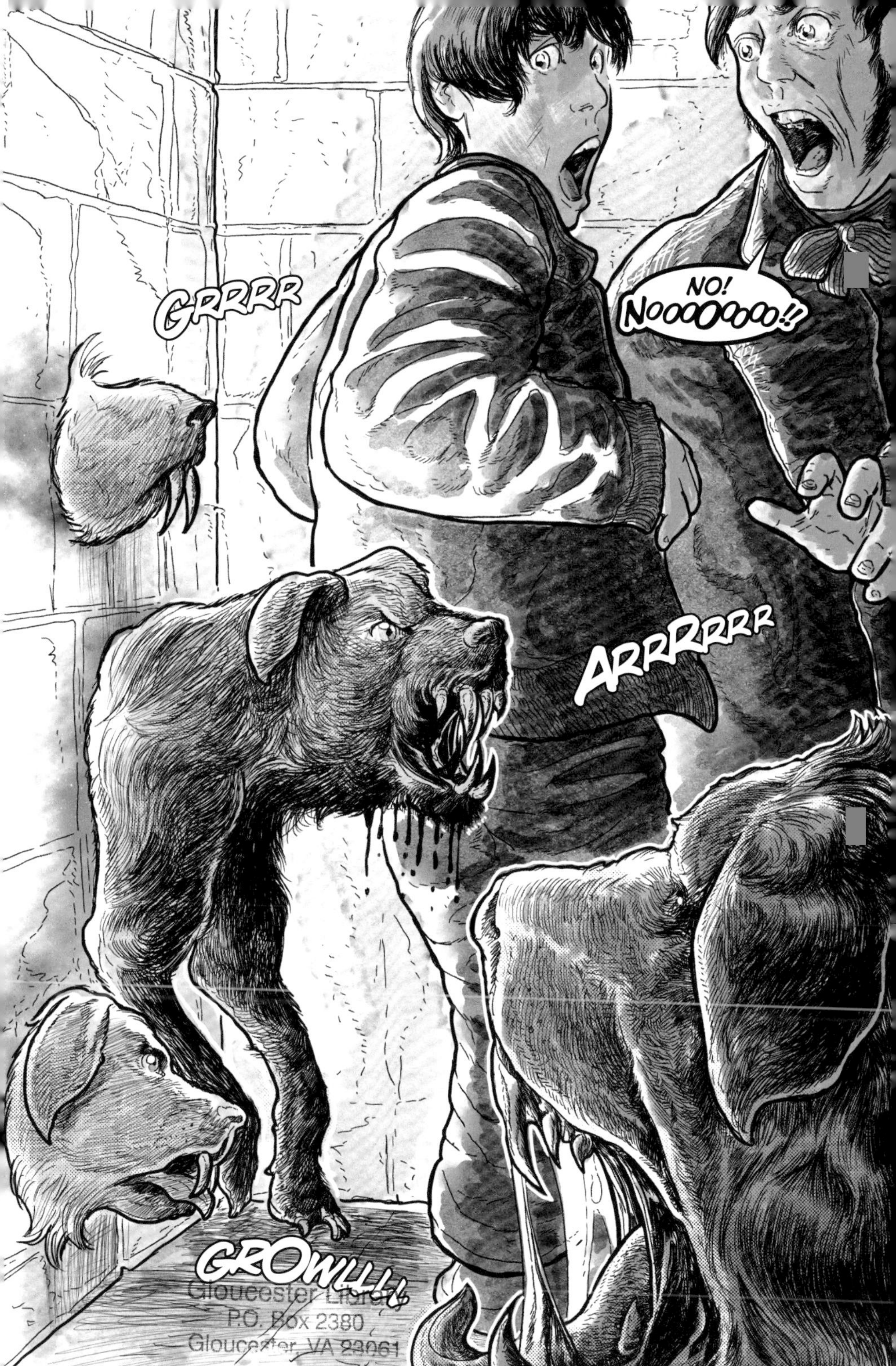
GRRRR
NO! NOOOOOOOO!!
ARRRRRRR
GROWLLLL

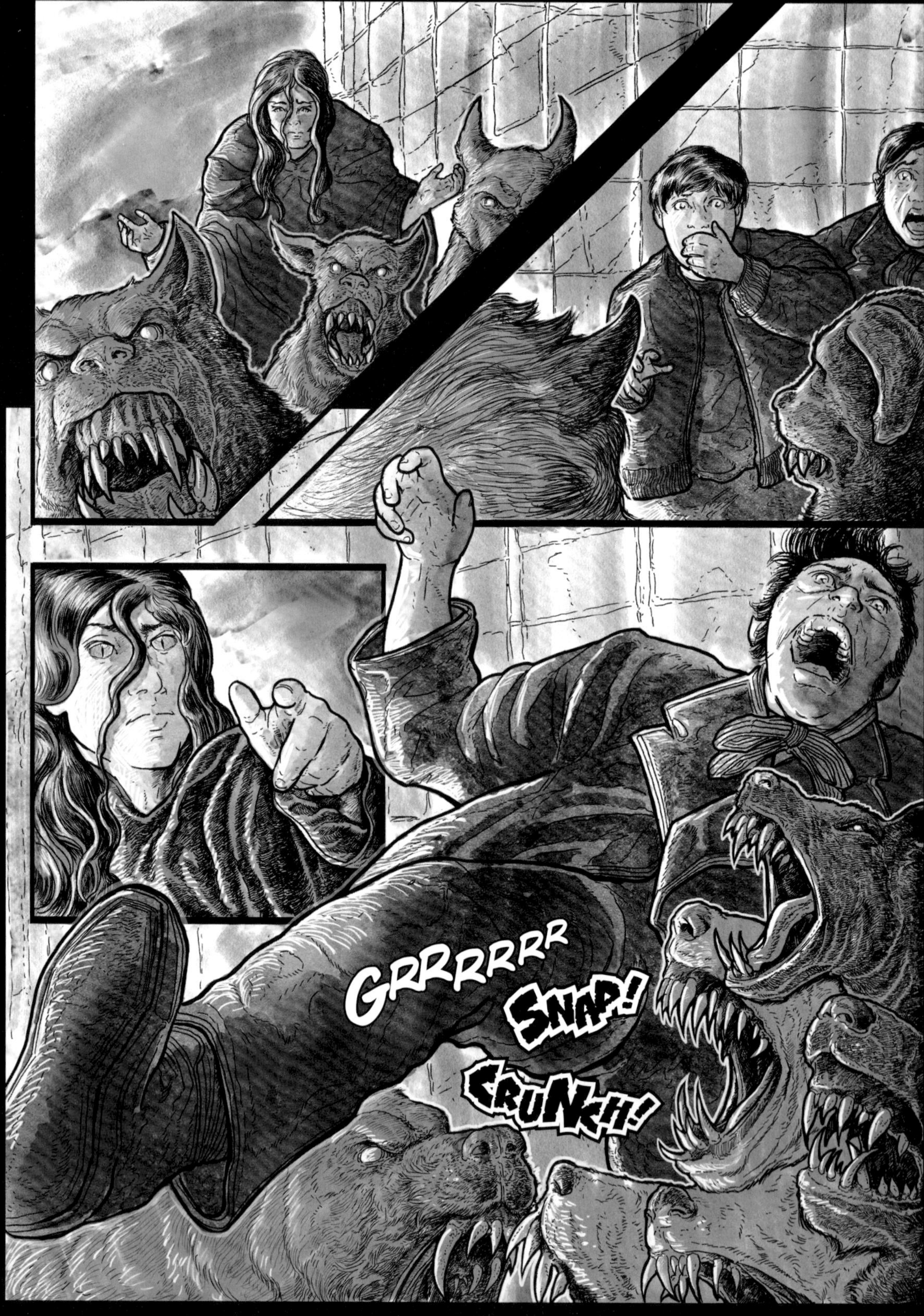
GRRRRRRR
SNAP!
CRUNCH!

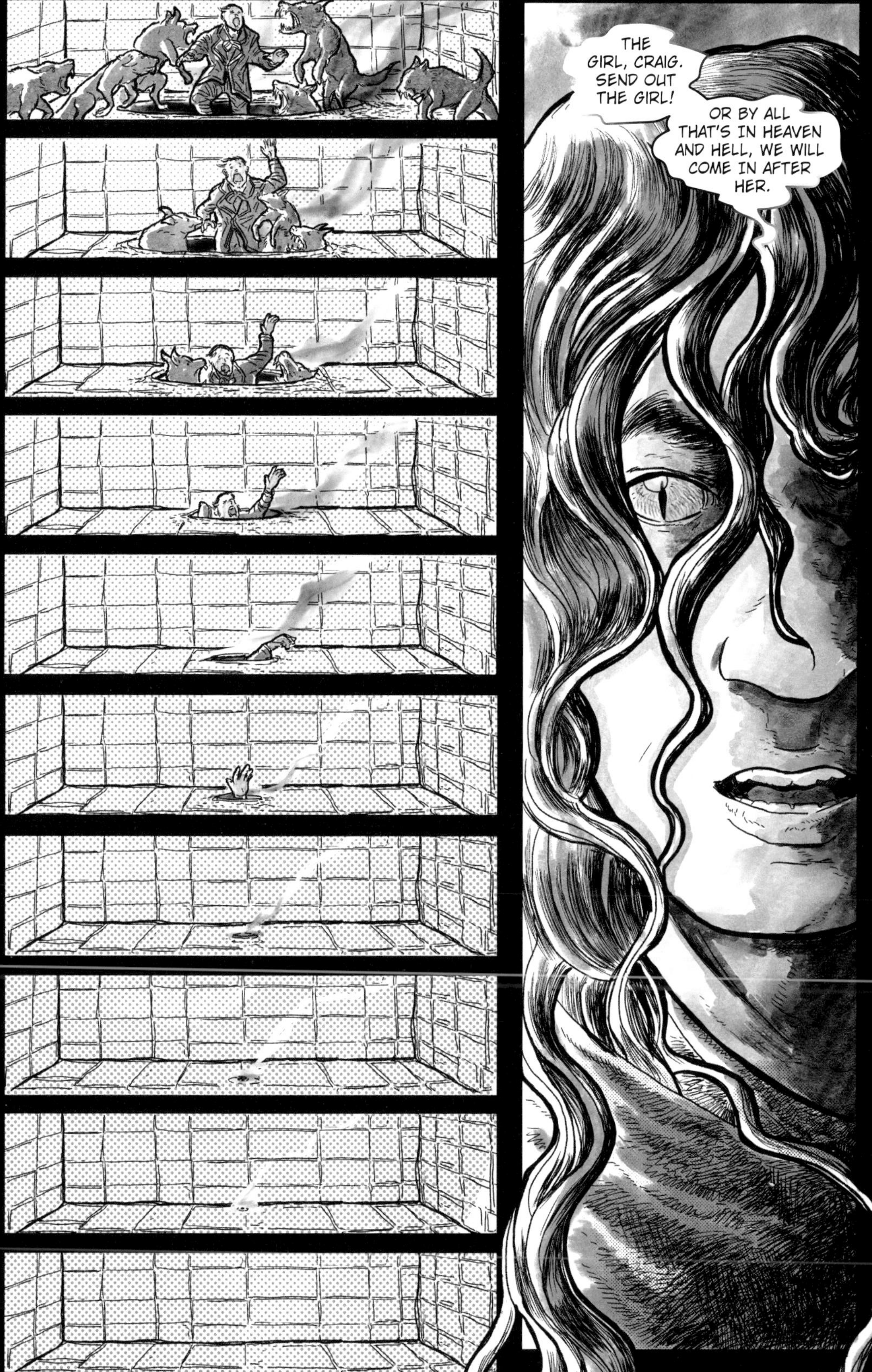
THE GIRL, CRAIG. SEND OUT THE GIRL!
OR BY ALL THAT'S IN HEAVEN AND HELL, WE WILL COME IN AFTER HER.

:huff!:

ouff!

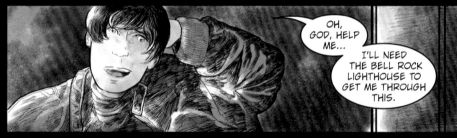

OH, GOD, HELP ME...

I'LL NEED THE BELL ROCK LIGHTHOUSE TO GET ME THROUGH THIS.

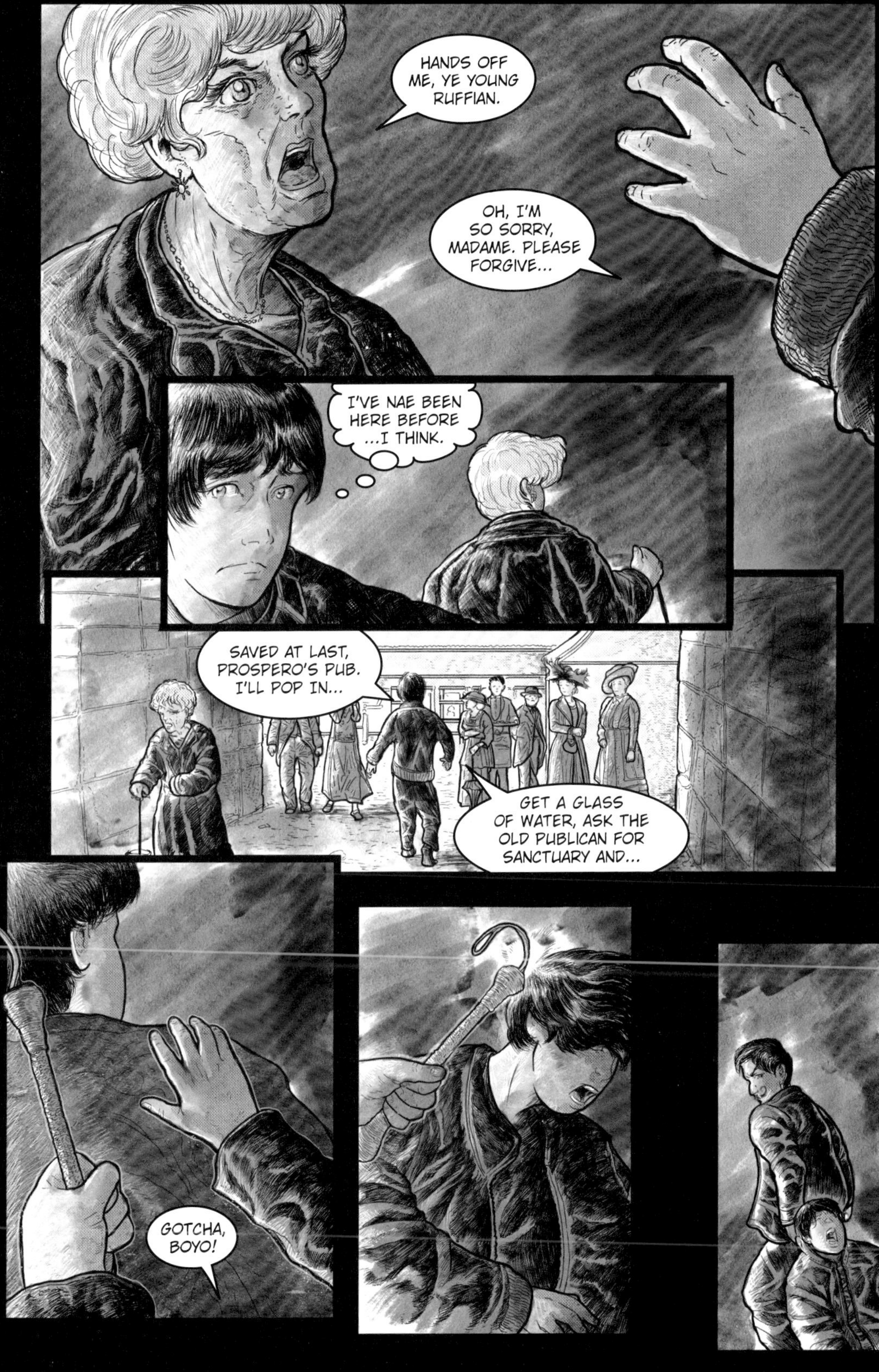
HANDS OFF ME, YE YOUNG RUFFIAN.
OH, I'M SO SORRY, MADAME. PLEASE FORGIVE...
I'VE NAE BEEN HERE BEFORE ...I THINK.
SAVED AT LAST, PROSPERO'S PUB. I'LL POP IN...
GET A GLASS OF WATER, ASK THE OLD PUBLICAN FOR SANCTUARY AND...
GOTCHA, BOYO!

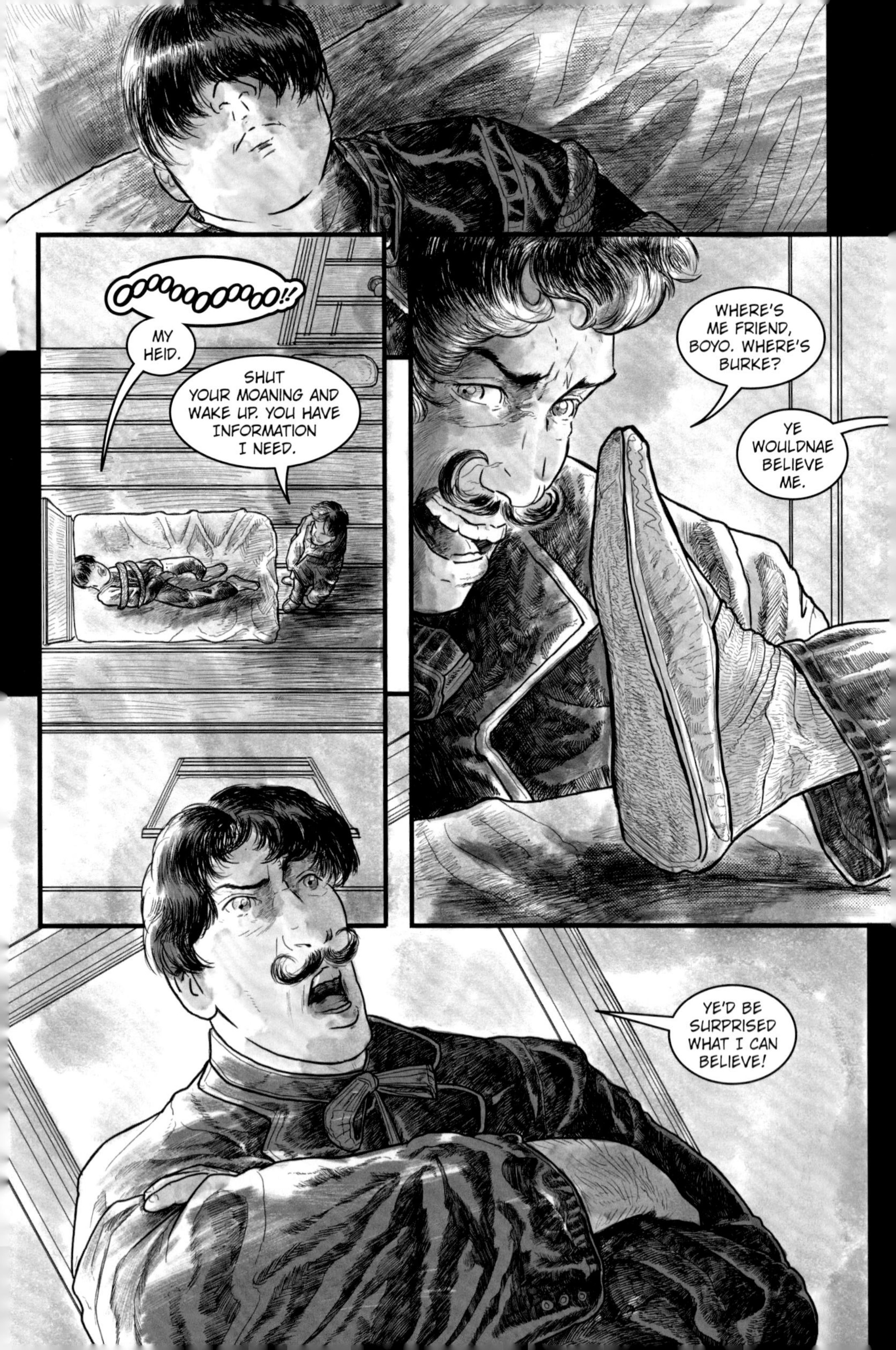
OOOOOOOOOOO!!
MY HEID.
SHUT YOUR MOANING AND WAKE UP. YOU HAVE INFORMATION I NEED.
WHERE'S ME FRIEND, BOYO. WHERE'S BURKE?
YE WOULDNAE BELIEVE ME.
YE'D BE SURPRISED WHAT I CAN BELIEVE!

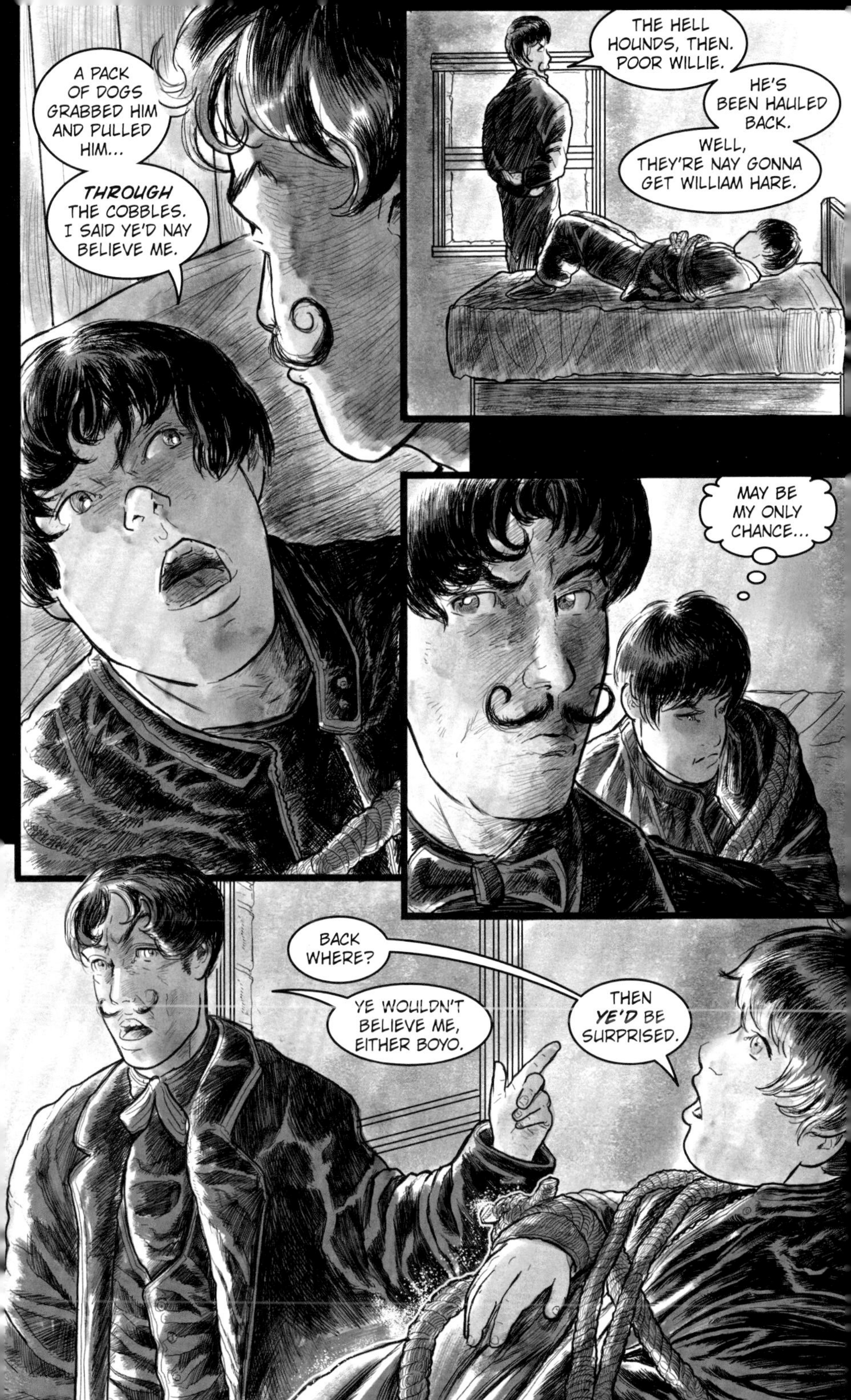
A PACK OF DOGS GRABBED HIM AND PULLED HIM...
THROUGH THE COBBLES. I SAID YE'D NAY BELIEVE ME.
THE HELL HOUNDS, THEN. POOR WILLIE.
HE'S BEEN HAULED BACK.
WELL, THEY'RE NAY GONNA GET WILLIAM HARE.
MAY BE MY ONLY CHANCE...
BACK WHERE?
YE WOULDN'T BELIEVE ME, EITHER BOYO.
THEN YE'D BE SURPRISED.

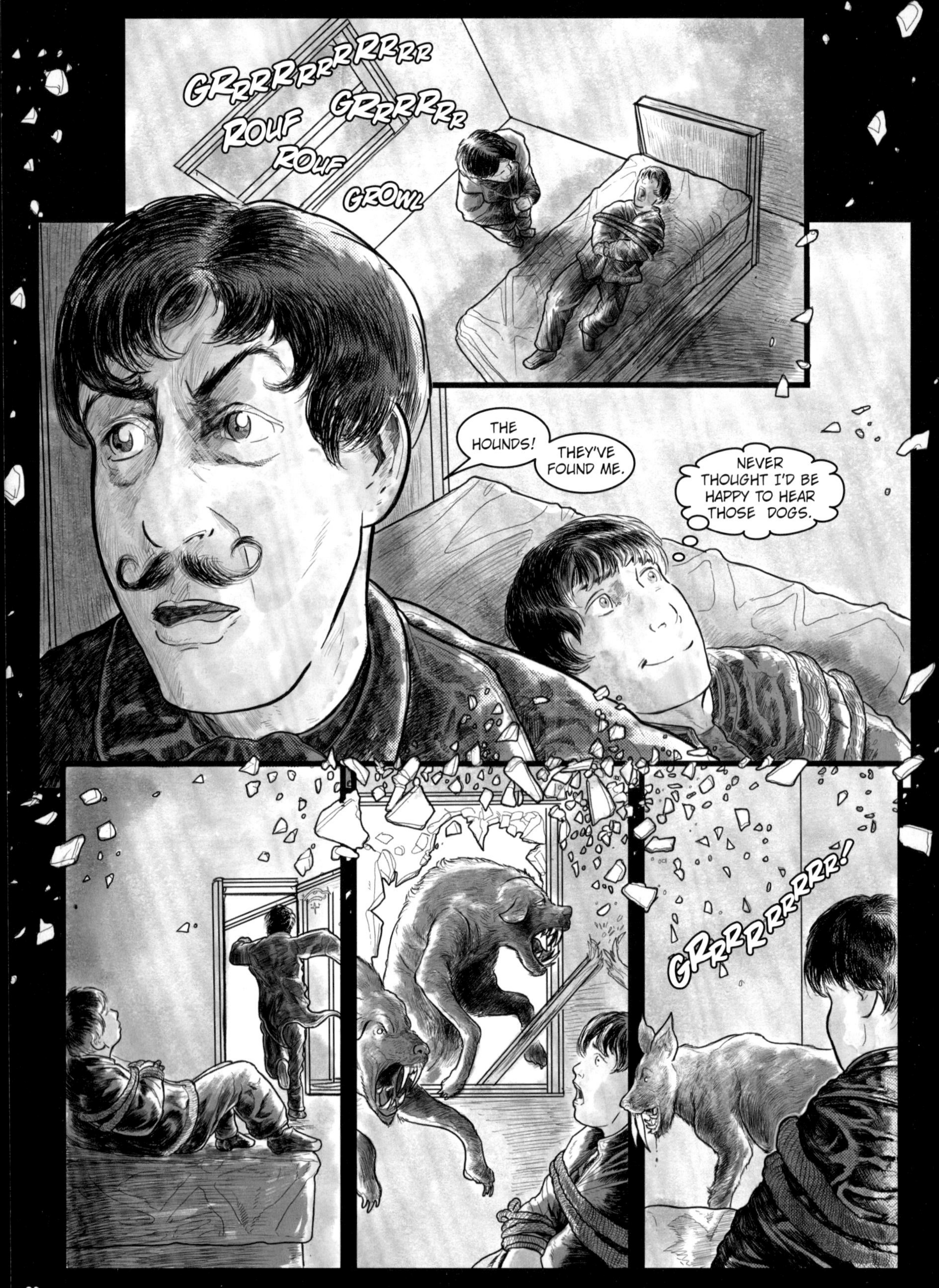

GRRRRRRRRRRRR
ROUF
GRRRRRRR
ROUF
GROWL
THE HOUNDS!
THEY'VE FOUND ME.
NEVER THOUGHT I'D BE HAPPY TO HEAR THOSE DOGS.
GRRRRRRRRR!

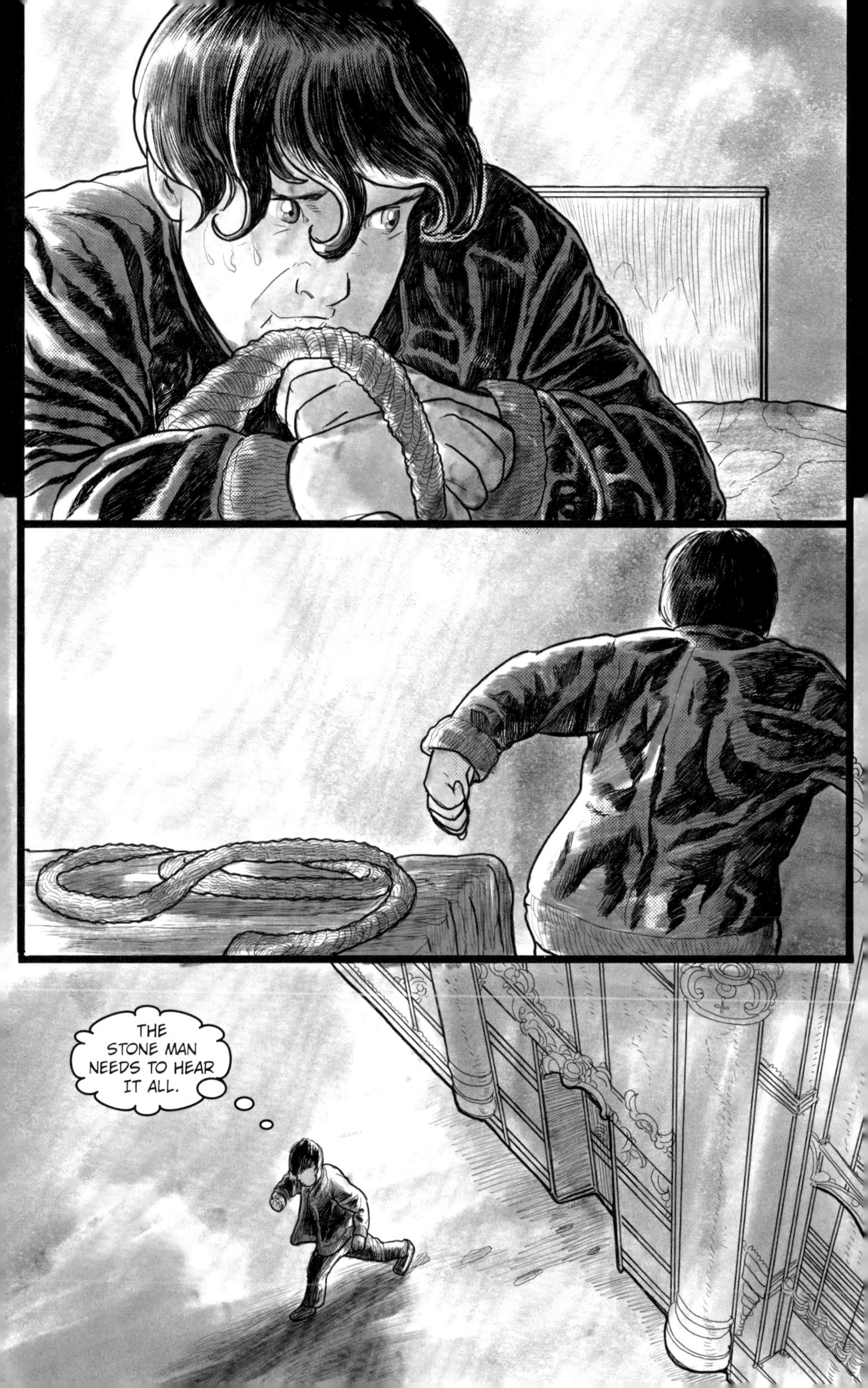
THE STONE MAN NEEDS TO HEAR IT ALL.

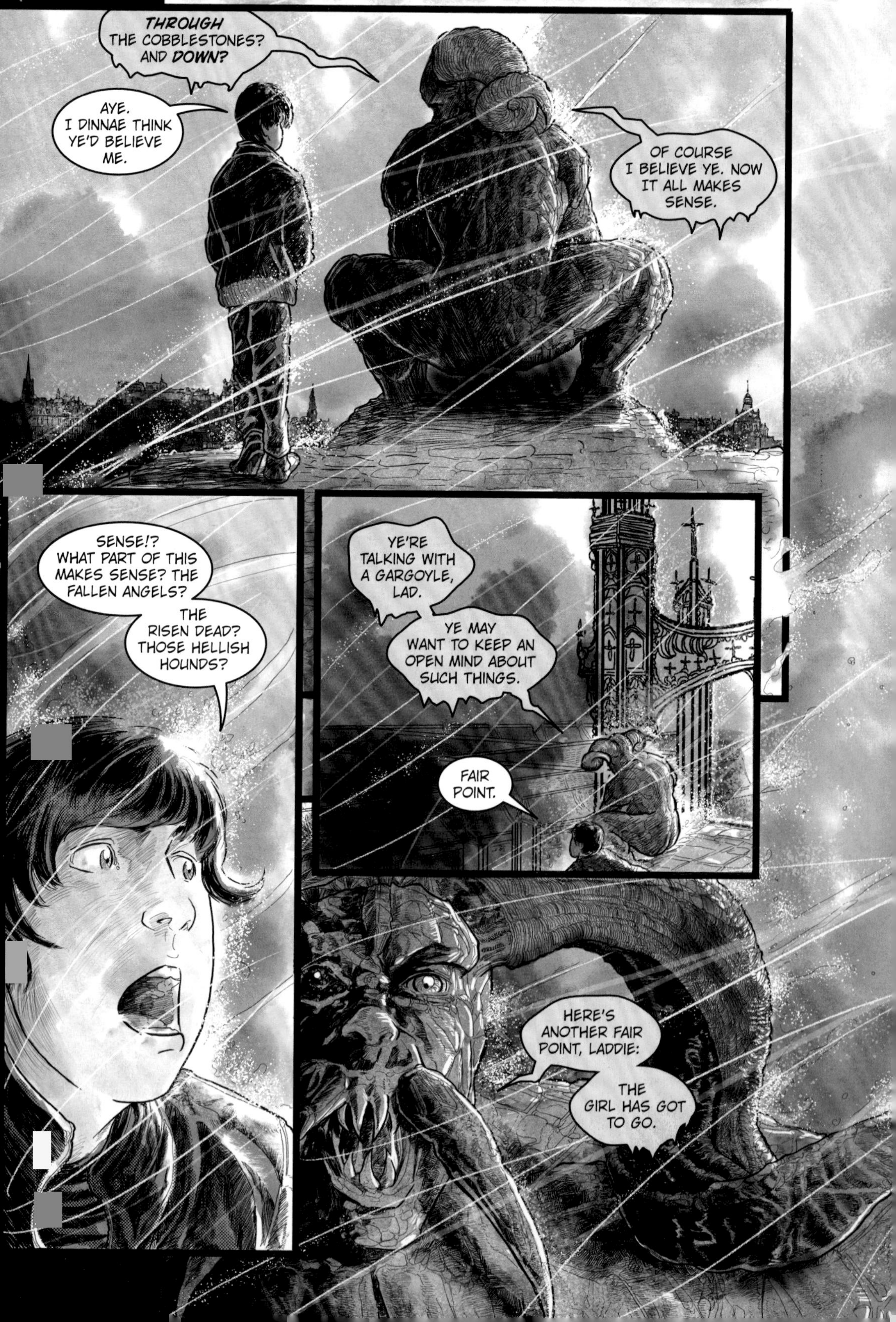
THROUGH THE COBBLESTONES? AND *DOWN?*
AYE. I DINNAE THINK YE'D BELIEVE ME.
OF COURSE I BELIEVE YE. NOW IT ALL MAKES SENSE.
SENSE!? WHAT PART OF THIS MAKES SENSE? THE FALLEN ANGELS?
THE RISEN DEAD? THOSE HELLISH HOUNDS?
YE'RE TALKING WITH A GARGOYLE, LAD.
YE MAY WANT TO KEEP AN OPEN MIND ABOUT SUCH THINGS.
FAIR POINT.
HERE'S ANOTHER FAIR POINT, LADDIE:
THE GIRL HAS GOT TO GO.

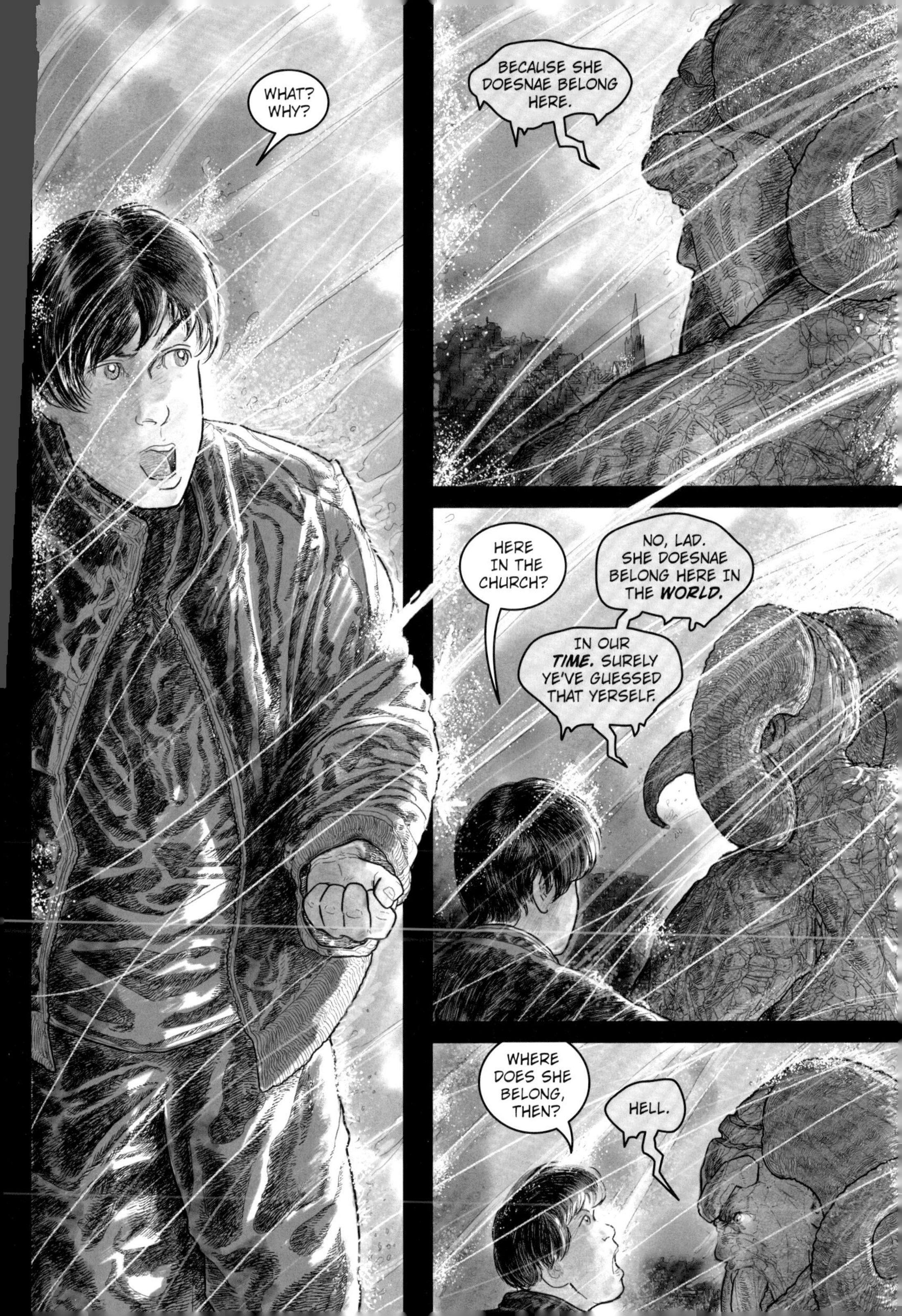
WHAT? WHY?
BECAUSE SHE DOESNAE BELONG HERE.
HERE IN THE CHURCH?
NO, LAD. SHE DOESNAE BELONG HERE IN THE ***WORLD.***
IN OUR ***TIME.*** SURELY YE'VE GUESSED THAT YERSELF.
WHERE DOES SHE BELONG, THEN?
HELL.

CHAPTER 8
CONFESSION

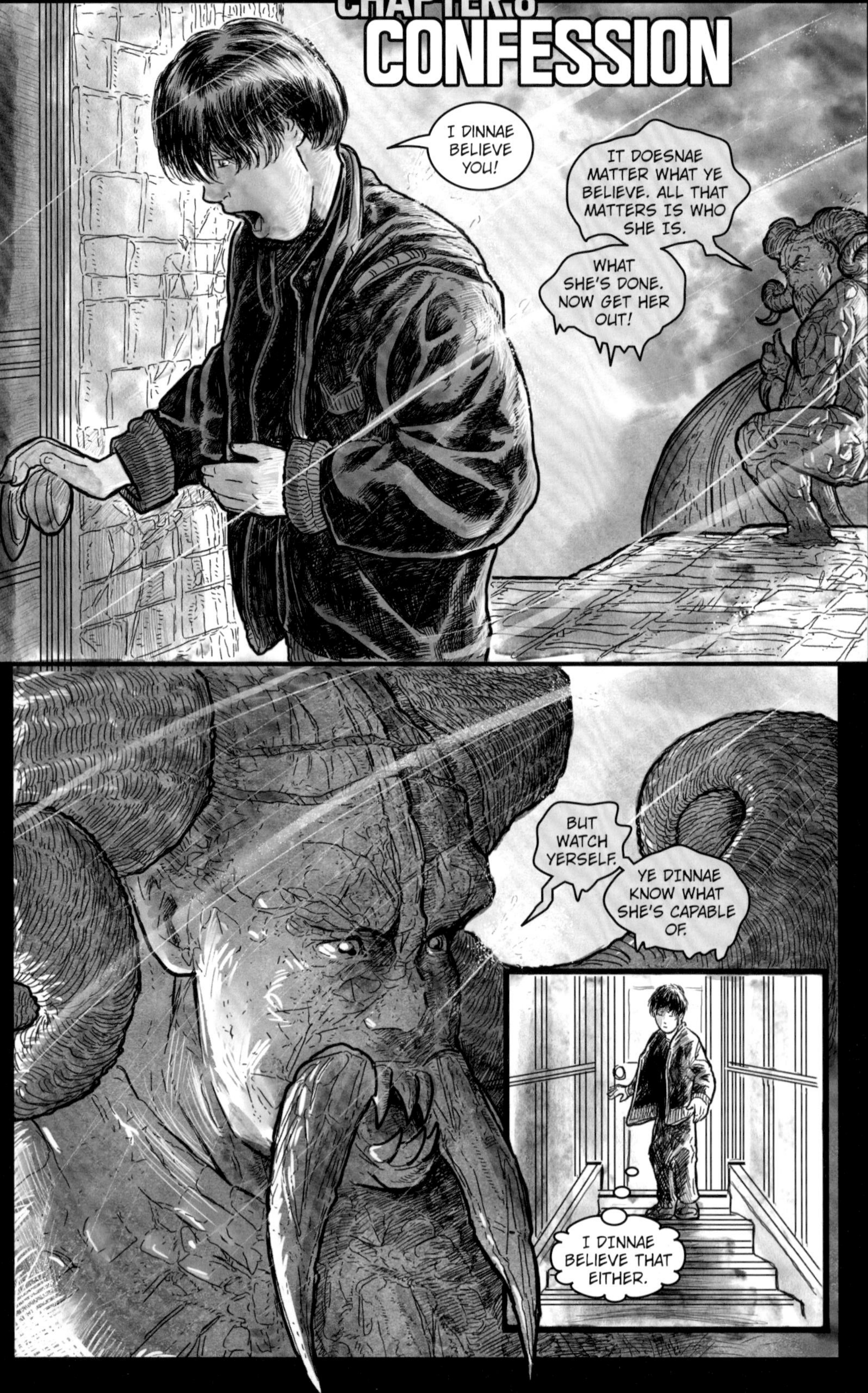
I DINNAE BELIEVE YOU!
IT DOESNAE MATTER WHAT YE BELIEVE. ALL THAT MATTERS IS WHO SHE IS.
WHAT SHE'S DONE. NOW GET HER OUT!
BUT WATCH YERSELF.
YE DINNAE KNOW WHAT SHE'S CAPABLE OF.
I DINNAE BELIEVE THAT EITHER.

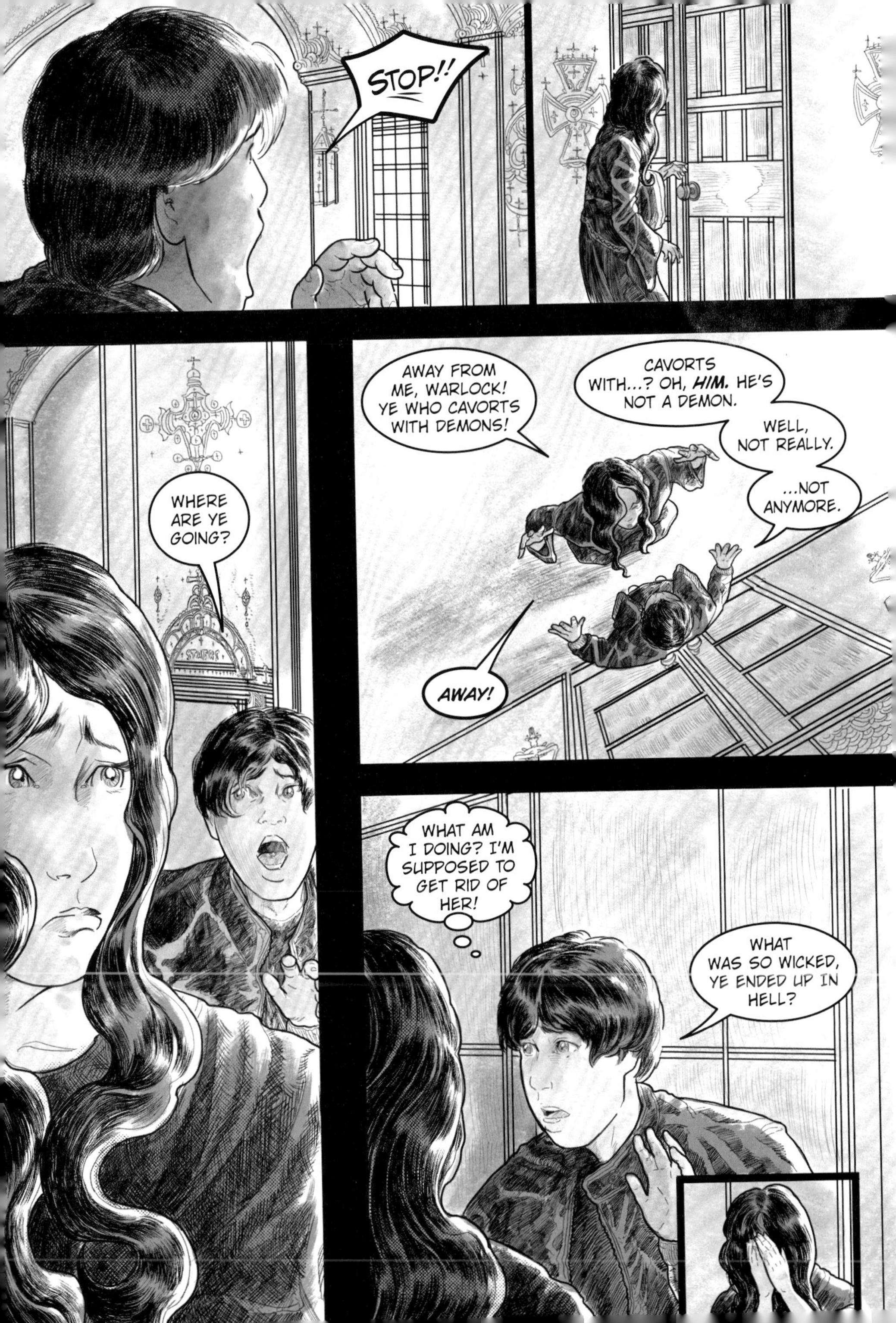
STOP!!
WHERE ARE YE GOING?
AWAY FROM ME, WARLOCK! YE WHO CAVORTS WITH DEMONS!
CAVORTS WITH...? OH, HIM. HE'S NOT A DEMON.
WELL, NOT REALLY.
...NOT ANYMORE.
AWAY!
WHAT AM I DOING? I'M SUPPOSED TO GET RID OF HER!
WHAT WAS SO WICKED, YE ENDED UP IN HELL?

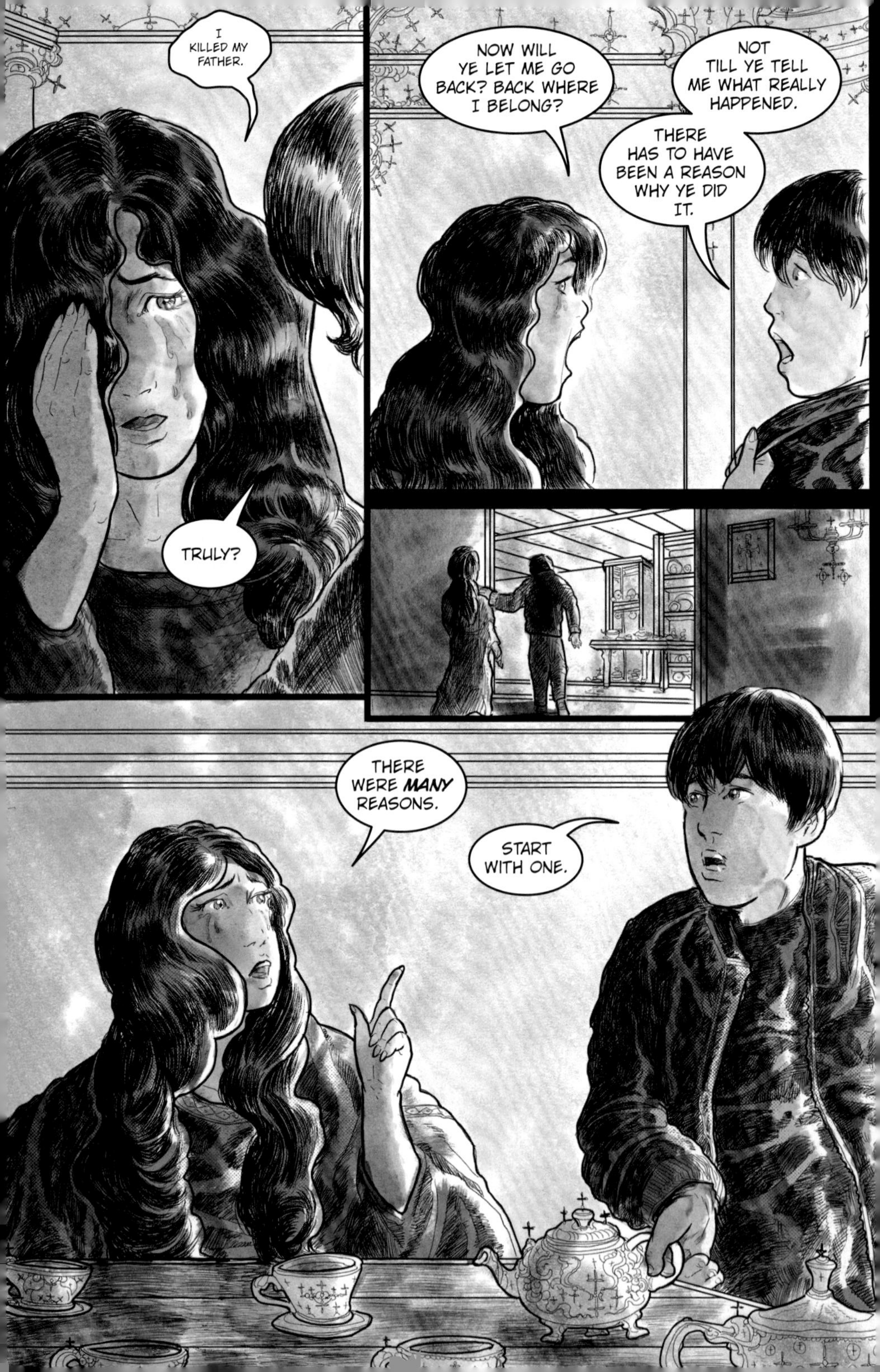
I KILLED MY FATHER.
TRULY?
NOW WILL YE LET ME GO BACK? BACK WHERE I BELONG?
NOT TILL YE TELL ME WHAT REALLY HAPPENED.
THERE HAS TO HAVE BEEN A REASON WHY YE DID IT.
THERE WERE **MANY** REASONS.
START WITH ONE.

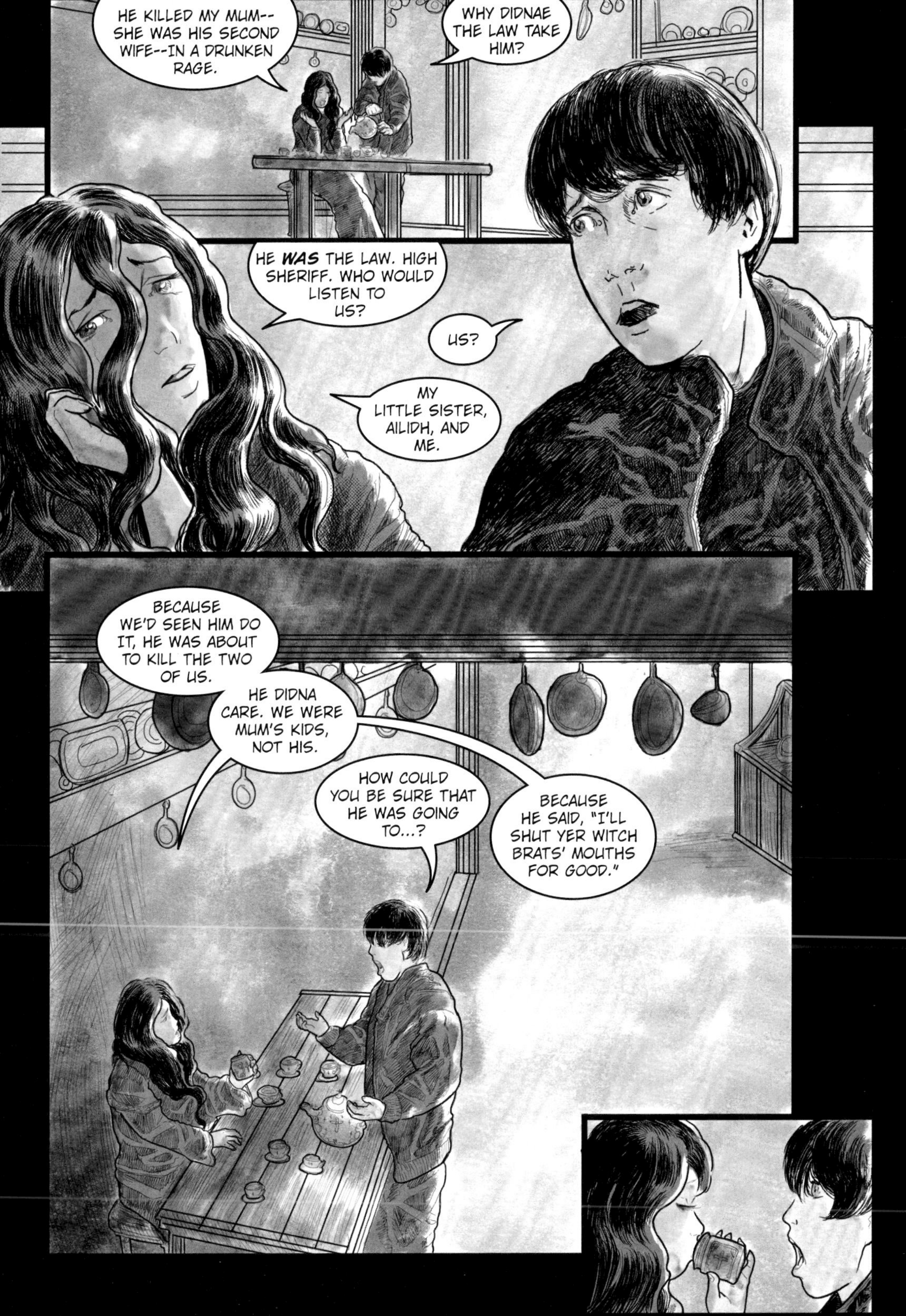
HE KILLED MY MUM--SHE WAS HIS SECOND WIFE--IN A DRUNKEN RAGE.
WHY DIDNAE THE LAW TAKE HIM?
HE **WAS** THE LAW. HIGH SHERIFF. WHO WOULD LISTEN TO US?
US?
MY LITTLE SISTER, AILIDH, AND ME.
BECAUSE WE'D SEEN HIM DO IT, HE WAS ABOUT TO KILL THE TWO OF US.
HE DIDNA CARE. WE WERE MUM'S KIDS, NOT HIS.
HOW COULD YOU BE SURE THAT HE WAS GOING TO...?
BECAUSE HE SAID, "I'LL SHUT YER WITCH BRATS' MOUTHS FOR GOOD."

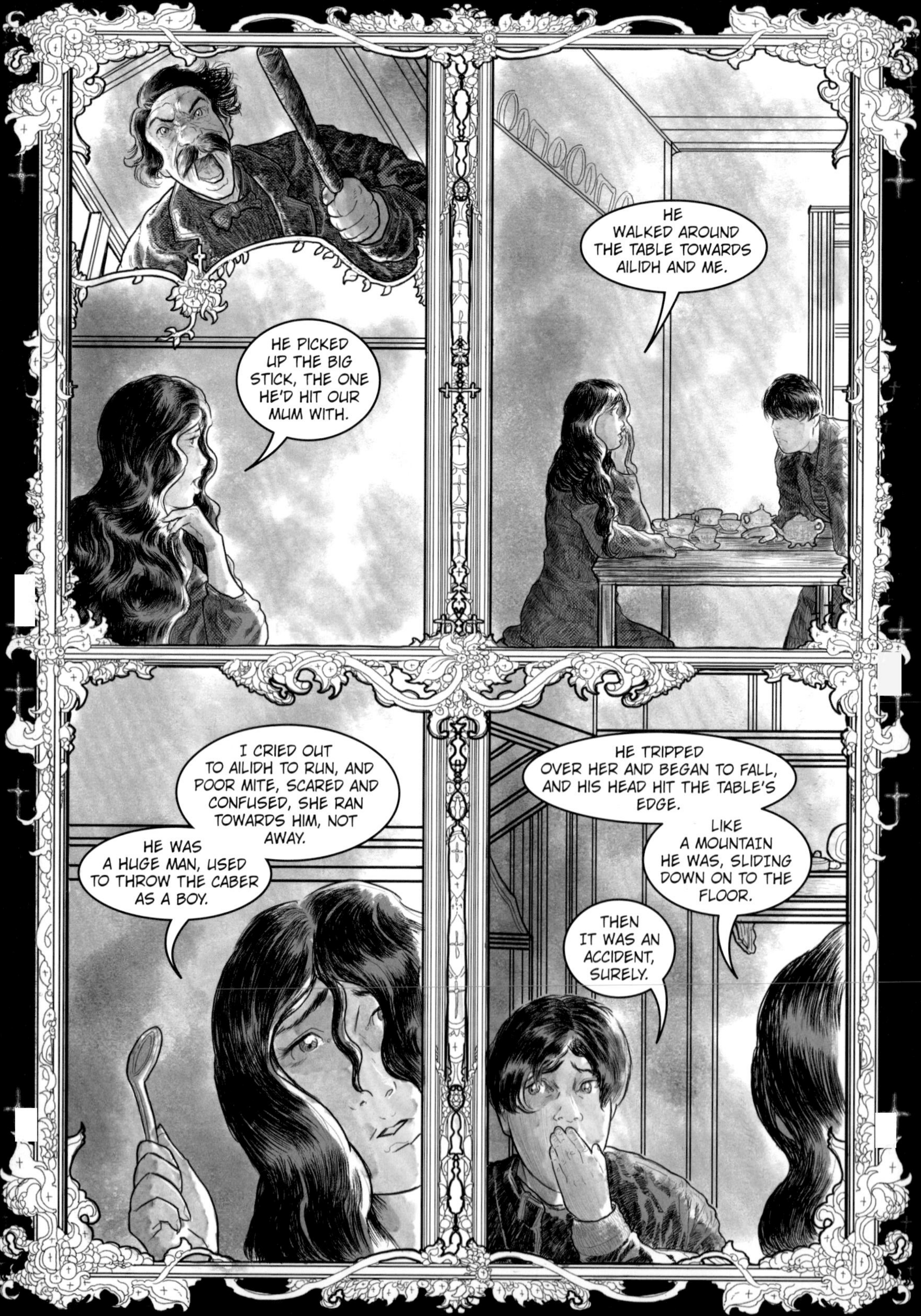
HE PICKED UP THE BIG STICK, THE ONE HE'D HIT OUR MUM WITH.
HE WALKED AROUND THE TABLE TOWARDS AILIDH AND ME.
I CRIED OUT TO AILIDH TO RUN, AND POOR MITE, SCARED AND CONFUSED, SHE RAN TOWARDS HIM, NOT AWAY.
HE WAS A HUGE MAN, USED TO THROW THE CABER AS A BOY.
HE TRIPPED OVER HER AND BEGAN TO FALL, AND HIS HEAD HIT THE TABLE'S EDGE.
LIKE A MOUNTAIN HE WAS, SLIDING DOWN ON TO THE FLOOR.
THEN IT WAS AN ACCIDENT, SURELY.

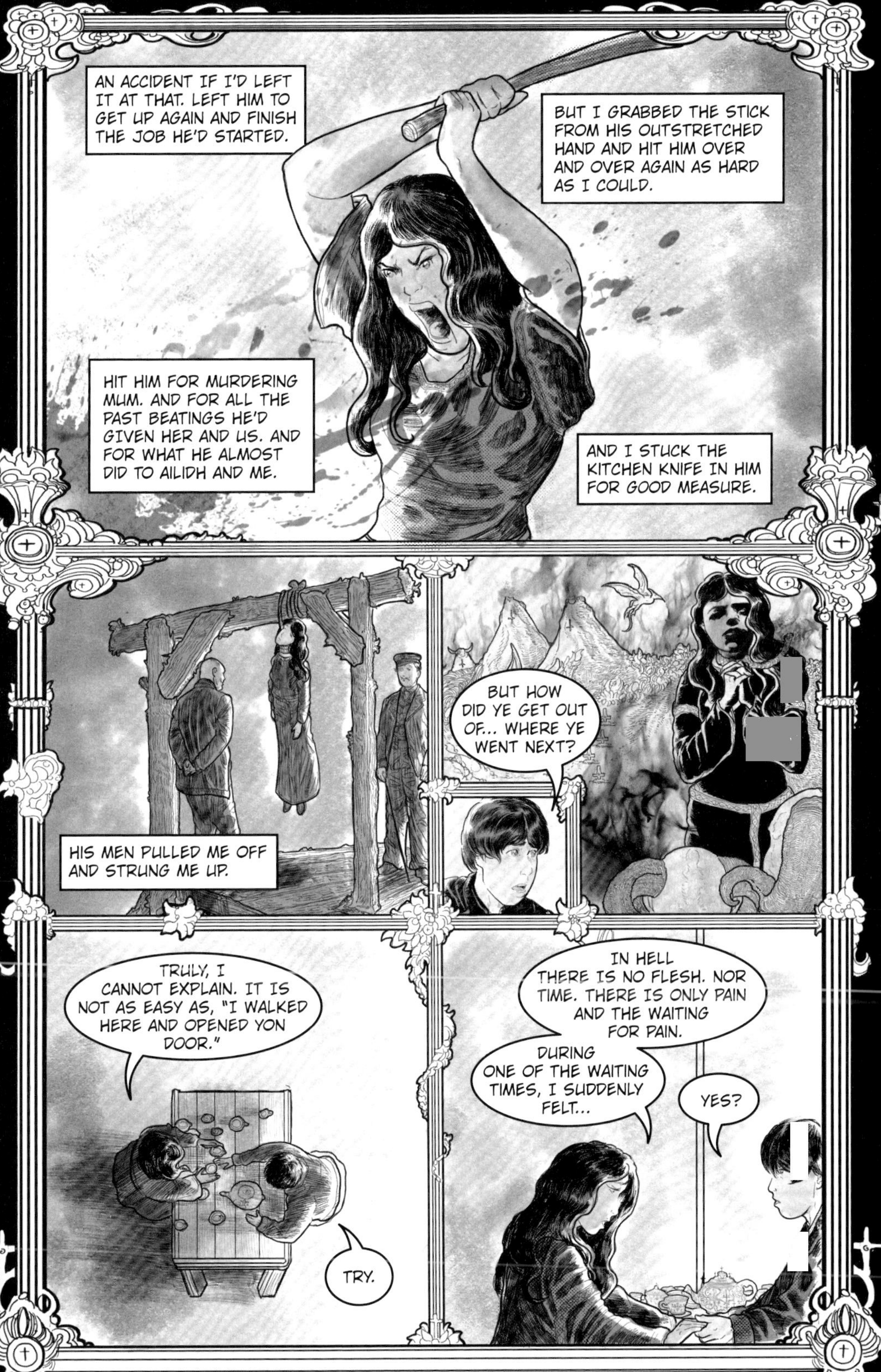
AN ACCIDENT IF I'D LEFT IT AT THAT. LEFT HIM TO GET UP AGAIN AND FINISH THE JOB HE'D STARTED.
BUT I GRABBED THE STICK FROM HIS OUTSTRETCHED HAND AND HIT HIM OVER AND OVER AGAIN AS HARD AS I COULD.
HIT HIM FOR MURDERING MUM. AND FOR ALL THE PAST BEATINGS HE'D GIVEN HER AND US. AND FOR WHAT HE ALMOST DID TO AILIDH AND ME.
AND I STUCK THE KITCHEN KNIFE IN HIM FOR GOOD MEASURE.
HIS MEN PULLED ME OFF AND STRUNG ME UP.
BUT HOW DID YE GET OUT OF... WHERE YE WENT NEXT?
TRULY, I CANNOT EXPLAIN. IT IS NOT AS EASY AS, "I WALKED HERE AND OPENED YON DOOR."
TRY.
IN HELL THERE IS NO FLESH. NOR TIME. THERE IS ONLY PAIN AND THE WAITING FOR PAIN.
DURING ONE OF THE WAITING TIMES, I SUDDENLY FELT...
YES?

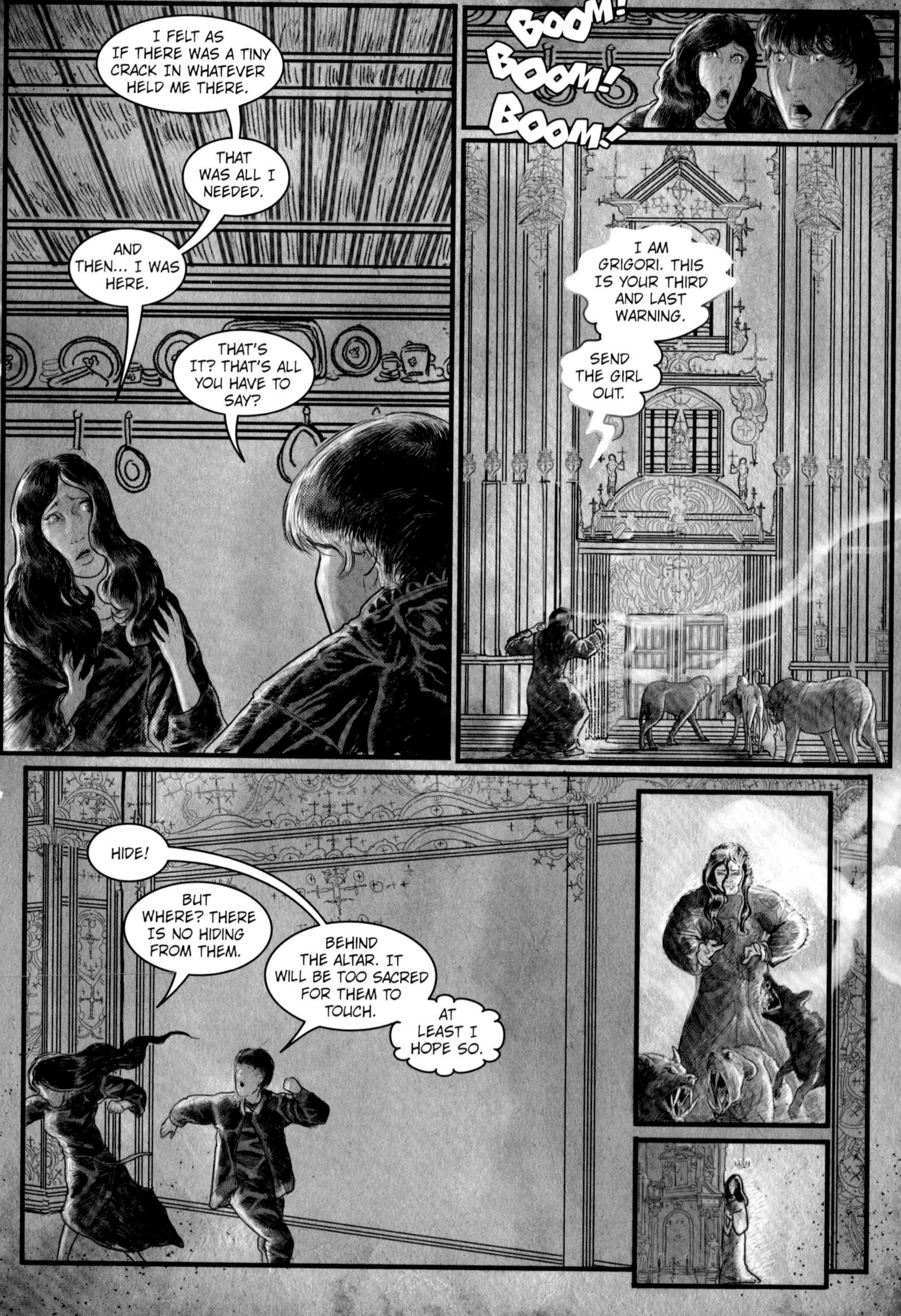
I FELT AS IF THERE WAS A TINY CRACK IN WHATEVER HELD ME THERE.
THAT WAS ALL I NEEDED.
AND THEN... I WAS HERE.
THAT'S IT? THAT'S ALL YOU HAVE TO SAY?
BOOM! BOOM! BOOM!
I AM GRIGORI. THIS IS YOUR THIRD AND LAST WARNING.
SEND THE GIRL OUT.
HIDE!
BUT WHERE? THERE IS NO HIDING FROM THEM.
BEHIND THE ALTAR. IT WILL BE TOO SACRED FOR THEM TO TOUCH.
AT LEAST I HOPE SO.

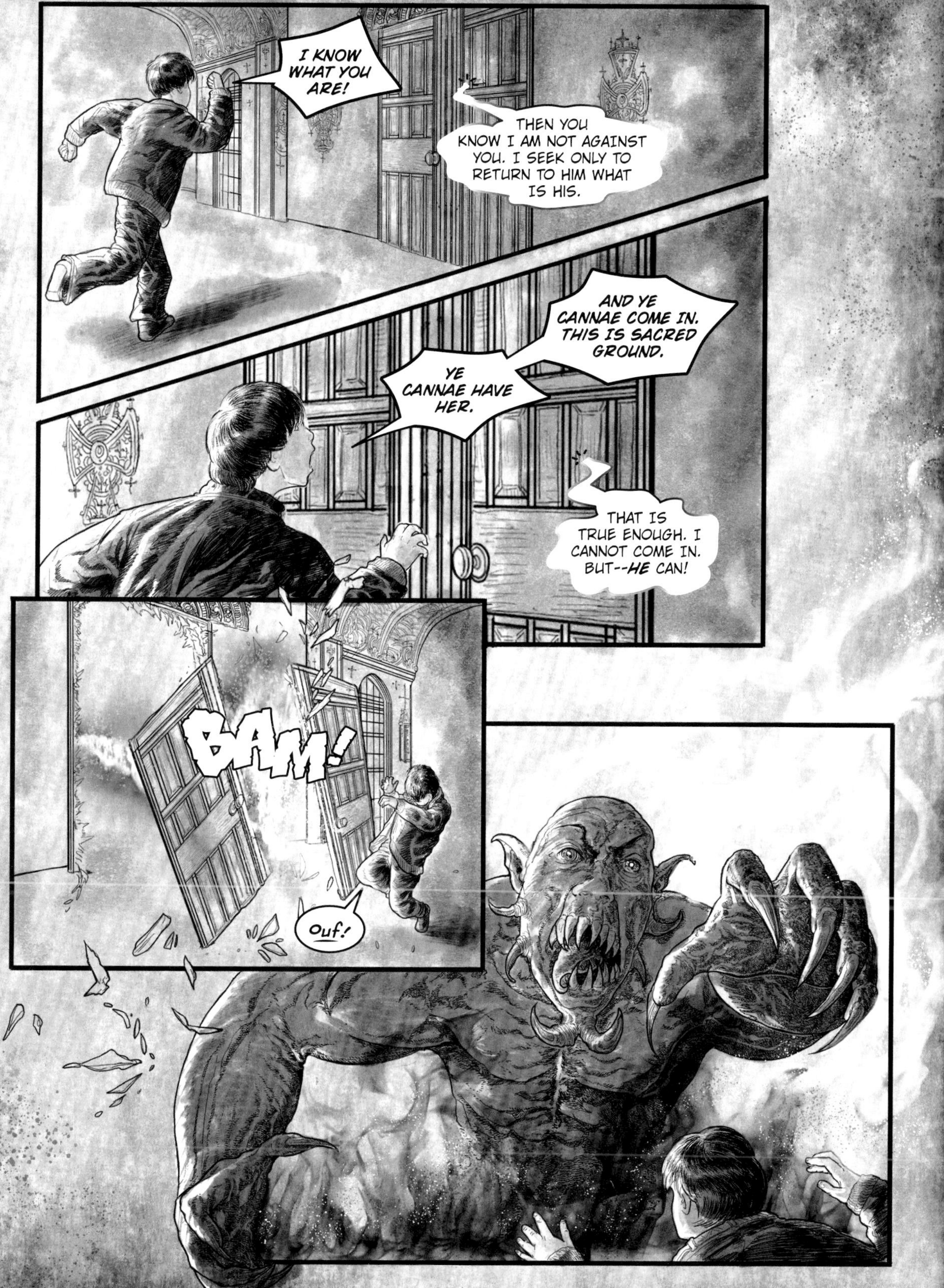
I KNOW WHAT YOU ARE!
THEN YOU KNOW I AM NOT AGAINST YOU. I SEEK ONLY TO RETURN TO HIM WHAT IS HIS.
AND YE CANNAE COME IN. THIS IS SACRED GROUND.
YE CANNAE HAVE HER.
THAT IS TRUE ENOUGH. I CANNOT COME IN. BUT--HE CAN!
BAM!
Ouf!

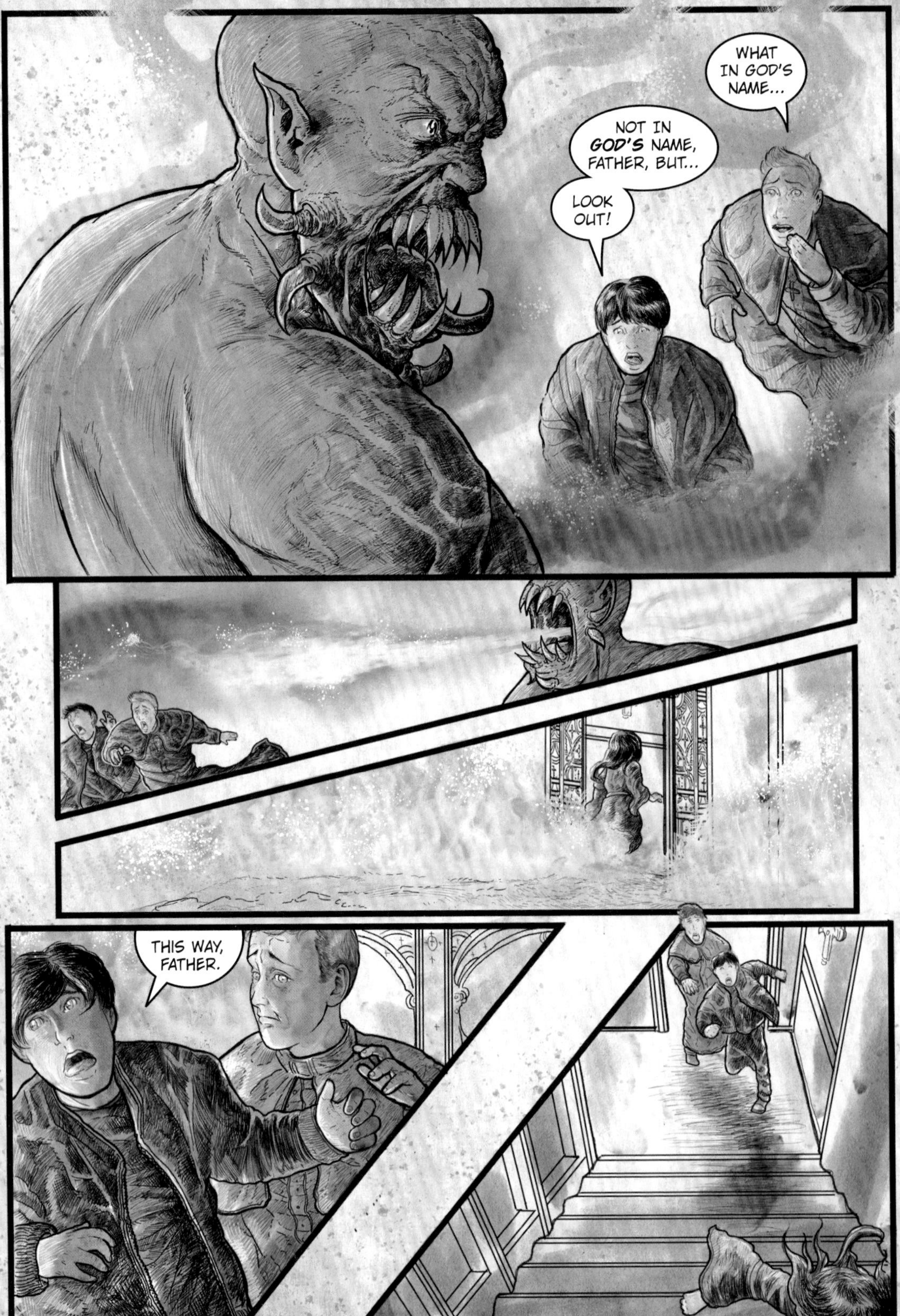
WHAT IN GOD'S NAME...
NOT IN **GOD'S** NAME, FATHER, BUT...
LOOK OUT!
THIS WAY, FATHER.

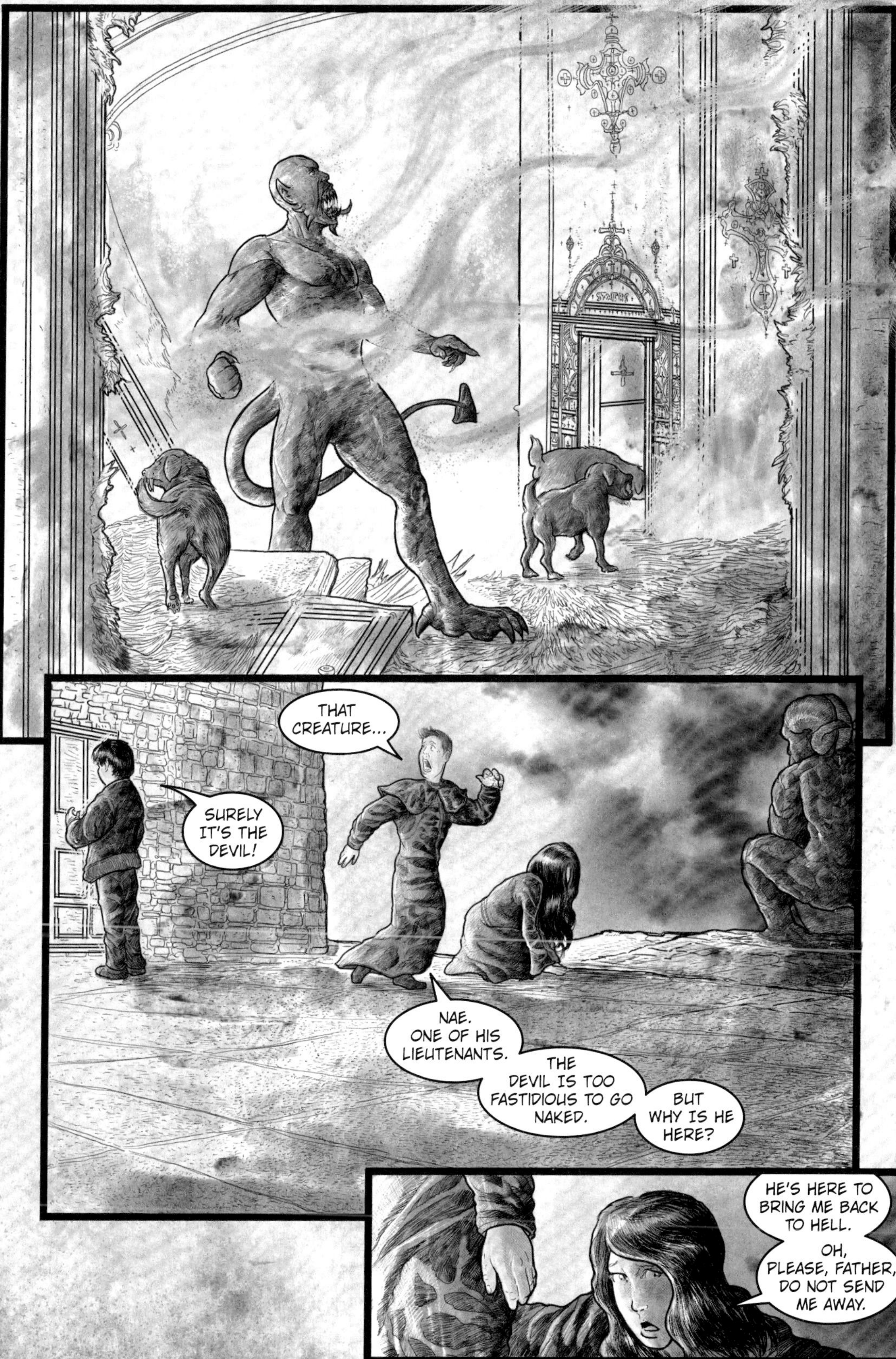
THAT CREATURE...
SURELY IT'S THE DEVIL!
NAE. ONE OF HIS LIEUTENANTS.
THE DEVIL IS TOO FASTIDIOUS TO GO NAKED.
BUT WHY IS HE HERE?
HE'S HERE TO BRING ME BACK TO HELL.
OH, PLEASE, FATHER, DO NOT SEND ME AWAY.

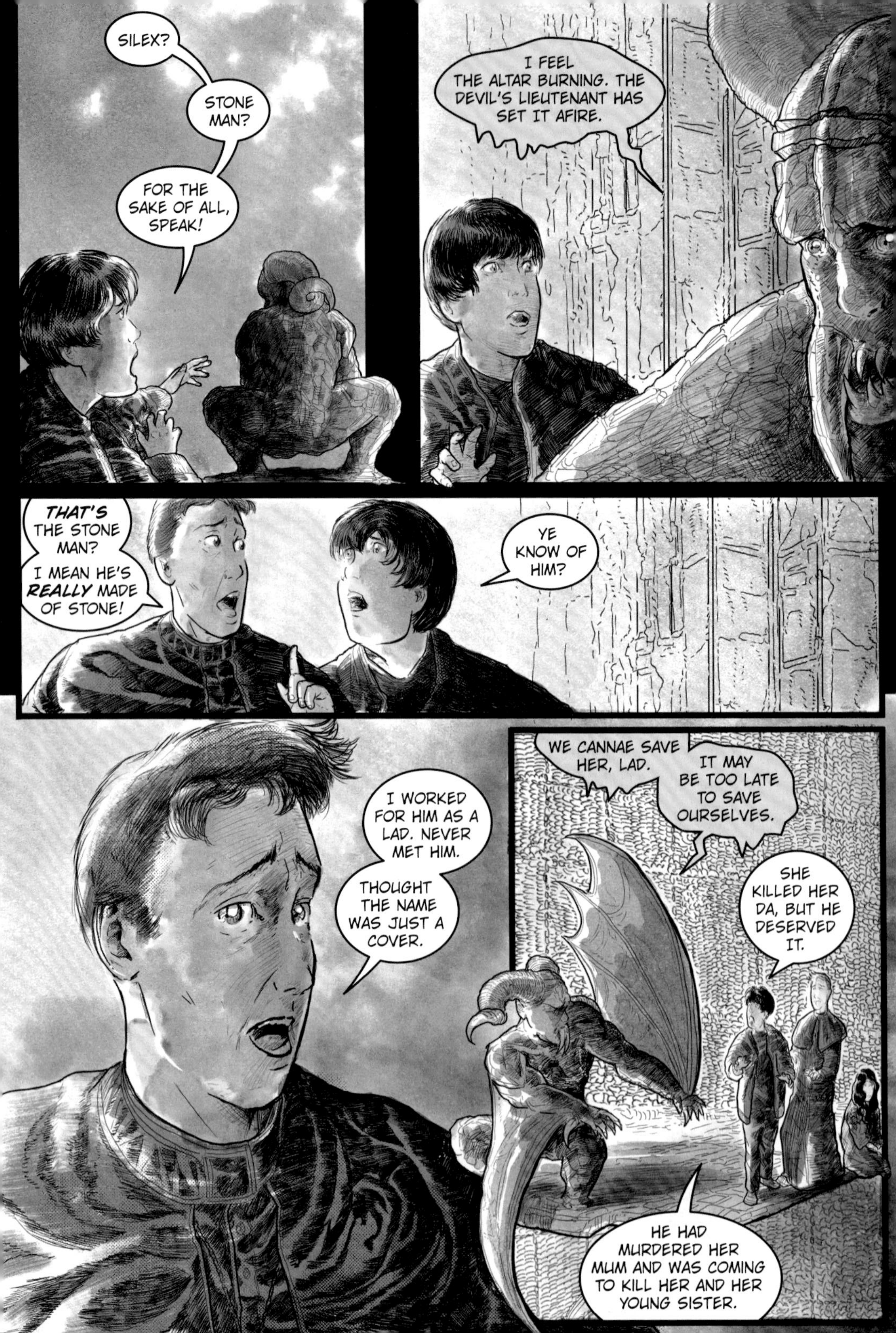

SILEX?
STONE MAN?
FOR THE SAKE OF ALL, SPEAK!
I FEEL THE ALTAR BURNING. THE DEVIL'S LIEUTENANT HAS SET IT AFIRE.
THAT'S THE STONE MAN?
I MEAN HE'S *REALLY* MADE OF STONE!
YE KNOW OF HIM?
I WORKED FOR HIM AS A LAD. NEVER MET HIM.
THOUGHT THE NAME WAS JUST A COVER.
WE CANNAE SAVE HER, LAD.
IT MAY BE TOO LATE TO SAVE OURSELVES.
SHE KILLED HER DA, BUT HE DESERVED IT.
HE HAD MURDERED HER MUM AND WAS COMING TO KILL HER AND HER YOUNG SISTER.

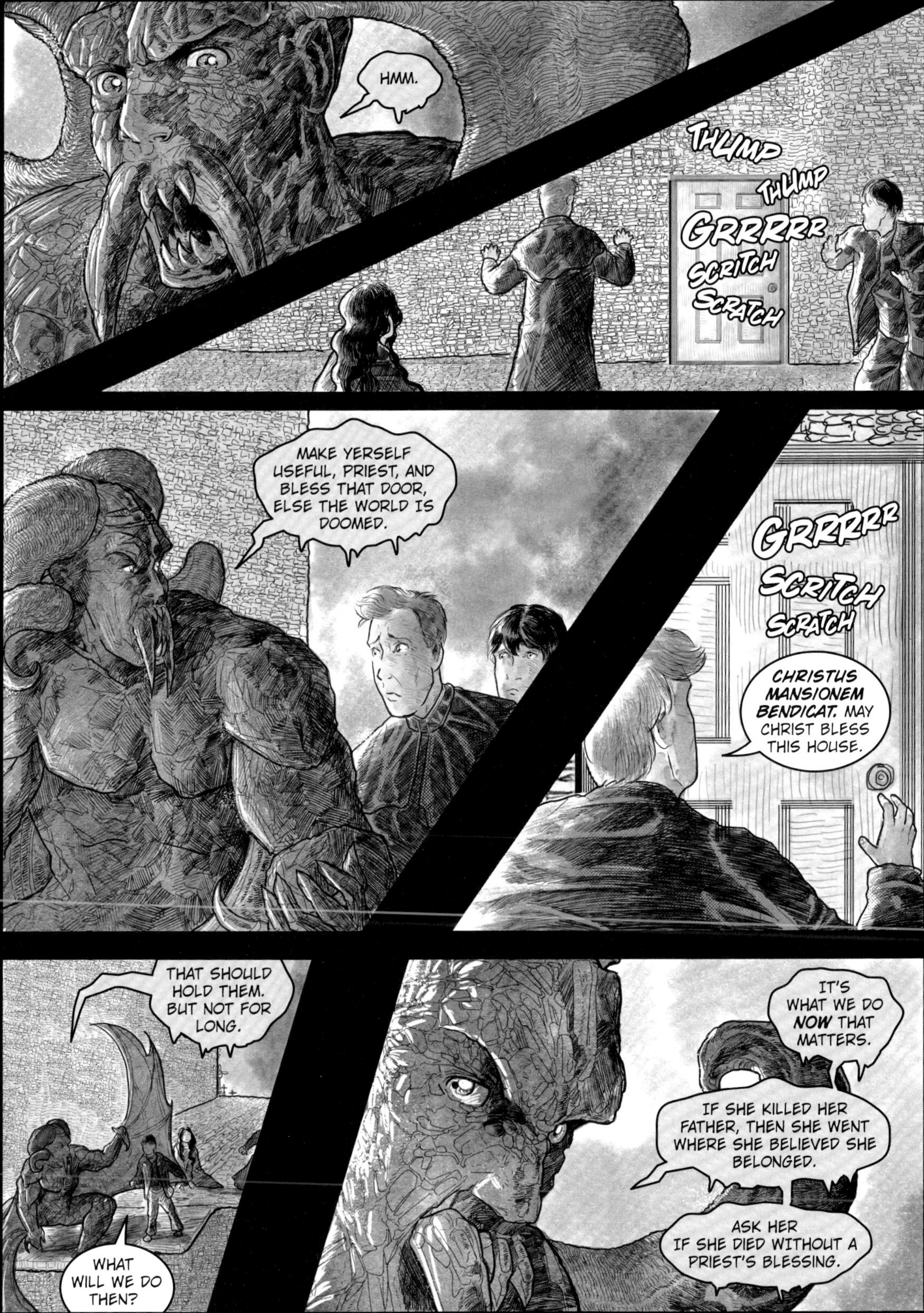
HMM.
THUMP
THUMP
GRRRRR
SCRITCH
SCRATCH
MAKE YERSELF USEFUL, PRIEST, AND BLESS THAT DOOR, ELSE THE WORLD IS DOOMED.
GRRRRR
SCRITCH
SCRATCH
CHRISTUS MANSIONEM BENDICAT. MAY CHRIST BLESS THIS HOUSE.
THAT SHOULD HOLD THEM. BUT NOT FOR LONG.
WHAT WILL WE DO THEN?
IT'S WHAT WE DO NOW THAT MATTERS.
IF SHE KILLED HER FATHER, THEN SHE WENT WHERE SHE BELIEVED SHE BELONGED.
ASK HER IF SHE DIED WITHOUT A PRIEST'S BLESSING.

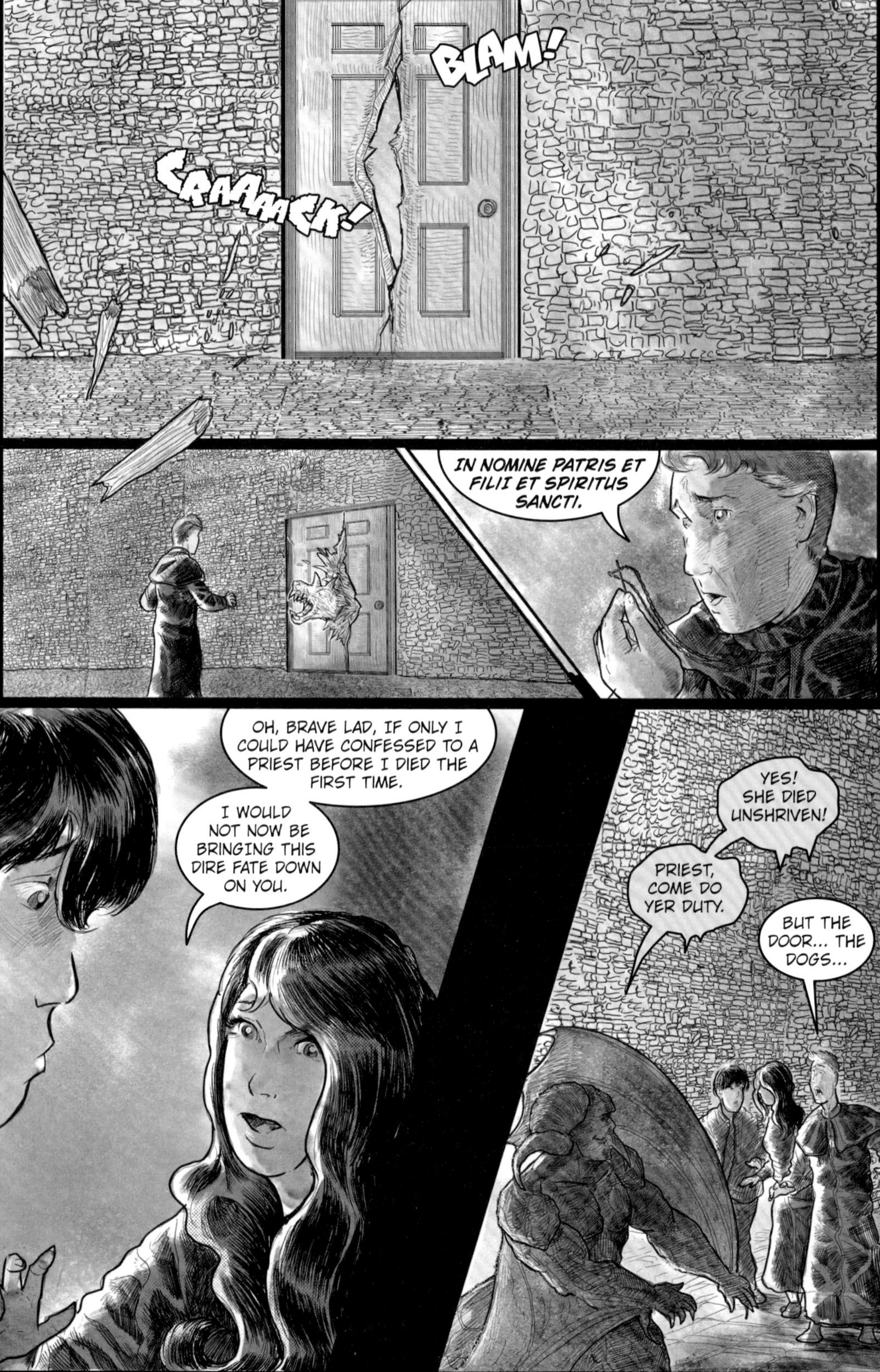
BLAM!
CRAAAACK!
IN NOMINE PATRIS ET FILII ET SPIRITUS SANCTI.
OH, BRAVE LAD, IF ONLY I COULD HAVE CONFESSED TO A PRIEST BEFORE I DIED THE FIRST TIME.
I WOULD NOT NOW BE BRINGING THIS DIRE FATE DOWN ON YOU.
YES! SHE DIED UNSHRIVEN!
PRIEST, COME DO YER DUTY.
BUT THE DOOR... THE DOGS...

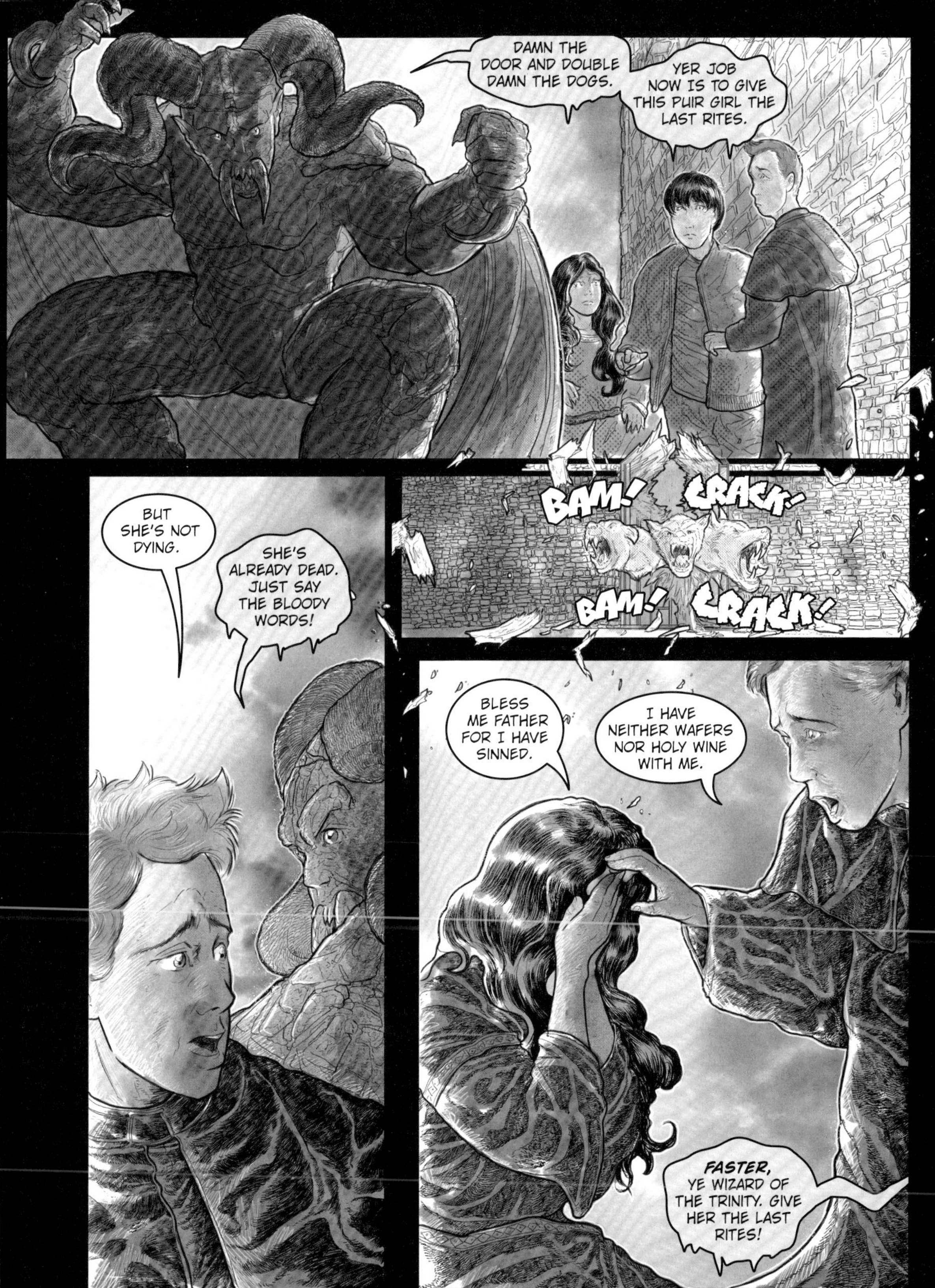
DAMN THE DOOR AND DOUBLE DAMN THE DOGS.
YER JOB NOW IS TO GIVE THIS PUIR GIRL THE LAST RITES.
BAM! CRACK!
BAM! CRACK!
BUT SHE'S NOT DYING.
SHE'S ALREADY DEAD. JUST SAY THE BLOODY WORDS!
BLESS ME FATHER FOR I HAVE SINNED.
I HAVE NEITHER WAFERS NOR HOLY WINE WITH ME.
FASTER, YE WIZARD OF THE TRINITY. GIVE HER THE LAST RITES!

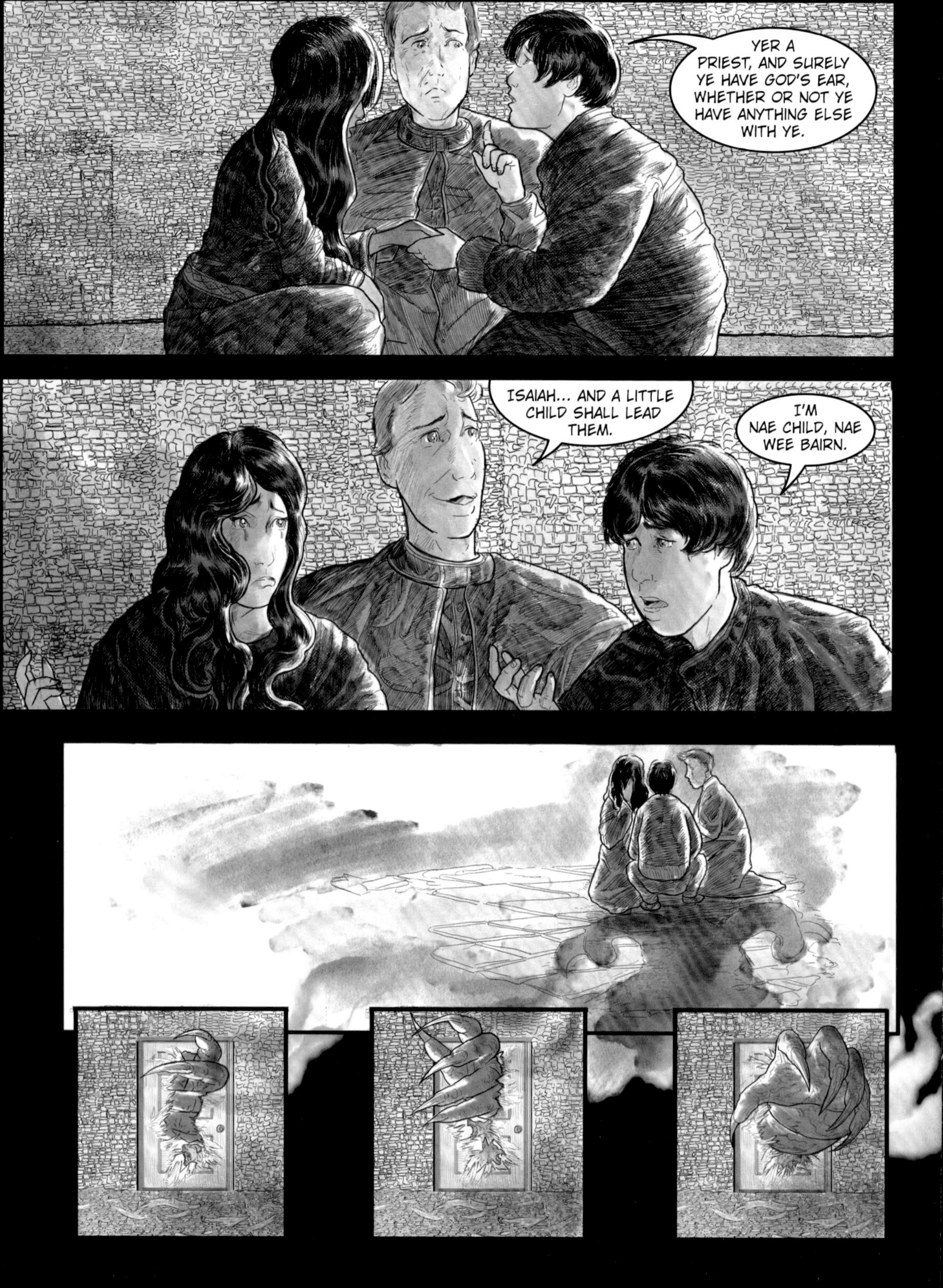
YER A PRIEST, AND SURELY YE HAVE GOD'S EAR, WHETHER OR NOT YE HAVE ANYTHING ELSE WITH YE.
ISAIAH... AND A LITTLE CHILD SHALL LEAD THEM.
I'M NAE CHILD, NAE WEE BAIRN.

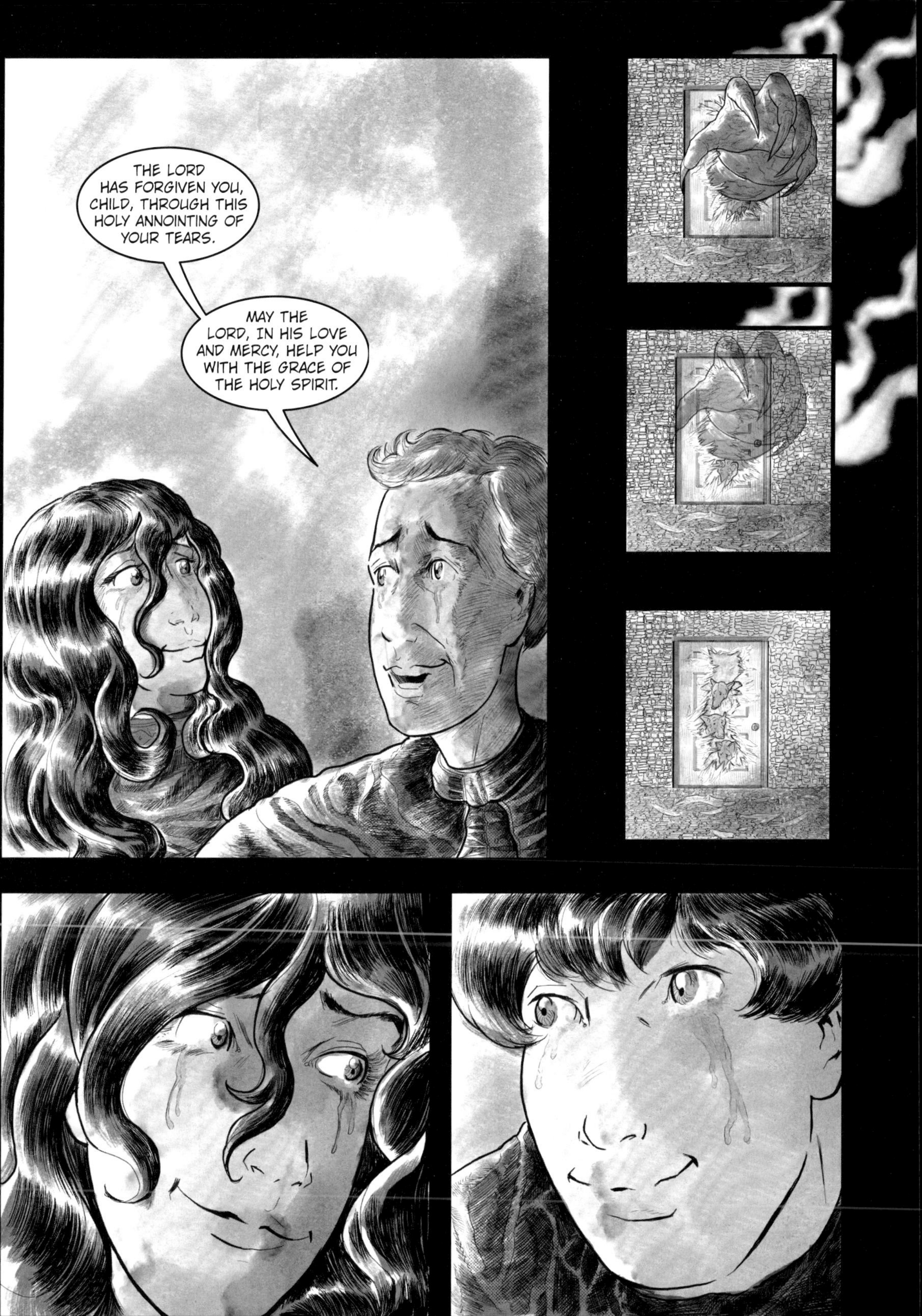
THE LORD HAS FORGIVEN YOU, CHILD, THROUGH THIS HOLY ANNOINTING OF YOUR TEARS.
MAY THE LORD, IN HIS LOVE AND MERCY, HELP YOU WITH THE GRACE OF THE HOLY SPIRIT.

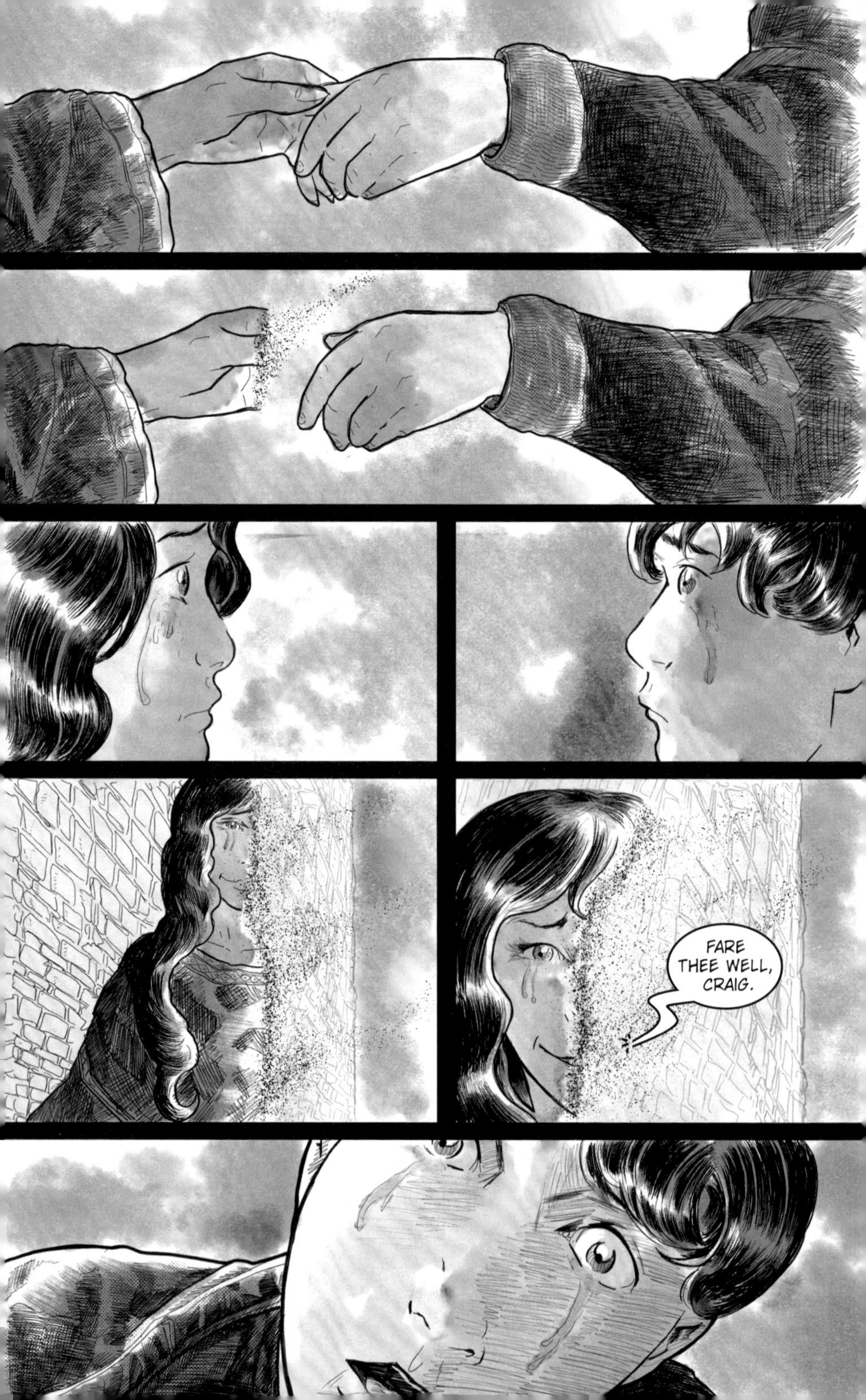
FARE THEE WELL, CRAIG.

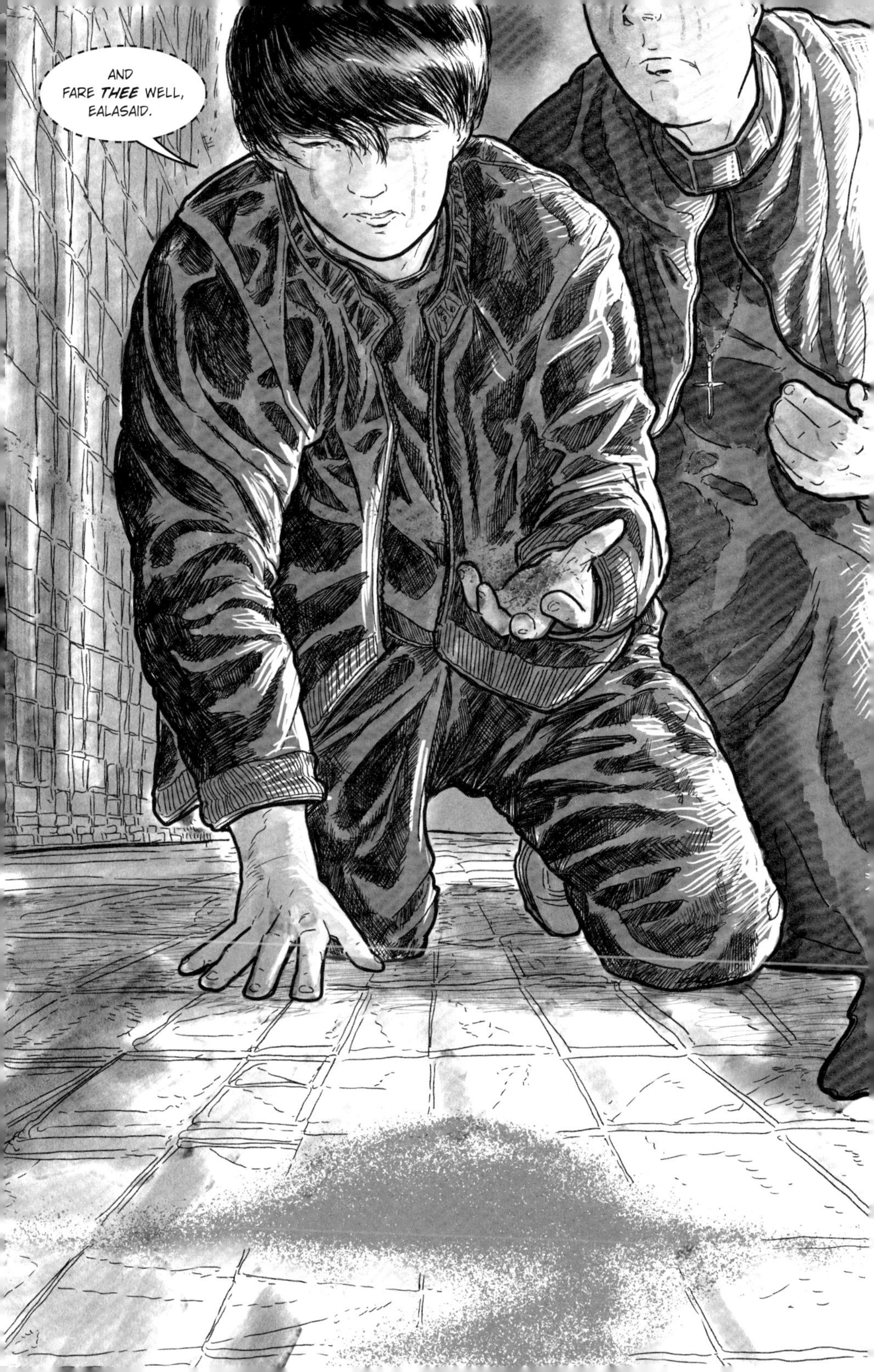
AND FARE THEE WELL, EALASAID.

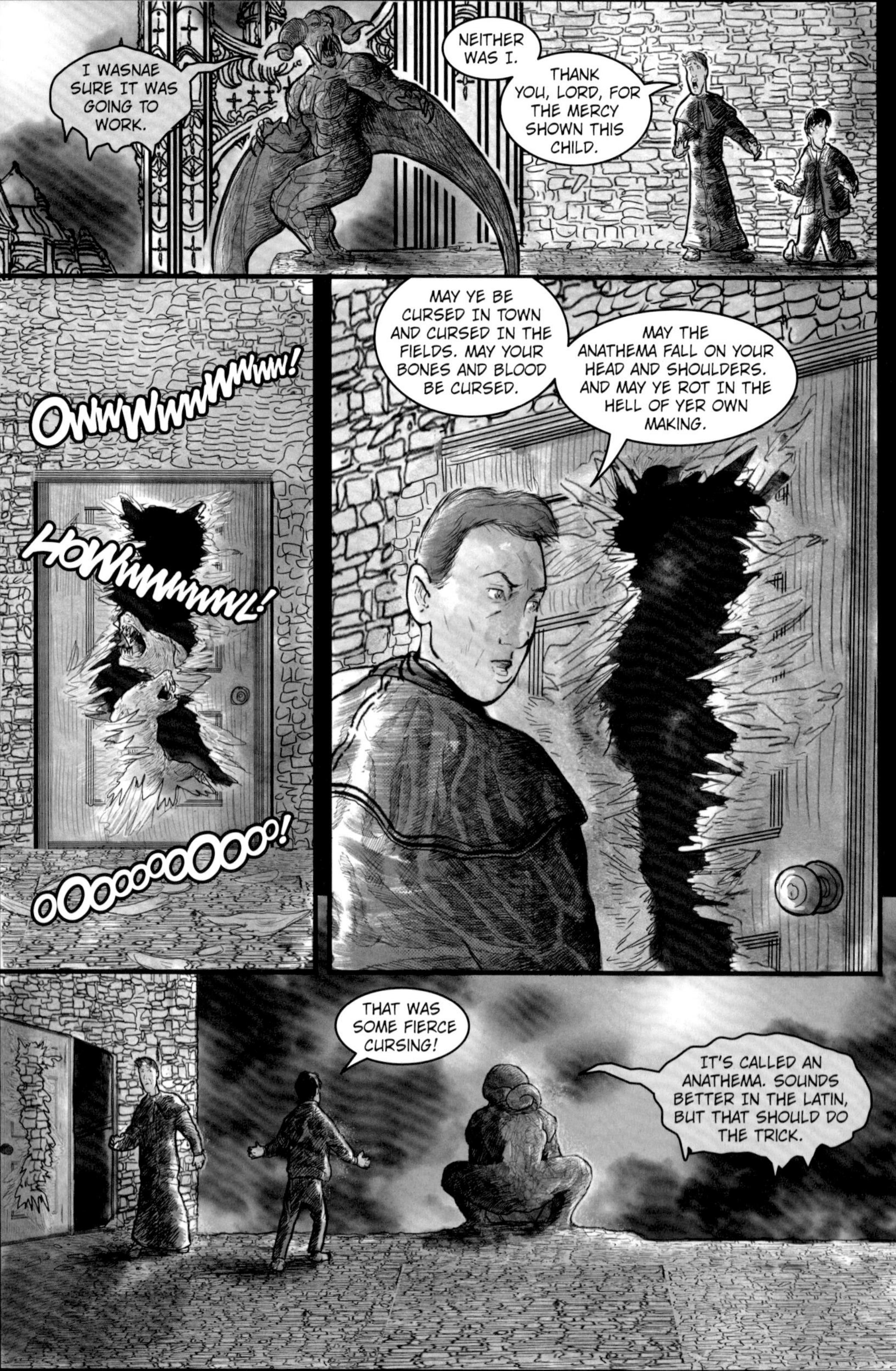
I WASNAE SURE IT WAS GOING TO WORK.
NEITHER WAS I.
THANK YOU, LORD, FOR THE MERCY SHOWN THIS CHILD.
OWWWWWWWW!
HOWWWWWWL!
OOOOOOOOOOO!
MAY YE BE CURSED IN TOWN AND CURSED IN THE FIELDS. MAY YOUR BONES AND BLOOD BE CURSED.
MAY THE ANATHEMA FALL ON YOUR HEAD AND SHOULDERS. AND MAY YE ROT IN THE HELL OF YER OWN MAKING.
THAT WAS SOME FIERCE CURSING!
IT'S CALLED AN ANATHEMA. SOUNDS BETTER IN THE LATIN, BUT THAT SHOULD DO THE TRICK.

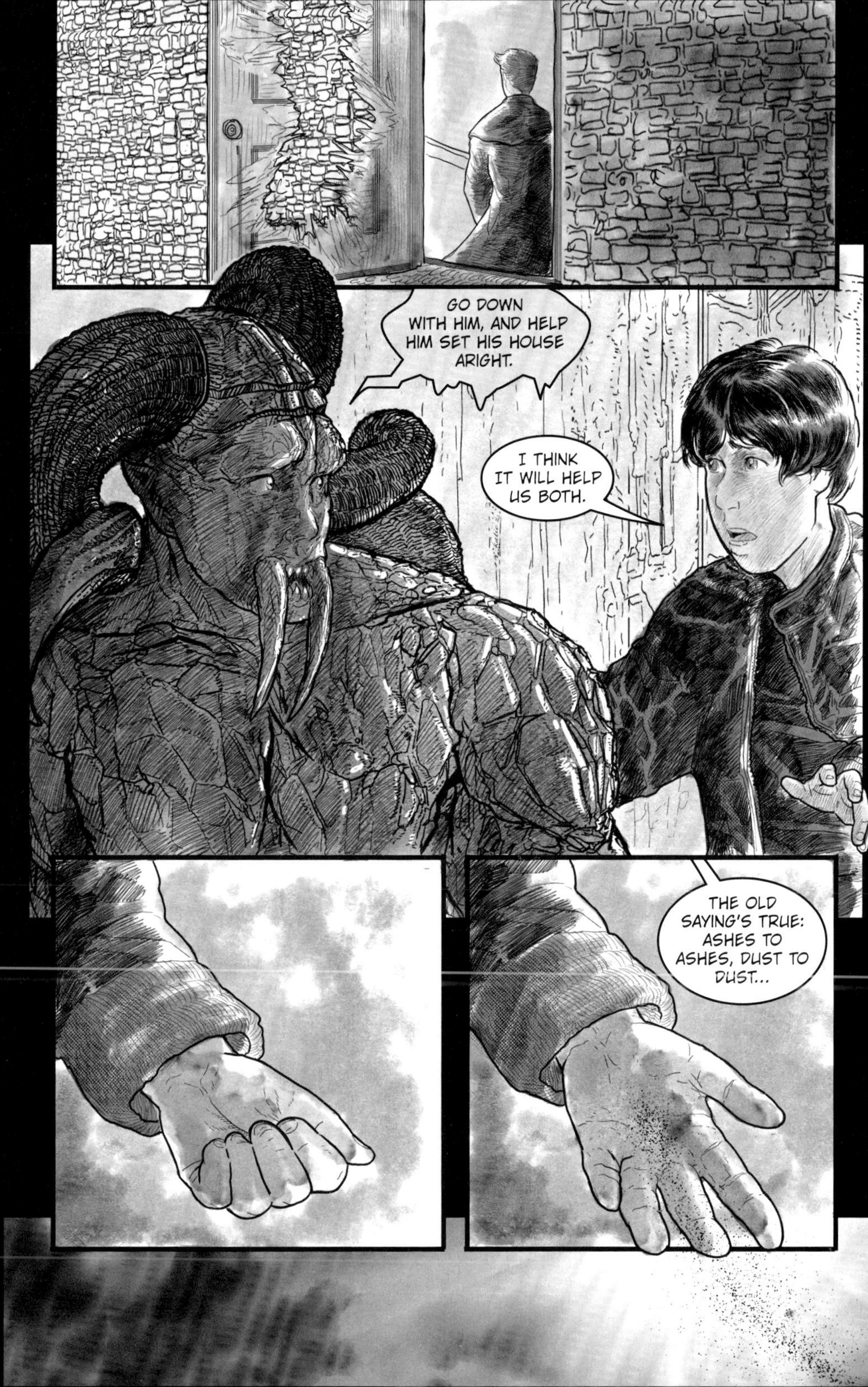
GO DOWN WITH HIM, AND HELP HIM SET HIS HOUSE ARIGHT.
I THINK IT WILL HELP US BOTH.
THE OLD SAYING'S TRUE: ASHES TO ASHES, DUST TO DUST...

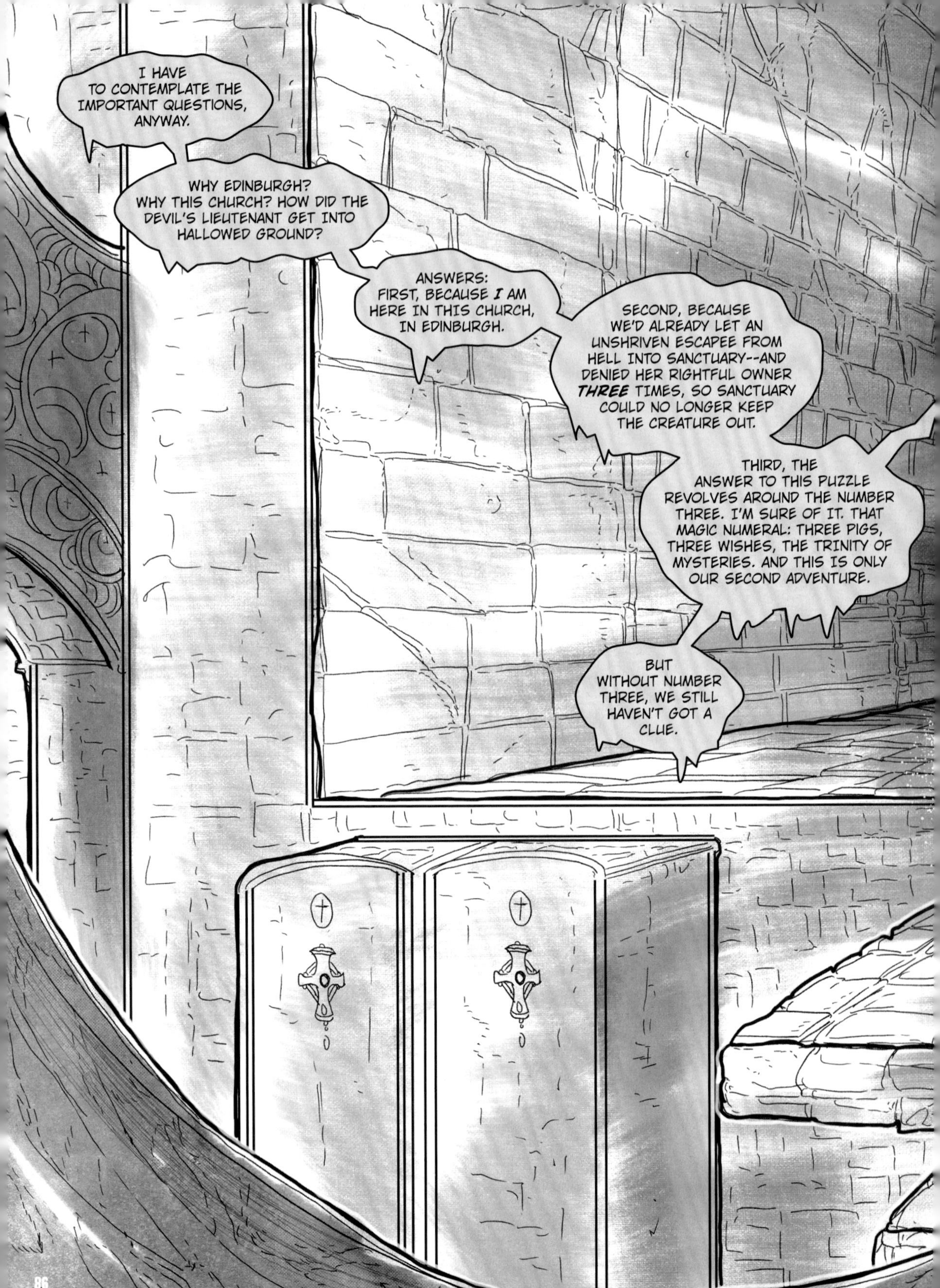
I HAVE TO CONTEMPLATE THE IMPORTANT QUESTIONS, ANYWAY.
WHY EDINBURGH? WHY THIS CHURCH? HOW DID THE DEVIL'S LIEUTENANT GET INTO HALLOWED GROUND?
ANSWERS: FIRST, BECAUSE *I* AM HERE IN THIS CHURCH, IN EDINBURGH.
SECOND, BECAUSE WE'D ALREADY LET AN UNSHRIVEN ESCAPEE FROM HELL INTO SANCTUARY--AND DENIED HER RIGHTFUL OWNER ***THREE*** TIMES, SO SANCTUARY COULD NO LONGER KEEP THE CREATURE OUT.
THIRD, THE ANSWER TO THIS PUZZLE REVOLVES AROUND THE NUMBER THREE. I'M SURE OF IT. THAT MAGIC NUMERAL: THREE PIGS, THREE WISHES, THE TRINITY OF MYSTERIES. AND THIS IS ONLY OUR SECOND ADVENTURE.
BUT WITHOUT NUMBER THREE, WE STILL HAVEN'T GOT A CLUE.

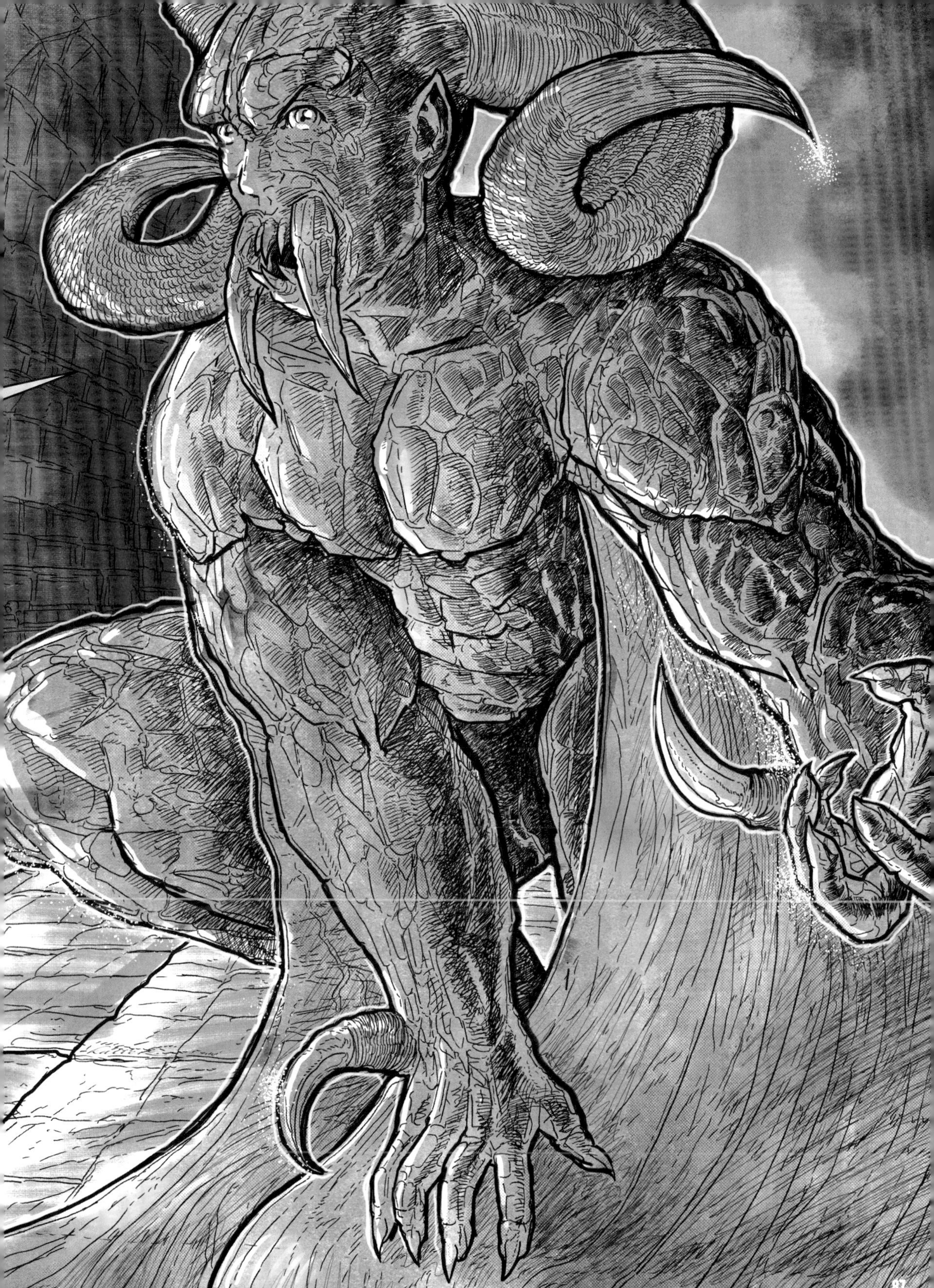

Jane Yolen is the author of more than 350 books, including *Owl Moon*, *The Devil's Arithmetic*, and the graphic novels *Foiled, Curses! Foiled Again*, and *The Last Dragon*. Her books and stories have won a Caldecott Medal, two Nebulas, and dozens of other awards. Six colleges and universities have given her honorary doctorates for her body of work. Also worthy of note: her Skylark Award—given by NESFA, the New England Science Fiction Association—set her good coat on fire. If you need to know more about her, visit her website at www.janeyolen.com.

Adam Stemple is the author of fantasy novels and short stories including *Singer of Souls* and *Steward of Song*. Stemple and Jane Yolen have previously coauthored the Rock 'n' Roll Fairy Tale and Seelie Wars book series. Stemple also performs Celtic-influenced American folk rock. He is based in Minneapolis and online at adamstemple.com.

Orion Zangara is an illustrator and comic book artist who lives in Sterling, Virginia. He is a graduate of the Kubert School, an art trade school with a concentration in sequential art, founded by his grandfather Joe Kubert. Currently, he is illustrating a soon-to-be-announced series for Image Comics. And he finds it very strange describing himself in the third person! You may reach him at www.orionzangara.com.